DUPLICITY

BAND OF BELIEVERS, BOOK 2

JAMIE LEE GREY

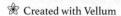

To the man I love...
Husband and best friend...
All my heart.

CONTENTS

Chapter 1	1
Chapter 2	16
Chapter 3	31
Chapter 4	40
Chapter 5	51
Chapter 6	60
Chapter 7	74
Chapter 8	81
Chapter 9	90
Chapter 10	100
Chapter 11	110
Chapter 12	123
Chapter 13	133
Chapter 14	143
Chapter 15	151
Chapter 16	158
Chapter 17	166
Chapter 18	175
Chapter 19	186
Chapter 20	195
Chapter 21	203
Chapter 22	213
Chapter 23	222
Chapter 24	229
Chapter 25	240
Epilogue	244
Excerpt from Book 3, Destruction	247
Letter To Readers	255
Acknowledgments	257
Books By Jamie Lee Grey	259
About the Author	261

CONTENTS

1

W hat was that dog barking about now?

Jennifer Price groaned and flopped over in bed, flinging her arm to waken Nathan. But he wasn't there.

Groggy, she reached for the lamp on the night stand. Flipped the switch, but it didn't come on.

Right. She sat up. The power had been off for three days. And Nathan hadn't returned from Missoula on the day it went off.

Titus barked incessantly in the barnyard.

Couldn't he just run off the coyotes and shut up?

Jennifer reached for the flashlight she'd left by her glass of water, fumbling in the dark until she found it. She pushed away the quilt and eased her bare feet onto the braided rug. If that dog would just quit barking, she could get back to sleep. She turned the flashlight beam on her watch. Just after 3 a.m.

The barking grew more ferocious. Maybe there were wolves out there.

Jennifer shoved her feet into her slippers and stood up, then made her way to the doorway and descended the stairs. She lit an oil lamp in the kitchen and moved to the living room. Stopping at the gun cabinet, she took out Nathan's 30-30 and made sure it was loaded, then set the oil lamp on the fireplace mantle and picked up the flashlight.

She unlocked the back door and swung it open. Titus stood on the stoop, hackles raised, snarling fiercely into the darkness. The huge black Newfoundland stepped in front of her, cutting off her forward motion. She paused.

What had gotten into him?

He yelped and stumbled.

Something slammed into her chest. Guns boomed. Pain!

Burning, awful pain in her ribs. Blood seeping down her white cotton nightgown.

Titus fell. He turned those big brown eyes on her as the light in them flickered out.

Her own breathing grew labored. Her knees wobbled.

She fell beside him, her arm flung over his neck.

Footsteps! Approaching fast.

She reached for the rifle she'd dropped when she fell. A black boot kicked it away from her fingers.

"Is she dead?" A deep male voice yelled from the darkness by the barn.

"Almost," a younger one answered above her.

Was she almost dead? She still felt pain. And cold. It was hard to breathe.

More footsteps approached. Flashlights flicked on.

"Hey! Why're you wearing camouflage?" The deep voice bellowed. "You're supposed to wear all black, like the rest of us."

"What's the big deal? This is stealthy."

"The big deal, fool, is we wear all black because we plan to do most of our hunting at night. That's always been the plan."

"So what? It's dark. Not like they're gonna see my camo when it's pitch black out."

"It's what we wear. All black. No exceptions."

"Whatever." The younger man stepped over Jennifer and walked into her living room.

The pain was pulling her under. She shivered. More men approached. All wearing black.

"Help me," she gasped.

A male voice laughed. "There's no help for you, lady. Or your dead dog."

"Get rid of that dog corpse," a strident voice ordered. "We'll bury the woman in the morning."

More men, maybe a half dozen, stepped over her and into her home.

"This is a nice little hidey hole," the strident voice said. "We could make this our new headquarters."

Another man laughed. "Ponderosa, Montana! Gotta love this place!"

Blood gurgled from Jennifer's mouth. Then everything faded to black.

THE TRUTH WAS, they'd probably starve if they didn't go to town for supplies. On the other hand, they'd probably be captured if they did go.

Willow Archer sighed and leaned back against a tree trunk. What should they do?

Her little group was at odds with the world and with each other. Rejecting the Mark of the Beast, they'd run to this Montana forest to evade the task force assigned to implant the I.D. chip in everyone. But now, they were arguing amongst themselves.

Raven Deepwater favored staying away from civilization and making do with what they had brought with them.

Willow's brother, Josh, agreed.

But his friend, Matt Daniels, wanted to return home for more supplies. At 15, he also wanted to see if his mom was okay – and if she'd changed her mind and wanted to escape the task force now.

Then there was Candy O'Connor. Willow rolled her eyes. She knew she had to love her enemies, but that Candy was a challenge. Anyway, the blonde Barbie wanted to go back for some things for herself and her toddler daughter, Maria. But there was no way that could happen anytime soon. Candy's ankle was getting better, but she'd sprained it bad enough that it'd be weeks before she'd be able to walk normally, much less hike ten or twelve miles through the mountains.

So, if they went back to town, Candy would have to stay here with Maria. And someone dependable would probably have to stay to babysit both of them.

Willow looked to the heavens. *Lord, what do we do?*

Everything was at stake: the freedom and survival of each member of the group, and the security and secrecy of this little cabin that God had given them. If one member were captured, they'd be forced to give up the location of this homestead. All the group members would be betrayed. The band of believers would be destroyed.

Willow could not afford to make a mistake.

KRISTIE DANIELS RAN a comb through her dirty hair. She, like all her neighbors, hadn't had a shower in four days. The EMP or solar flare, or whatever it was, had knocked out the power and fried everything that had electrical circuitry.

The lights went out. Cars stopped running. Trucks didn't bring food to Ponderosa, Montana, anymore. Maybe they didn't bring food anywhere. Telephones, radios and TVs didn't work, so who could know?

But the worst of it – the very worst, was losing indoor plumbing. Well, sure, the plumbing was still there, but no water was pumped through the pipes.

She couldn't flush her stupid toilet!

Or take a shower and wash her hair.

How long would this go on? No one knew. Rumors abounded, of course, in tiny Ponderosa.

Her neighbor, Jim Hill, said it would be at least a year or two. He said that America didn't manufacture electrical transformers anymore, and didn't keep them in stock, either. And each one cost many thousands of dollars, and thousands of transformers would have to be imported from China – if China wasn't the one that EMP'd the United States – and little ole Ponderosa would be last on the list to have power restored. New York and D.C. and California would probably be the first to be fixed.

But what did he know? He was just a retired truck driver.

The police said the power could be restored in a few months. Maybe they had better intel, or maybe they were just more optimistic. Trying to restore calm, and all that.

She didn't trust the cops, though – they'd hurried down to the only grocery store in town on the first day the power went out, and they requisitioned all the food. Sure, they'd distributed the perishables that first day, but they locked up the rest and put guards on it. Using it to feed themselves and their families, no doubt.

Not to mention, before the EMP, they'd failed to find her son, Matt, and bring him home after he'd run off to the woods with Raven and Willow and Josh.

Then the police had forced her to get the I.D. chip! They'd threatened her physically, and she'd caved. She still felt sick about that.

But what could she do? Without it, she'd starve. It was required to buy or sell anything. How would she feed herself?

It was a moot point now. There was no food to buy. And there were no functional scanners in Ponderosa to scan the I.D. chips anyway. She glanced at her right hand. There had been a small mark the first few days where the chip was implanted, but it was invisible now.

She could feel it, but just barely, when she ran her fingers over the injection site.

In hindsight, maybe Matt had been right to escape to the forest with his friends. The odds of survival out there might soon be better than here in civilization. Things were taking a nasty turn. At first, it was mostly the Christians' homes that were looted. But now, any house that looked vacant was vulnerable. And lots of occupied houses, like hers, could appear vacant because the lights were all out even though she was home.

A few old cars from the 1970s still ran, and she'd seen young hoodlums cruising around neighborhoods, casing the houses. It was a matter of time until they came here. And she was alone. No dog. No gun. No family. Really, no friends.

She swiped at her damp eyes with a grubby hand. Could it get any worse?

A glance out the window revealed a stunning sunset. She'd better hurry to get a few things done before dark. She only had three candles left.

Stepping out the back door, she looked toward the trees at the north end of her property. It had become a habit over the past two weeks. Matt was out there somewhere. Maybe one day soon, he'd appear at the edge of the forest.

In fact, there *was* something there. Something small and white. Was she imagining it? She strained her eyes, staring, trying to make it out.

Did it just move?

"Matt?" She bounded down the steps and ran toward the forest. "Matthew, is that you?"

The white spot disappeared. Kristie stopped to catch her breath.

"Matt? Matt?"

Could it have been him? What else could it be?

A hoodlum?

"Matthew, are you there?"

A young man in a white t-shirt appeared from behind some trees, moving swiftly toward her.

She ran toward him. "Matthew!"

They met at the edge of the forest, crashing into a bear hug.

Kristie pulled back and stared at him. He looked taller. And skinnier. Older, somehow. She crushed him in another hug. Then planted a mom kiss on his cheek.

He brushed it away, looking sheepish.

Her mind reeled with the reality of his return. Joy, relief and anger swirled together in her heart.

"Are you okay? Where have you been? I'm so glad to see you. And you're in so much trouble, young man! Grounded is just the beginning of it!"

"I can't stay, mom." He pulled out of her embrace.

"What! What do you mean? Of course you're staying!"

"I just came to check on you. And get some stuff."

"No." She stared at him. "No! I'm not losing you again. Not with all that's going on!"

"We need to get out of sight." He slipped back toward the forest. She followed.

"Matthew, you cannot leave. I forbid it!"

"What did you mean, all that's going on?" He turned those steady blue eyes on her. He looked so grown up.

For some reason, she didn't want to tell him the whole story.

She needed him. Needed him to stay with her. He was her only family.

"You know, they've been making people get chipped."

"Did you get chipped?"

"No." She flat lied, but only because she had to. What would he think if she admitted the truth? He'd leave her again. After all, he'd run away to avoid what he thought was the Mark of the Beast.

"Then you should come with us."

"Us?" She peered into the trees behind him. Didn't see anybody.

"You know, Raven and Willow and Josh."

"Are they here? Where are they?"

"Will you come with us? We have a place to live. We just need to get more supplies."

"Maybe...." Because really, what was the point in staying? She was low on food, with no means of getting more. In the forest, at least they could hunt and fish. And it was summertime. It'd be like camping.

At home, there was no running water, no electricity, and no means of heat because she didn't have a wood stove. And the new threat of thefts and burglaries. There were worse things than living in the woods for a while.

"Good." Matt headed for the house. "I need to get some stuff. And you should pack everything important that you can carry."

Matt took the back steps two at a time. He held the door open for her, then reached for the light switch. Nothing happened. He flicked it down and back up, then looked at her.

"Did you forget to pay the electric bill again?"

"No. The power's out." It was a half-truth, but who cared? It wasn't like he would be sticking around, and she probably wouldn't, either. She wasn't sure why she didn't want to tell him about the EMP, but she knew she didn't. Not yet.

But she really didn't want him to know about her getting chipped. Ever.

KRISTIE HURRIED to fill her backpack with the stuff Matt told her to bring – hiking gear, mostly. It'd been a few years since she'd actually gone hiking, but she still had all the basics. At his insistence, she also brought some winter outerwear and wool socks. Not that she'd need them. She was planning to be home well before winter fell in the mountains. But since he had such strong feelings about it, she went along to avoid a fight with him.

He was rattling around in the kitchen, filling his nearly empty pack with who-knows-what. There wasn't any camping gear in the kitchen! And not a lot of food left there, either.

Matt stepped into the doorway of her bedroom.

"There's hardly anything to eat," he said. "When's the last time you went shopping?"

It wasn't possible to go shopping. But he didn't need to know that.

"I don't know. A week ago, maybe?"

"Geez, Mom!" He shot her a disgusted look. "Are you about ready? And do we have any garden seeds?"

"Don't give me that look. And yes, there are some seeds in the drawer by the washing machine."

He left, and she packed some lip balm and moisturizing lotion. Then grabbed all her gold and silver jewelry and stuffed it in a satin travel bag. She added a travel-sized sewing kit and full sized scissors. And a photo of her parents, and one of her and Matt when he was a baby. She looked great in that photo, if she did say so herself.

"Are you ready yet?" Matt stomped into her room. "We gotta go, Mom!"

"Okay, okay." Her pack was overflowing already. And weighed a ton. "Just let me get my rain jacket."

On their way out, Matt grabbed a hammer and a bag of nails from a remodeling project she hadn't gotten around to yet.

They walked back to the woods just as darkness enveloped the valley. In the trees, Matt turned on his headlamp.

"Guys?" He called quietly. "Hey, guys?"

There was no response.

"Josh and Raven are supposed to meet me here. They both went to their houses to see what they could salvage."

He shrugged out of his pack and set it on the ground.

"I'm gonna go find them. They can probably use an extra hand."

What? No. He might never make it back. Things were dangerous now. Houses were ransacked, squatters moved in... and everyone was armed.

"Let's wait a few minutes."

"Why? I can help them carry stuff back here. We need everything we can get."

"You might miss them in the woods. And then you might get caught, even as they safely make their way back here. Let's give them ten minutes. After that, I'll go with you."

Because there was no way she was staying here in these woods alone, and there was no way she was letting him out of her sight again.

"Fine. Ten minutes, then we're going." He sat on a stump and turned out his headlamp. "You might as well take off your pack."

Kristie was happy to unburden herself. She rolled her shoulders, then stretched.

"Since we've got a few minutes, you can tell me all about your past couple of weeks now. Starting with, where's Willow?"

"She stayed behind to take care of the animals and Candy."

"Candy?"

"Candy O'Connor. She joined us the second day with her little girl, Maria."

"So why does Willow have to take care of her?"

"Candy sprained her ankle. Can't really hike on it. Plus, Maria slows us down." Matt yawned. "Anyway, we've got a nice cabin now, so we're all set. Especially after we get this extra gear back to the mountain, and the seeds and stuff."

"So we'll have a garden. That's nice."

"It's way more than nice. We need food to get through the winter."

But how would they preserve it? It's not like they'd have freezers at the cabin, or probably even cans and canners. Some of it could be dried, maybe, and maybe they could make a – what were those underground food pantries called? Well, anyway, one of those things. For potatoes and whatnot. If they had potatoes and whatnot. A root cellar.

A light flitted off a nearby tree, and Matt put his hand on Kristie's shoulder.

"Shhhh..." he whispered in her ear.

The light continued approaching them.

"It's probably Raven and Josh," Matt whispered.

The light stopped about a hundred feet away, then turned and slowly lit up different sections of the forest as it revolved. Matt and Kristie stayed behind a big pine tree.

"Matt?" The low, hushed voice clearly belonged to Josh.

Kristie let out a breath she hadn't realized she'd been holding.

"Over here," Matt called back quietly. He stepped out from behind the tree.

"Is Raven with you?"

"No. I thought she would be here by now." Josh made his way to them. "I was sure I'd be the last one."

"You're not." Kristie stepped out into the light of his headlamp.

"Mrs. Daniels!" Josh sounded shocked. "You're here!"

"Of course. I've been worried sick about you guys."

"But – are you coming back with us? Or did you take the mark?"

"Yes, I'm coming with you. And no, I didn't take the mark." Another lie, but what did it matter?

"Wow, that is great!"

Kristie smiled. "Thanks, Josh. I'm glad you're all okay."

"So far," Josh agreed. He shined his light on Matt, illuminating his golden blond hair. "We should go help Raven."

"Let's give her a few minutes," Kristie interjected.

"Okay. Five minutes, then we'll go." Josh dropped his pack and sat on a log. He turned off his headlamp. "So, what did you get, Matt? Any food?"

"Yeah, I pretty much cleared out the kitchen. But Mom was low on food."

She thought about defending herself, but decided to let it go. For now.

"But he also got seeds and some tools and nails," she told Josh.

"Awesome!" Josh said. "I got some stuff Willow asked for, and some more ammo, and stuff for the chickens and goats. And I got this roll of chicken wire, and a garden spade and hand tools."

"Was it weird being back at your house?"

"The power was out. And it'd been ransacked." His voice sounded sad. "The door was hanging open when I got there, so I didn't know if someone was inside. But no one was there, thank God!"

Kristie's heart fluttered. Josh was lucky. He didn't know how lucky. Crazy things had happened since the EMP.

"Did you get any food?"

"Just a little. There wasn't much in there. Looked like someone had gone through all our stuff. Drawers were turned over on the floor, stuff thrown all over the place. A real mess."

"But it sounds like you still got some good supplies," Kristie said.

A light seared through the woods and hit her eyes. She shielded her face as it blinded her.

"I hope that's Raven."

WILLOW MILKED THE GOATS SLOWLY, careful to keep every drop in the pail. A mist rose from the dewy meadow below as the sun's early rays broke over the mountain. But the serene scene did nothing to calm her anxiety.

Where were they? Should she go look for them? She should have made Josh stay here at the cabin with her and Candy.

Raven, Josh and Matt had left for supplies two mornings ago. They should have spent most of that first day hiking out of the mountains, then a few hours in the evening gathering whatever food, seeds, tools and supplies they could find and carry. The plan was, they'd spend the first night in the forest near town, and strike out for the cabin by first light. So they should have been home by dark yesterday.

When they didn't return, Willow didn't sleep.

And now it was morning, and she needed to make a decision – stay here with Candy and Maria, or head out to find Josh and the others.

The goat kicked, nearly knocking over the pail of milk. Willow grabbed it, sloshing just a tiny bit out of the bucket. Gilligan, Raven's border collie, hurried over to lap the spilled milk off the grass.

It was possible that they hadn't made it back yet because

they were carrying a lot of supplies, which would be great. A heavy load would definitely slow down their return hike, and that could explain the delay. Maybe they were just a couple miles from the cabin when darkness fell last night, and they'd made camp somewhere. In that case, they could be home in the next few hours.

But what if things hadn't gone so well?

They might have all been captured. They might have suffered an attack from a bear or cougar or wolves. Willow shuddered, remembering the howling she'd heard during the night. What if – no, she wouldn't consider that possibility.

She took a deep breath and let it out slowly. God had brought them this far, and she had to keep trusting Him.

She glanced over at the cabin. It was small, sure, but it kept the rain out and the heat in, and there'd been some supplies in it when Raven's Uncle Tony led them here. Tony had known the guy who'd supposedly owned the place and brought the canned goods, and Tony said he'd died of cancer.

It wasn't much to look at – just an old homestead cabin, about twelve by eighteen feet, with two sets of bunk beds in the back, a half loft above them, and a wood stove. Two chairs and a small table beneath one of three windows completed the furniture. The guys happily moved into the loft, leaving the bunks for the girls.

Out behind the cabin sat a rickety outhouse, and beyond that was a shed that they'd turned into a barn for the goats and chickens. It was small, but it worked for now. Willow hoped the guys and Raven had been able to retrieve some chicken wire from the pen at their former home, so they'd be able to make a run or portable pen for the chickens here.

How long should she wait before she went looking for them? Another hour? Two?

Maybe she should just stay home. The odds of her crossing

paths with them in the forest was slim. They'd be skirting or avoiding roads, to avoid being spotted and captured.

There was still volcanic ash on the ground from the recent eruption, although the rain had washed a lot of it down into low spots and creeks. She could probably follow their tracks out, though, and maybe they were taking the same path home.

Of course, if she could follow their tracks, anyone could, which was a risk they'd discussed before they left. For that reason, they'd planned to stay to higher ground and rocky areas where the ash had blown or washed off the ground. Still, they would leave some tracks even there, or when they had to cross a draw or valley.

The cabin door swung open, and Candy hobbled out, leaning on a big tree limb they'd fashioned into a crutch of sorts. Maria burst out the door after her. Gilligan wagged his tail as he ran to greet the child.

"Are there any eggs?" Candy asked.

Willow nodded. "Five this morning."

The hens had started laying better after they'd arrived at the cabin. They spent their days scratching around the barn and cabin, finding ants, spiders, grubs and seeds.

"Good. We're starved," Candy said. "I'll get a fire going in the stove."

"Actually, let's save them for Raven and the guys. They'll be famished when they get home," Willow said.

If they get home. Willow rejected the thought. *When*. When they get home.

illow poked a stick in the dirt. It was nearly noon. She should go find her brother and the rest of the group. Shouldn't she?

Stay.

It was a soft voice, almost a whisper, in her head. She'd probably imagined it.

Josh might be in trouble. Maybe stranded somewhere, or lost, or injured. She could help, if she could find him.

But that was the problem – how could she find him? It'd be so easy to pass within a quarter mile of the group, and never know it. The forest was dense as it crawled over mountains and valleys, hills and dips. Josh and the team would be traveling quietly, so she wouldn't hear them, either.

With limited noise and visibility, they'd be very difficult to locate. She threw the stick at a tree.

She had to do something. She closed her eyes. Lord, please help me find my brother and my friends.

Striding back to the cabin, she made up her mind. It was time to go look.

Candy sat at the table with Maria on her lap. She ran a comb through the child's hair.

"Shouldn't they be back by now?"

"Yep." Willow grabbed her backpack. "I'm going to see if I can find them."

"You're leaving me?"

"You'll be okay. Stay close to the cabin." Willow reached for her water bottle and a portable water filter, and pushed them into the pack. She grabbed two full magazines for her handgun. Those went into her back pocket. The holstered weapon was part of her daily uniform. It went on as soon as she put on her jeans every morning.

"But what if – what if you get lost?" Candy's voice trembled. "What if nobody finds their way back here?"

"I won't get lost. And everyone will find their way back."

"You should stay. I have a bum ankle, and a baby – "

"I'll be back by dark. Keep a close eye on the chickens and goats. We can't afford to lose any to hawks or coyotes. Pay attention to Gilligan. He'll alert if there's a problem."

Willow scratched the dog's ears, then let herself out the door, closing it before Gilligan could follow or Candy could protest further.

You should stay. It was that quiet voice in her head again.

No, she shouldn't. She'd taken on this group as her responsibility. Her leadership skills had kept them safe and together. Well, that and the Lord, of course.

She couldn't let them down now.

Heading for the edge of the clearing, she glanced toward the sun. High noon. She had four hours to search, then she should head back to the cabin in order to make it home by dark.

Scattered footprints were visible in the volcanic ash. She still didn't know which volcano had gone off. Mt. Saint Helens? Rainier? Yellowstone?

Probably not Yellowstone. It was a super volcano, and she'd heard that most of the United States would be wiped out if it ever went off.

Maybe the group had found out, if they spoke to Matt's mom. She would've heard on the news.

It'd been weeks since Willow had seen a news broadcast or gotten any news of the outside world, or even of her own hometown. She'd probably never see a television again, unless she got captured. And that was still a possibility, so she needed to pay attention to her surroundings. It wouldn't be good to stumble into a patrol out here and get herself caught.

Stopping under a big larch tree, she pulled out her water bottle and took a sip. The late June sun had warmed the forest, bringing out all the early summer fragrances. On the hill above her, a syringa bush cloaked itself in delicate white blooms. No wonder the air smelled so sweet. She drank in the scent with another sip of water, then moved on.

An hour later, she came to a small creek. Wiping the perspiration from her brow, she decided to take a break and cool her feet. But first, she needed to refill her water bottle.

She filtered the cold, clear water into her bottle and took a long drink. The cold water was so much more refreshing than the lukewarm water she'd been carrying. She drank her fill, then filtered more into the bottle, refilling it.

Sunlight cut through the cedar trees on the banks of the creek, sparkling like diamonds in the water as it played over rounded rocks on the bottom. As she took off her hiking boots, Willow saw a trout swim into a deep pool just a few yards downstream. Too bad she didn't have her fishing pole. She might have had a good lunch, right here on the banks of this beautiful creek.

She pulled off her socks, rolled up her jeans, and stepped into the water. She gasped. Cold! But her feet were hot and the water felt great. She took a deep breath and let it out slow, then rolled her shoulders and closed her eyes, letting the sun warm her eyelids as the water iced her feet.

Snap!

Her eyes flew open as her hand streaked toward her holster.

"Freeze! Hands up!" A man's voice, off to her left.

She froze, all except her gaze, which zipped along the trees. There, just across the creek. A guy in hunting gear, dark hair and tanned face, pointing a big scoped rifle at her.

"I said, 'Hands up!'"

Slowly, almost involuntarily, Willow's hands rose to shoulder height.

What could she do? She didn't even have her boots on! What was she thinking, letting down her guard like this? Stupid, stupid, stupid!

This was why God had told her to stay at the cabin. If only she'd listened!

Think! Willow swallowed hard.

"Don't shoot. I'm just a kid."

"You don't look like a kid from here."

The guy didn't look very old himself. Just a few years older than she was.

"A teenager," she clarified, letting her hands slowly drop.

"Keep your hands up!" He kept that rifle trained on her chest. "What, nineteen?"

"Eighteen." More or less. She lifted her hands a little. Since they'd been on the run, she'd lost track of the days. Had her birthday come and gone already? Was it today? Tomorrow?

"Where's your parents?"

She was tempted to correct his grammar, but thought better of that.

"They're gone."

"Gone where?"

"None of your business." He wasn't wearing a uniform, so he

probably wasn't on patrol looking for her. "Would you please point that thing somewhere else?"

His gun barrel dropped a little to the left.

"Are you out here alone?"

At the moment. "Yeah."

What was he hunting, anyway? It wasn't deer season or elk season or moose season. Bear? Was bear season in June?

"I'm going to put on my boots." Willow slowly lowered her hands. "Don't shoot me, okay?"

"I won't shoot if you don't reach for that pistol."

"Deal."

She slowly backed out of the water, then eased down on the bank and put her socks on, keeping a careful eye on him. Once she had her boots on, she'd run. And then what?

"What're you doing out here all by yourself?"

"Camping."

"Way out here?" He narrowed his eyes. "By yourself?"

"What's it to you?"

"Well, I'm not going to leave a kid miles from civilization in the woods by herself."

"I'm a legal adult." Well, probably. Or close, anyway. "You can't do anything about it."

"Fine. I'll just let the Forest Service know where you are, so your family can find you."

Government officials? Oh, no, that was not good. The I.D. task force would be on her group as soon as the Forest Service staff notified them about Willow.

"And I'll let Fish, Wildlife and Parks know you're hunting out of season."

His lips tightened, then relaxed. "Yeah, good luck with that."

Huh? What did he mean? What did he know that she didn't? She pulled on her left boot and tightened the laces. Should she run? Would he report her?

Was there a way to just make him leave and forget he'd seen her?

She rolled down her pants legs and stood up slowly, then pulled on her backpack.

"Say... you don't have the I.D. chip, do you?"

Her heart pounded wildly against her ribs. She studied his face. It was a mask. Was there a bounty on Christians? Was he a bounty hunter? Or an agent, just wearing civilian clothing?

She whirled around and raced up the hill. Just as she found her stride, her toe caught a tree root and she fell, sprawling headlong to the forest floor. Her head smashed into something hard.

Stars. Flashing across her eyes. Then darkness.

PAIN. Her head throbbed. Her neck ached. Slowly, Willow opened her eyes. Green fabric floated above her. She felt constricted. Couldn't move, couldn't stand up.

A wild look around revealed she was in a tent. The light was very dim. Dusk, or dawn?

Her hands were tied in front of her with a cotton rope. She had Dad's old multi-tool and a knife in her pack. Where was it?

How did she get here?

The man. At the creek. Running away, falling, pain. The memories came back in fits and starts.

Her throat was achingly dry. A long strand of her auburn hair curtained her vision. She lifted her head, glanced around quickly, then let it back down. Hurt so bad. Even her eyes ached, and her jaw.

The glance told her she was in a mummy sleeping bag. Her pack was nowhere in sight, but her boots were at the opposite end of the tent. And he'd tied her up. Why? To harm her? To turn her in to the authorities?

She had to get free. Get out of here. She wriggled her hands, then her wrists. Too tight. She couldn't loosen the rope. So she'd have to cut it. Without her knife.

The tent flap opened. Willow shuddered.

The hunter pulled back the flap and looked in on her.

"You're awake. That's good." He held her water bottle out to her. "Thirsty?"

"Untie my hands." She stretched them out toward him.

"Later. I don't trust you." He crouched and entered the tent, then eased over to her like she was a wounded animal.

He didn't trust *her*? Hello! She was the one who was all tied up!

"Let's get you sitting up so you can drink." He slid his arm under her shoulders and pulled gently forward.

Her head pounded. She slumped against his chest. Taking the water bottle in her tied hands, she lifted it to her lips and gulped. Lukewarm, ugh. How long had she been out?

"What time is it?"

"After seven. You've been in and out a long time. Took a pretty bad blow on your noggin."

"Where am I?"

"In my camp. Not far from the creek where I found you."

"You can untie my hands."

He moved away and she laid her head down on the pillow. He turned and met her eyes.

"I don't have the mark, either."

Oh. That.

"I never said I didn't have it."

"But you ran." A slow smile lit his face, clear to his deep brown eyes. "Besides, I checked when I brought you here."

"Untie me."

"Okay, but don't get all psycho on me."

Willow held out her hands. She couldn't get all psycho. It was all she could do to keep her eyes open and drink a bit of water. But once she got rested....

He whipped out a hunting knife and cut the knot, then pulled the rope free of her wrists. She rubbed them and closed her eyes.

"You're welcome."

What, she was supposed to thank him for letting her loose? Right.

"Do you have any aspirin?"

"I think so. I'll go look." He crawled out the tent flap, leaving her alone.

Time to get out of here! She unzipped the sleeping bag and sat up.

Whoa... the tent spun. She braced herself with her hands. Her vision darkened. Not good! She lowered herself back to the pillow and watched the tent spin in crazy circles above her.

She wasn't about to go anywhere. Her eyes moistened. Until her head sorted itself out, she was stuck here with this hunter.

The tent flap flew back and he crawled in, a bottle of aspirin in his hand.

"Here. Take two. Then I'll bring you some venison stew."

"It's not deer season." Maybe she shouldn't have pointed that out. Might make him mad, and then he might do something crazy. Crazier than tying her up.

His eyes stared hard at hers.

"So you don't want any, then?"

Willow swallowed the aspirin with a gulp of water. "Yes, please."

He took the bottle and retreated.

It didn't make any sense. Why was he way the heck out here, hunting deer in June? Oh, right. He didn't have the mark. He was living like she was, and her group. Off the land. Hunting and fishing anything they could catch.

If he didn't have the mark, he was a Christian, right? Because by now, who else didn't have it? The philosophical and political holdouts had given in when their bank accounts were frozen.

He returned with a mug and a spoon. She tried to sit up, but the tent started spinning again.

"Here. Lean against me. I just brought some of the broth." He sat beside her, slid his hand under her shoulders, and pulled her up gently so she could lean back against his chest. She leaned her head against his shoulder, and reached for the mug.

The broth smelled delicious. Her stomach rumbled.

She tasted a spoonful. Oh, it was so good! In no time, the mug was empty.

"Thank you."

"Sure. If you keep that down, I'll bring you something meatier later." He shifted her back to the pillow.

A hunter. A cook. A nurse. Who was this guy?

"What's your name?" She met his gaze as he glanced back at her.

"Jacob. You?"

"Willow."

"Okay, Willow. You get some rest. I'll check on you in a while."

Her eyes closed, and when she opened them, sunlight played on the tent wall. So bright!

Slowly, she sat up. Her head throbbed, but the tent only spun a couple of times. Good. Much better than yesterday. Pushing the sleeping bag away, she inched toward her boots. Her stomach lurched, then settled.

She eased her left boot on, then her right one. That headache was a doozy! She touched her temple and found a very tender lump.

Her pack wasn't in the tent. Neither were her holster and handgun. She grabbed her water bottle and slowly, quietly unzipped the tent flap. If Jacob hadn't stolen everything, she needed to get her stuff and get out of here.

Peering out, she saw the remnants of a camp fire with a pot near it, a pile of dry wood a few feet away, and not much else.

Where were her things? Where was Jacob? She crawled from the tent and stood up. Too fast. As the trees spun, she lowered herself to her knees. And caught a whiff of venison stew. It was in the pot beside the fire, and there was a spoon in it.

Tentatively, she stood up again. Then slowly shuffled to the stew pot, eased down beside it, and reached for the spoon. Jacob must have eaten most of it. There was less than a pint left.

She dug in.

As she ate, she looked around camp. There was an axe that she hadn't noticed before, leaning against a tree. But where were her gun and her pack? And all of Jacob's things?

"I see you found breakfast."

She jumped, then settled herself. "I didn't hear you coming. Where were you?"

"Fishing, but no luck. How are you feeling?"

"Massive headache, but other than that, I'm good to go." She met his deep brown eyes. "Where's my stuff?"

"Behind the tent." He looked at the knot on her temple, reaching out to touch it, but Willow pulled away.

"It hurts. Can I have some more aspirin?"

"Yeah. And then I'll take you home."

What? No. She couldn't bring a stranger to the cabin. Her group's security rested on the secrecy of that place.

"No need. I'll be fine."

"You're far from fine. And there's no way I'm letting a kid with a head injury wander alone in the woods."

"I'm not a kid." She hated that he thought of her like that. Their eyes met in a challenge. Jacob looked away first.

"Whatever you say." He snorted. "I'm still taking you home."

She finished the stew and set down the pot.

"Aspirin?"

"Right." He stood up, walked around the tent, and returned with his backpack. Pulling the bottle from a side pocket, he handed it to her.

Willow downed two pills with water. "Thanks."

She stood up. Almost too fast again. She steadied herself with her hands on her knees until the ground seemed stationary.

Feeling queasy, she rethought her bullheadedness. Maybe she should let him walk her part of the way home. She wasn't safe alone. Couldn't run from danger, might get lost, or fall again... if only she'd stayed at the cabin yesterday and waited for the others to return!

"You okay?" Jacob gently took her elbow. "Maybe you should lie down for a while."

"No!" She straightened. "I'm fine."

"Yeah, you look it." He chuckled, releasing her arm.

He actually had a nice smile. And he'd taken care of her. As much as she hated it, she still needed help.

Slowly, she walked behind the tent. Her pack leaned against a shrub.

"Where's my gun?"

"Top of the main compartment."

She unzipped the zipper and found her gun and holster. Securing them in place, she glanced over at him. He was dousing the fire. In camo pants and a black t-shirt, he looked like he fit in the woods. He went in the tent and she could hear him rolling up the sleeping bag. She'd slept in his bed. Where had he slept?

Slowly, she hoisted her pack and eased it onto her back. It was light, since she hadn't planned on being away past dinner yesterday. She wondered how things were at the cabin. Had Candy taken care of the animals? Had Josh and the others made it back from town? Was everyone worried about her?

Jacob emerged from the tent, and released the guy lines and pegs. She wanted to offer to help, but felt too woozy. Anyway, he had it rolled and packed in less than two minutes.

She sat down as he finished packing all his gear. Finally, he shrugged into his pack – it looked like it weighed fifty pounds – and he offered a hand to help her up. She took it. It was strong and warm and a little calloused. She glanced around the forest.

"I'm not sure where we are. Can you take me back to the creek?"

"Sure thing, Missy."

"It's Willow."

"Okay, Missy." He smiled mischievously, and started through the woods. "Follow me."

What was up with the Missy thing? Jacob was odd.

She hoped she could trust him. For now, there was nothing else to do. She was lost. But when they got back to the creek, she'd part ways with him.

Slowly, he made his way through the trees, stopping once in a while to hold back a branch that would block Willow's path. He was sort of chivalrous. What was his story, anyway?

She didn't pay much attention to the forest or landmarks, just kept her eyes on Jacob and the game trail in front of her feet. The last thing she needed was to take another fall.

Jacob walked slowly in sturdy black leather boots, pausing to glance back at her occasionally.

"Doing okay?"

"Yeah." Her head still ached, and her stomach was a little

upset, but she needed to keep going. Get home to her friends and family.

"Let me know if you need a break."

They walked another ten minutes or so, and came to a creek. It was the one where she'd filled her water bottle yesterday and "met" Jacob. Relief poured over her as she realized where she was. Not lost anymore!

He led her upstream and around a bend to a large log that straddled the banks. A natural bridge. She hoped it wasn't slippery. He crossed first. The log didn't creak or sag. It looked safe.

Willow started across cautiously. The last thing she wanted was to slip and fall into the icy cold water. And her balance was way off this morning. At last, she neared the far side and Jacob held out a hand to help her. She took it, and stepped down, then stumbled into him. He caught her before she fell, wrapping one arm around her.

"Whoa, there, Missy." He kept a hand on her waist as he studied her eyes. "You okay? You don't look so good."

She didn't feel so good, either. Vertigo and nausea competed for her attention. She swallowed hard. Took a deep breath. Then stepped away from him.

"I'm alright."

"I'm not so sure." He watched her face. "Let's take a break."

That sounded good. She sat on the end of the big log she'd just crossed, and took out her water bottle. Man, how long was she gonna feel so terrible? The aspirin had barely made a dent in her headache. And the lightheadedness, and the dizziness, and now nausea – maybe she shouldn't have eaten that stew this morning. The thought of food made her stomach turn.

Was she going to be able to get home safely? She didn't feel so sure. But she had to! Had to get there, make sure her brother was home with the others, make sure the animals were okay, find out about the venture into town and what goods they might have brought back. Yeah, she had to get home. Soon.

She felt his eyes on her. Studying her. She glanced over, caught him looking away. Yep. He was wondering if she was going to make it. Well, she would. She took another sip from her water bottle, then stowed it in the pack and stood up.

"I can find my way from here. Thank you for bringing me back to the creek."

He smiled, a long, slow smile that brought out dimples in his cheeks.

"You're a crazy chick, you know that? You're white as a sheet, with a goose egg on your noggin, barely able to keep your feet under you, and you're gonna go hiking out in grizzly territory by yourself." He paused, then chuckled. "I don't think so."

She knew he was right. But she had to get home.

"It's not too far. I'll be okay."

"Yeah, you will. Because I'm going with you."

"You can't."

His gaze met hers. "Why in the world not?"

"Because –" she wasn't sure what to tell him.

"You got a super-secret gold mine? Your family will shoot me? What?"

"Where I live is a secret."

He held up his hands in mock surrender. "I promise not to tell anybody."

"But I can't tell you."

"You're a piece of work, Missy, you know that?"

"Why do you keep calling me Missy? It's Willow, for crying out loud!"

A wide smile lit his face and brightened his eyes. "There. Now I think you're feeling better. Let's get going."

He turned and started walking, and there was nothing she could do but follow him downstream to the location where she'd taken off her boots yesterday. Once they got there, her tracks in the scattered volcanic ash were easy to follow. He moved easily through the trees, backtracking the way she'd come yesterday from the cabin. At the top of a rise, he stopped and waited for her.

"Look, I don't mean you any harm, and I don't want to scare you. I just want to make sure you get home safe, understand?"

She swallowed. And nodded. "But I can't bring you home."

"That's okay. When we get close, so that you can walk the last little bit on your own, you just let me know. Deal?"

The truth was, she wasn't in good shape. Every hundred yards or so, the dizziness crowded in on her head, and she felt like she'd black out. Losing consciousness in the forest would be a terribly dangerous thing. She couldn't afford it.

"Okay." She paused. "Can we take another break?"

After a few minutes, she was ready to move on. As they walked, the sun heated the slopes and made her feel sick. She perspired. Maybe had a fever. They stopped often, and it seemed to take hours to cover ground she felt sure she'd hiked in an hour yesterday.

Finally, she thought they were almost to the cabin's clearing. She stopped.

"Jacob?"

He turned around. Looked at her, then hurried back to her side.

"Are you alright?"

She nodded, but the trees spun. Then darkened. She felt his hands grab her arms as her knees buckled and the lights went out.

3

W hen she opened her eyes, she was on a bunk at the cabin. Home. And hungry. She started to sit up, then thought better of it. Felt sick and dizzy.

"Hey, there, Missy. You're awake."

Jacob. What? He was *here*?

Oh, no.

She turned her head. He was here, all right, sitting on a chair beside her bunk. Holding her water bottle out to her, with two aspirin. All smiles.

She reached for the pills. "What happened?"

"Well, you conked your head, I took you to my camp and took care of you –"

"I remember that part. I mean, how did you get here?"

"Better question is how did *you* get here? I carried you."

"Oh." She swallowed the aspirin. "When?"

"Yesterday."

"What? I've been out all night?"

"You got it, Missy!" Another smile.

Ugh. Willow, you idiot. What was the matter with him? And

how was she going to get rid of him now? Figure that out later. What about Josh?

"My brother – "

"Josh is fine. He's out milking the goats. Raven's fine, Matt's fine, Candy and her daughter are fine, Kristie's fine."

Huh? Kristie?

"Kristie is here? Matt's mom?" Crazy. She didn't really expect that one. Thought the woman would have taken the mark by now.

"Yep, she came back from town with everybody."

"Were they here when you brought me in?"

"Sure were." Jacob rubbed his hands together. "Hungry? I made venison soup."

"Perfect." Willow struggled to sit up. Touched her temple. "Ow!"

"Yeah, you'll probably want to leave that knot alone. It looks impressive."

He went to the wood stove and ladled soup into a bowl, then brought it back to her. The fragrance had a mixed effect – making her both hungry and nauseated. Slowly, she raised the spoon to her lips. Not bad. She was more hungry than sick.

In silence, she finished the soup and handed him the bowl.

"Thanks."

"Want more?"

"Not now." She slid back down on her pillow. "I just need to rest."

~

POLICE CAPTAIN MARCUS LARAMIE stood at the back of the Ponderosa City Council chamber, keeping an eye on the boisterous crowd. He'd never seen a turnout like this for a council meeting. Not that he attended them regularly. Just when there was a particularly hot topic on the agenda. When things got heated, it was good to have a police presence on site.

Today's was the hottest topic ever: when would power be restored to Ponderosa?

Mayor Danielle Challis gaveled the meeting to order. Preliminaries including roll call, the pledge of allegiance, and approving the previous meeting's minutes were completed quickly.

"In order to allow as many people as possible to hear us, I'm going to suggest we take this meeting down the street to the public square," she announced.

No one objected, so Marcus squeezed his way out to the overflowing hallway.

"We're moving to the public square. Please make your way down the street," he ordered.

The sea of faces in the hallway turned around and headed for the exit. In ten minutes, everyone was assembled at the square. The mayor and council brought folding chairs, which were set up on the bandstand platform. Mayor Challis' grey hair glinted in the sunlight.

"We've already called the meeting to order and did the pledge of allegiance. So let's move on to new business."

The first item on the agenda was the one everyone cared about, so the mayor called the public works director up to the platform.

"Tom, why don't you explain where we're at?"

Tom Higgins cleared his throat and looked out over the crowd.

"As you know, Ponderosa has two things going for it that much of the rest of the country doesn't have – a power-generating dam on the Bethel River, and gravity-fed water from Clearwater Creek."

The crowd murmured.

"So why don't we have power and water?" Someone shouted from the back of the crowd. The murmuring grew louder.

Tom held up his hand for silence. And waited for nearly a full minute as the crowd simmered down.

"The transformers blew during the EMP. The dam is still capable of generating electricity, but without replacing the transformers, we have no way of bringing that power into town."

The crowd buzzed. Many voices yelled questions about water.

"Now, hold on. If you'll just quiet down, I'll explain as much as I can."

The noise level dropped several decibels.

"Without power to run the treatment plant, we'd be bringing polluted creek water to your taps. Folks would get all kinds of illness. Think beaver fever, people. And without medical supplies, particularly antibiotics, people might die from complications."

"We'll die without water, too," someone yelled. "We're running out of the bottled stuff!"

The crowd roared to life. Soon a chant began.

"Water! Water! Water! Water!"

Tom looked at the mayor and shook his head. She stood up and held both hands in the air for silence.

Finally, the crowd quieted. Mayor Challis glared at the assembly.

"Now, if you don't let Tom talk, you'll never hear our plan! And if you don't settle down, right this minute, we will hold all future council meetings in the chambers, which only seats thirty people. And we'll enforce the fire code's room limit!"

KRISTIE DANIELS PICKED up the shovel and turned over another scoop of soil, letting the volcanic ash sift into the dirt. Soon, they'd have a row of prepared earth so they could plant some of the seeds they'd brought to the mountain. Tomorrow, they'd make another row and plant it. Within the week, they'd have a full garden planted.

She wiped her brow. The afternoon sun was unforgiving. But it felt good to be out here in the fresh air, doing work that might prove useful, and being with her son again.

Guilt niggled at her for keeping Matt in the dark about the EMP. On the other hand, it wasn't like he or the others needed to know about it. It had no effect on them... did it? They were banned from buying or selling without the I.D. chip, which they didn't have – which also didn't matter, because there was no way to scan it anymore.

So what was the point of telling him about the EMP?

Now, as for her own I.D. chip, she'd never tell him about that. They'd see her as a traitor or something. Certainly as a fallen Christian. Never to be loved or trusted.

She plunged her shovel into the ground and stomped on it, driving it deeper.

And why shouldn't she be loved and trusted? She was Matthew's mother. All she wanted was to love and take care of him, and protect him from harm.

Kristie turned the soil over and spotted an earthworm. Bending down, she picked it up and dropped it in the old coffee can the kids had found in the shed. They'd put a big scoop of dirt in there.

It was a nice fat worm. It'd make good fishing bait this evening or tomorrow morning when the boys went fishing again. Maybe catch a nice fat trout.

She wiped her hands on her pants. Not long ago, there was no way she'd touch a worm. Alive or dead. Now, she barely thought about it.

A wry smile turned her lips. My, how things had changed!

WILLOW OPENED HER EYES. She was alone in the cabin. Hopefully, everyone else was out doing something productive.

Slowly, she sat up. No nausea. That was a good sign.

She swung her feet off the bed and found her boots. Who had taken them off her? Raven? Jacob?

What were they going to do about Jacob now? He knew where they lived. He could expose them to the authorities.

But why would he do that? He didn't have the mark, either. He'd be endangering himself if he betrayed her.

Should they let him stay at the cabin? Did he have a family to go home to? Willow swallowed. A wife, maybe?

Or a band of believers like this one? Were there any others out there?

Slowly, she pulled on her boots. Her headache had let up, but she felt so fatigued. Unbelievably tired, like she'd just had a terrible bout of stomach flu or something.

Holding onto the bunk post, she stood up. A moment of dizziness came and went. Carefully, she made her way to the door and pushed it open.

Josh. Where was he?

Late afternoon sun lit up the clearing, but no one was in sight. Where was everyone? Willow eased around the corner of the cabin and headed for the outhouse.

When she emerged, she walked to the shed barn. Voices filtered through the back. She made her way around, and found everyone.

The guys were building a portable chicken run from some chicken wire that no doubt had come from Willow and Josh's old home. Raven, Candy and Kristie were planting seeds in a row of freshly turned earth. Just beyond them, little Maria played with Raven's dog Gilligan in the shade of a bull pine.

Willow's shoulders relaxed. She hadn't realized they were so taut. Everyone was fine, and they were accomplishing quite a bit without her.

Josh saw her first. His face beamed into a smile as he stood up and walked toward her.

"I'm glad you're okay."

"Mostly. Still a little sore." She smiled and messed his hair. He'd seen her yesterday and this morning, no doubt, but this was the first time she'd seen him in – how many days? Three? Four?

"Jacob's helping us build a chicken tractor." Josh grinned. "You're gonna like it!"

"A chicken tractor?"

"Yeah, that's what these portable pens are called."

"Huh." Willow eyed it. They'd found a couple of 2x4 boards that looked about six feet long, which they'd used for the base of the long sides, and some short, mismatched 2x6s, which were attached to the ends of the 2x4s to form the base of the short sides. Jacob was stretching the chicken wire in a big arch over the boards, forming a long dome about three feet tall along the center line.

"We're gonna close off one end, and leave a flap on the other end that we can use as a gate to put the chickens in and bring them out," Josh said. "We'll use this wire to secure the flap when they're inside. See?"

"Yeah. That's real nice."

Jacob glanced up from his work. "Twice a day, we'll move them, so they get fresh greens and grubs. This will keep them from running off, and keep the hawks from getting them as they forage."

"Perfect." Willow smiled.

Kristie stood from her planting and came over. A motherly look of concern wrinkled her brow.

"Hi, Willow. Are you feeling okay?"

"Yeah. I think so." She relaxed into Kristie's embrace. It made her miss her own mom. Where was she? Was she still alive? Had she possibly escaped the I.D. task force that had captured her at the church in Missoula? That was so unlikely, but Willow tried to hold onto hope.

She pulled away.

"How are things in town? We haven't heard any news in weeks. Well, I haven't, anyway!"

Kristie pursed her lips, then glanced at the ground.

"Well, I – "

"Hallo, the cabin!" The shout came from the forest behind them.

Willow's breath caught in her throat. She reached for her gun. Where was it? Oh, no, she'd forgotten to put it on when she put on her boots. And now her whole group was standing out in the open, defenseless! So stupid!

"Hallo, the cabin." The call came again, and this time, the shouter stepped out of the trees. A grizzled old guy in a faded black t-shirt.

Raven leapt to her feet.

"Uncle Tony!" She raced toward him. He set his rifle on the ground before she reached him and wrapped him in a hug.

Willow found her breath. They were safe. This time. Next time, she promised herself, they'd not be caught off guard or unarmed if someone approached their retreat.

Tony picked up his rifle and let Raven loop her arm through his, bringing him down to the group. His bright eyes scanned them quickly.

"I see you've got a couple new folks here."

"Yes." Raven motioned to Kristie. "This is Matt's mom, Kristie Daniels. Kristie, this is my uncle Tony."

They shook hands and exchanged greetings.

"And this is Jacob Myers, who rescued Willow."

He'd rescued her? Is that what he'd told everyone? Willow's gaze shot toward Jacob as he stepped forward to shake Tony's hand.

Sure, he'd brought her home – but only after he held her at gunpoint and then tied her up! Still, she might not have gotten back to the cabin without him.

Raven beamed at her uncle.

"It's so wonderful to see you!" She gave him one more hug. "Are you going to stay with us? We could sure use the help and all your knowledge."

"No, I can't stay. But I brought you something."

"More bear meat?"

"Better than that. News!"

"Let's get out of this sun and hear all about it," Willow said. She led them to a shady spot near where Maria played. "Don't keep us guessing, now."

"Yeah, spit it out!" Raven added.

"All right. Here it is: I located another Christian group, like yours, and they want to meet you."

Willow froze. Another group? Where? Did they have a cabin, too? Did they want to join up? Did *she* want anyone else to join her group? How would they feed any more mouths? It was exciting. Frightening. She had a million questions. And before Tony left, she'd make him answer them all.

4

"Where are they?" Raven asked. "When can we meet them?"

"Do they have any cute girls?" Matt wanted to know.

"If they have running water, I'm moving in with them!" Candy announced.

"Oh, yeah!" Kristie laughed.

Everyone seemed to have as many questions as Willow did. Except Jacob. He stood at the edge of the group, arms crossed in silence.

"Okay, now." Uncle Tony chuckled. "One at a time."

"Why don't you start by telling us how you met them, and what you know?" Willow suggested.

"Yeah," Josh agreed.

"Alright, I will." Uncle Tony drew a deep breath. "I've actually only met one of them, John Anderson. I was out one morning, scouting for a new hunting area, just around dawn. I'm standing at the edge of a clearing, just behind the tree line, and I see something move at the far side. Maybe a hundred yards or less.

"So this guy walks into the clearing, and he's wearing hunting gear – all camo – and he's got a nice rifle. I decide to stay quiet and just let him wander off. I'm not in a hurry to meet new folks, you know."

"But you did meet him," Raven urged.

"Yeah, I'm getting there," Tony continued. "The guy ends up coming straight across the clearing. Right at me! I couldn't disappear. He'd have heard me or seen me. So when he gets about ten yards from where I'm standing, I call out. 'Hey!'"

Tony mimicked the man's reaction. Wide eyes, stunned face, looked like he'd been hit. "Don't shoot, I'm a friendly!"

Tony smiled, remembering. "So I call back, 'So am I.' And I step out to meet him. We shake hands, I tell him a little about me, and he asks me to meet him there again the next morning. Says it's important. So, next morning, I show up, same time, same place. He's there early, sitting in the clearing. I scout the whole perimeter to make sure it's not some kind of trap. Nobody else is there, so I go out and say hi.

"He tells me he wanted me to come back that morning because he's part of a group and he wanted to tell them about me. They want me to join their group because of my years of living in the woods, hunting and fishing and all. Think I would be a huge asset.

"I ask what they're offering in return. He says I'd live at an off-grid retreat with a small group of other Christians. He knew right away when we met that I was a Christian because of my Ragamuffin Band t-shirt. Says the retreat has good running water from a spring above the house, propane stove and fridge, a big woodshed, fenced-in garden, and so on."

Kristie clapped her hands.

"That's it, we're going!" She grinned at Matt. "Running water!"

"I imagine there's a lot more than he told me. Probably a big supply of stored food. Maybe barns and animals. He did say his Bible study group had been preparing together for several years. They sensed bad stuff coming, and tried to get ready like the parable of the wise virgins."

Jacob coughed. "I don't remember that one."

Willow looked at him before explaining.

"If I remember right, there was going to be this big wedding feast, and the guests were waiting for the groom or the wedding party. The virgins all brought lamps because they knew it would be a while. The foolish virgins ran out of oil for their lamps, but the wise brought extra oil to re-fill their lamps. The foolish asked the wise to share their lamp oil, but the wise said they'd all run out if they did that. So the foolish went to buy oil, and while they were gone, the groom arrived and they went in to the party and shut the door. And the foolish were never allowed to enter."

She gazed at Uncle Tony.

"Is that about right?"

"That about sums it up. Now, where was I? Right – they've been prepping for a while. Anyway, John talked to his group, and they wanted me to join. I told him I'd give it some thought, but I'd already turned down another group. And I explained that I'm a loner. Liked my peace and quiet.

"Well, he was disappointed. I didn't tell him flat out no, mind you, but I didn't say yes, either. So he asked about this other group I'd turned down. And it was you, of course."

Tony looked at his niece.

"I told him I didn't feel free to say too much, in order to protect everyone's privacy, but that you're good Christian young-sters who fled from the I.D. task force. And you're likely to make it, because you've got skills and whatnot."

Willow's head hurt again. She touched her temple and winced.

"Got quite a shiner there," Tony said. "You okay?"

"I'll be fine. Got a lot of questions, though."

"Shoot."

"So you never met the rest of the group? Don't know how many there are, or where they live?"

"Right. But they want to meet you guys."

"All of them are going to meet all of us?" She wasn't sure if that was a good idea.

"We can set up whatever you want," Tony said. "Except not at their retreat. They want to keep that location secure. Unless you join, of course."

"We won't meet here, either," Willow said. "Maybe at that clearing where you first met John Anderson?"

"That'd be fine, I guess," Tony agreed.

"And I don't want all of us to go. Maybe just two. Or three." She glanced around the group, then back to Tony. "Could you set that up for two mornings from now?"

"No problem." He stretched his back. "I told John I'd meet him tomorrow morning and give him an answer from you. I'll be back here tomorrow in time for dinner, which hopefully will be pretty good, and then the next morning we'll get a very early start for that clearing."

THAT NIGHT, Willow called a meeting of her group. There were two items on the agenda. First, what to do about Jacob. And second, Tony's revelation about the other Christian group.

"Jacob, let's talk about you first," Willow said. "You arrived here yesterday, and I assume you talked with everyone about yourself then, but I don't know any of that. Do you have a place to live? A family to return home to? A group of friends that you'll be meeting up with?"

Jacob turned those big dark eyes on her.

"I was on my own. My family lives in Billings, so I won't be going back anytime soon. It's too far. I was just planning to live in the woods. A hunter gatherer, I guess."

"So, is that what you want to do?"

"Be a hunter?" He glanced quizzically at her. "Sure, something like that."

"No, I mean, do you intend to go live alone in the woods, in your tent?"

His eyes turned serious.

"I'd rather not." Jacob looked from one person to another. "I would like to stay here and become part of the group. Do what I can to help out."

"Alright, then," Willow said. "We'll have you step out for a while so we can discuss that."

He cocked an eyebrow. "Really?"

"Yes." She stood and opened the cabin door. "Really."

Jacob stood and walked out, and Willow closed the door behind him. She turned to her friends.

"Okay, you guys. Tell me what you think."

Josh spoke up first. "We should keep Jacob. I like him."

"Me, too," Matt said. "And, he's a hunter. We've been eating good venison since he arrived."

"He's a hard worker," Candy added. "It's nice to have a man around."

Willow shot a glance at her. Did Candy have a crush on Jacob? She had to be several years older than him!

"We should pray about it." Raven looked from one face to another. "But I'd have a hard time sending him away now. He's seen our place, and he knows what animals, supplies and gear we have here."

"If we told him to leave, you think he'd betray us?" Willow asked.

"Not necessarily." A slight frown wrinkled Raven's face. "But if he got caught... who knows? And he might feel that we betrayed him first, by sending him away after he helped you."

Josh looked at Willow. "What do you think?"

"I'm not sure. Raven is right, we do need to pray about it." She picked a piece of lint off her sleeve.

"Do you like him, though?" Josh persisted.

Her cheeks warmed at the question. Like him? Like him like what?

"He's okay, I guess," she replied. "I don't really know him."

She went on to explain how Jacob had held her at gunpoint when they met, and later tied up her hands.

"I certainly didn't like him then, but I might have done the same to someone, if I were in his position at the time." She took a deep breath. "You can't just have strangers hanging around your camp, obviously. And I was a little out of my head after I smashed my temple. So I forgive him for that. Plus, he carried me home. But I don't trust him yet."

She stood and glanced out the window. Jacob sat beside a larch tree at the edge of the clearing. It looked like he was whittling a stick.

"How about this – we'll tell him we're praying about it, and he can stay for a day or two, until we get some clarity on whether we're supposed to add him to our group. As a Christian, he will understand that."

WILLOW BARELY SLEPT the night before the meeting with the other group of Christians. Her mind whirled and wheeled. She couldn't wait to meet them. How many were there? Did they want to combine groups? Did she?

Lord, what do you have for us?

Maybe they could combine resources or work groups for big projects. How far away did they live? Even Uncle Tony didn't know that.

She'd take Raven and Josh with her. The others could take care of the animals and continue working on the garden. Maybe catch some fish.

Finally, pale light filtered through the cabin windows, and she got up and rousted Raven. She climbed the ladder to the guys' loft and grabbed Josh's foot in his sleeping bag. He grunted.

"Wake up and get ready to go." She shook his foot.

"Okay, okay!" He sat up. "I'm awake."

"Get ready." She descended the ladder, then lit a fire in the stove. They'd have a breakfast before they went on this morning's hike. Scrambled eggs, and some of Jacob's venison.

A glance out the side window revealed Tony rolling up his bedroll. He'd wanted to sleep under the stars instead of inside the cabin. She didn't blame him. The cabin was crowded and stuffy since they'd added two new people this week. Kristie had taken a lower bunk across from Candy, who had doubled up with her little girl, while Raven and Willow had moved to the top bunks.

Jacob made his way down the ladder. The little half loft was getting crowded with three guys up there now.

"Is my brother getting up?" She asked Jacob.

"Yeah, he's putting on his boots." Jacob ran his hands through his short dark hair. "Want me to come with you?"

"No." She put the cast iron pan on the top of the stove. "I'd love it if you'd catch some fish today, though."

His smile faded as he turned away and picked up his hat. He let himself out the door.

When breakfast was ready, Willow stepped outside and called Tony. She held the door open for him.

"Have you seen Jacob?"

"Yep. He went fishing."

"He could have had breakfast first."

Tony shrugged. "He didn't seem too happy when I saw him."

Willow frowned. So, was Jacob super sensitive? Pouting because he didn't get to go meet with the other group?

Whatever. She didn't have time to worry about his feelings.

She dished up breakfast for herself, Raven, Josh and Tony. The others were still sound asleep when they let themselves out of the cabin.

The sun's first rays brightened the tops of the trees on the hills. Tony took the lead, and they fell in single file behind him. They all carried their weapons and light packs with water, filters, a lunch of smoked trout, and rain gear.

Willow pushed a lock of hair away from her face and accidentally brushed her temple. Wow, that still hurt! But all the nausea and dizziness had cleared up. She'd spent most of the previous day close to the cabin recuperating and resting. Today she felt almost normal. As long as she didn't touch her head.

After an hour, Tony led the group down to a creek.

"Let's take a short break," he said. "We're not too far now. You might want to re-fill your bottles if you're getting low."

Josh and Willow filtered more water and filled their bottles, but Raven's bottle was mostly full still.

The rest of the hike was less than thirty minutes. They waited in the woods at the edge of the clearing. The fragrance of grass and wildflowers filled the air. Willow drummed her fingers on her pants. Where were the other guys? Were they here? On their way? Waiting in the woods?

Finally, motion caught her attention at the far edge of the clearing.

"That's John. Wait here for a minute." Tony stepped forward, moving out from the tree cover into the sunlit clearing. The two men met in the middle.

After a minute, Tony looked back toward Willow's group, and motioned for them to join him. Willow smiled. At last, they were meeting other believers who didn't take the mark! It felt like meeting distant family you didn't know yet.

Long strides took her swiftly to Tony's side. Raven and Josh were steps behind her.

Tony set his hand on Raven's shoulder.

"Raven, I'd like you to meet John Anderson. John, this is my niece, Raven."

They shook hands, then Tony introduced Willow and Josh.

"It's so nice to meet you, John." Willow couldn't stop smiling. "Did you bring anyone with you?"

"Not this time." John's eyes were clear and blue. Grey hair blended into brown in his close cropped style. He appeared to be about her height, 5'10" or so. "But next time, I hope. My wife can't wait to meet you."

"Why didn't she come today?" She didn't hide the disappointment in her voice.

"She has a migraine."

"Oh, I'm sorry. That must be miserable."

"It is, and the sunlight makes it worse, so she stayed at home."

Willow glanced around the clearing. It felt exposed.

"Do you mind if we move to the trees?"

"Not at all. That's a good idea." John followed them toward the forest. "So, how many are in your group?"

"We started out as four, but now we have eight," Willow answered.

"Young? Old? In between?"

"We have a toddler, and a woman in her forties. But the rest of us are teens and twenties. You?"

"We're a bit older than that. Our youngest member is in his forties. I'm fifty-one, and my wife is fifty. Then we've got some friends in their sixties and two in their seventies."

Whoa. They were way older, not *a bit.* They were all grand-parent age.

That was okay, though. She could use extra grandparents. Who couldn't?

"We started preparing for bad times and persecution when most of us were in our thirties and forties," John explained. "So we've been getting ready for decades. Now that it's bad, we're old."

He winked, and Willow smiled. He struck her as a nice guy. And Tony wouldn't have set up this meeting if he didn't have some confidence in John.

They talked a little longer, and agreed to meet again at the same location in two days. They all had a lot to think and pray about. The two groups' strengths and weaknesses seemed obvious: Willow's group was lacking in food and supplies, but they were young and strong. John's group had packed in the food and gear, but they were getting older and weaker. They didn't have the strength and stamina for work that Willow's group had.

There were some good reasons to combine the groups, Willow thought as they hiked back to the cabin. It'd be really nice to sleep in a real house with running water again. She smiled.

But more than that, her group could supply labor – chopping wood, gardening, and so on – while John's group could supply resources like tools, materials and food.

On the other hand, combining groups posed some problems, as well. Leadership, for one. John was clearly the kind of guy who was used to being in charge – and at his retreat, that made sense. But she was the leader of her group. The others looked to her and followed her decisions. Usually.

She didn't want a power struggle, and she was okay with being under another leader. But what if God told her something and John disagreed with it? How would they handle that?

Also, it might be risky to combine the groups from a security standpoint. If John Anderson's retreat location were compromised, everyone would be at risk – her and her group, as well as his. If they had to flee, they could return to the cabin, but nothing would be there for them. They would have moved the goats and chickens to John's place, and the garden would have died for lack of care.

These were all things to think and pray about for a few days. And they would be discussed in both groups, too. It was possible that John or his group wouldn't want anything to do with an outside group after they spent time considering it.

But for now, there was a more urgent matter: what to do about Jacob? Let him stay, or make him go?

5

As soon as <u>Willow</u> stepped into the clearing below the cabin, Matt whooped.

"They're back!" He yelled, blond hair blazing in the early afternoon sunshine.

Moments later, everyone gathered in front of the cabin.

"Well? How did it go?" Kristie could barely contain her enthusiasm. "Are we moving over to their place?"

"It went fine. But no, we're not moving yet."

"Where's Tony?" Candy asked.

Raven answered that one. "Uncle Tony headed off to do his own thing, as usual."

"Are we moving later?" Matt glanced from Raven to Willow.

"We don't know," Willow said. "We need to pray about what to do, and so do they."

"Are there any girls? Are they nice?" Matt looked pointedly at Josh.

"They're all really old," Josh answered. "We're *so* out of luck."

Disappointment drooped Matt's face. "That stinks!"

Willow laughed, then recounted the meeting, with Josh and Raven filling in details. Finally, Jacob spoke.

"What was your take on the guy? Can we trust him?"

"I think so, yes," Willow said. Raven and Josh nodded their agreement. After the questions wound down, Willow took up the other subject.

"A couple of days ago, we agreed to pray about you, Jacob. It's time for us to discuss that, so if you don't mind –"

He held up his hands in feigned surrender.

"I know, I know... I'll leave." He turned and walked toward the barn. Willow faced those remaining.

"Okay, what did you hear from the Lord?"

"I think he should stay," Kristie said.

"Me, too," Candy agreed. Matt and Josh nodded.

"Raven?" Willow studied her friend's face. Raven hesitated. Then slowly shook her head.

"I can't quite put my finger on it, but... I think he's a nice guy, but I think he should go."

"Why?" Candy demanded. "If he's a nice guy, why should he leave? We need the extra help."

"Right," Kristie said. "And what's he gonna do all alone out in the wilderness? Imagine if it was one of you. How would you feel? It's practically a death sentence!"

"What do you think, Willow?" Josh asked.

Willow sighed. She wasn't sure. Her prayers felt like they'd been falling short of Heaven lately, like they didn't quite make it to God's attention. Or like He'd stopped talking to her. It was puzzling and troubling.

In spite of that, she believed Raven was right, that Jacob should leave. But that didn't make any sense. He was strong and a good hunter, and they really could use his help. And kicking him out could be a death sentence – for him, or for the group, if he betrayed their location.

Personally, she was getting used to having him around. It was good for the boys to have a role model. And he was flat-out easy on the eyes.

Everyone was staring at her.

"I don't know."

Raven's eyebrows tightened. "What did God tell you?"

"I'm not sure." Willow wavered. "Maybe, since we don't seem to have a definite consensus, we should leave it alone for now and revisit it later."

Raven snorted. "Like the Israelites, when they went to spy out the Promised Land? Ten said it was too scary, and two trusted God? Consensus means nothing."

"Who's to say you're right?" Kristie challenged. "We all prayed about it, and four of us say it's okay for him to stay. You're the only one opposed."

"Now, hold on," Willow held up her hand before the meeting could get uglier. Her head hurt. Raven was maybe the strongest believer in the group. So her opinion rated higher than say, Kristie's or Candy's, for sure. But anyone could be wrong. Even Raven.

She just couldn't, in good conscience, send Jacob away right now. It was too dangerous for him, too dangerous for the group, and besides, she owed him for bringing her home safely the other day.

She rubbed her eyebrow and accidentally brushed her temple. Oh, ow! Had to stop doing that!

"Okay, here's what we're going to do: everybody is going to pray about it again. We'll have another meeting to make a decision."

"When?" Raven looked at Willow like she was a coward.

"Soon."

Police Captain Marcus Laramie picked a location at the rear of the crowd, where he could keep an eye on everyone. He planted his feet and crossed his arms. Mayor Danielle Challis was just calling the special City Council meeting to order in the town square as the sun began sliding down behind Deadman's Peak.

The Council whizzed through the preliminaries and got right down to the good stuff. Power and water.

"As some of you have already heard, water service will begin tomorrow," Mayor Challis said.

Cheers rose from the crowd. She lifted her hand for silence.

"Now, hold on – there are important things to keep in mind. We've been having the police go around to all the neighborhoods, and asking you to tell all your neighbors, too – this is not pure, treated water. It's creek water."

A few voices murmured.

"So boil it before you use it for drinking or cooking or brushing your teeth."

The mayor's gaze swept across the crowd.

"If you fail to do that, you are likely to get very sick. Old folks and little ones are most vulnerable. People could die."

"But we'd definitely die without the water," a baritone voice yelled. Marcus turned his attention on the man standing at the far edge of the crowd. A tall guy, brown cowboy hat, grey hair, probably packing... someone to keep an eye on, for sure.

"That's why we're turning it on," the mayor said. "But it's up to you to use it safely and make sure all your neighbors know to boil it first. Otherwise...."

She threw her hands up in the air.

"Well, you've been warned."

Marcus almost smiled. Tomorrow, he'd heat up a bunch of water on his wood stove and take a bath. Get really clean for the first time in weeks.

A woman in the front row raised her hand, and the mayor called on her.

"What about the sewage? I mean, if we're all using water again, flushing it down our drains and toilets, what happens to it?"

"That's a very good question, and we have more good news about that," the mayor said. "I'm going to have our public works director, Tom Higgins, explain how we're going to handle it."

Tom made his way to the front and climbed up on the bandstand with the mayor and council.

"First of all, you should know we found some old transformers in the shop, and crews are installing them as we speak."

The crowd roared in approval.

"We're gonna have power, too!" Mr. Cowboy Hat yelled.

"Now, hold on – I didn't say anything about that," Tom countered.

"But you just said you're installing transformers."

"Those are very old, sixty, seventy years old," Tom said. "We don't even know if they can handle the load and still work. These were the old ones that we replaced about fifteen years ago."

The crowd murmured, but Tom held up his hand and continued.

"We're installing them on a direct line from the dam to the sewage treatment plant. If all goes as planned, we'll have enough power to treat the sewage before it's released into the river."

The lady in the front row raised her hand again.

"And if there's not enough power... then what?"

Tom looked at the mayor for guidance. She stood up.

"As a last resort, if the treatment plant can't be brought online, then, well... it'll go into the river anyway."

"Raw sewage? Dumped into the Bethel?" The front row woman yelled. "You can't be serious."

Marcus moved from his position at the rear of the crowd and made his way up along the left edge. If this lady didn't settle down, he wanted to be closer if he needed to intervene.

"We hope not," the mayor said. "But if it comes down to that or no water to the residents – that's what might have to happen."

"It'll destroy the ecosystem," the woman huffed. "The EPA –"

The mayor laughed.

"If you can get the EPA here, I'll be the first to kiss their feet." She stared into the crowd. "We're on our own, folks. Nobody is coming to help Ponderosa. Or the State of Montana, for that matter.

"But we're incredibly fortunate here. We have a good, strong community. And unlike most towns, we have our own power generating dam, and gravity-fed water. How many other towns can say that?

"Almost none, that's how many!"

WILLOW TURNED RESTLESSLY in her sleeping bag. Trouble stirred around her, disturbing her sleep and her dreams. But she couldn't recall the dreams, just that they seemed... weird. She opened her eyes.

The full moon shone in the front window, casting a cold, pale light on the table and chairs. Above her head, she heard one of the boys rustling in the loft. Maybe they had a bad dream, too.

A lonesome howl, then another, then a third filled the night air. Wolves. And they sounded close!

Were the chickens okay? The goats? Gilligan was outside, and he was no match for wolves. Wide awake but weary, Willow unzipped her sleeping bag.

A figure climbed silently down the loft ladder. Bigger than

Josh and Matt. It was Jacob. Willow was about to get out of her bunk, but she stopped.

In the dim moonlight, she watched Jacob pick up his rifle. The door opened, he stepped out, and then it closed quietly and the latch clicked.

Willow lay back on her pillow. Jacob must have heard the wolves, too, and had done what she was going to do – make sure the barn was secure and the animals were okay. She zipped up her sleeping bag and closed her eyes.

The others were right. It was really nice having a man around.

The next thing she knew, sunlight streamed in where the moonbeams had been. Raven was up, stoking a fire for breakfast. Willow climbed down from her bunk and dressed quickly. Candy, Kristie, and little Maria were still sound asleep.

Willow picked up the water pail.

"I'll go fill this," she said as she opened the door.

Raven looked at her, but said nothing.

She was probably still mad that Willow hadn't been ready to send Jacob away. And now she had one less reason to. She walked around the corner of the cabin and smacked right into Jacob.

"Whoa, there, Missy," he said, pulling his rifle out of her way. "Where you going in such a hurry?"

"Why do you keep calling me Missy?" It was beyond annoying.

A slow smile turned his lips and brought out his dimples.

"When you officially met me, I told you my name was Jacob. But by then, I'd nursed you through an afternoon and evening, when I didn't know your name. You looked like a Missy to me, so that's what I called you."

"You called me Missy when you didn't know me?" That was

so weird. "Why don't you call me Willow now? You know my name."

The dimples deepened.

"You'll always be Missy to me. That's how I first knew you."

She couldn't look into those deep brown eyes any longer. Turning aside, she stepped out of his way.

"I'm going to the creek." She swung the pail like a goofy kid. Ugh.

"There's wolves around. I'll go with you." He fell in step beside her.

She wanted to argue, but there wasn't much room for argument. She'd forgotten to holster her sidearm when she got dressed, again. Well, it'd be the last time she did that. Foolish mistake!

"Are the animals okay?" She decided not to mention that she'd seen him go out in the middle of the night.

"They're fine." He shouldered his weapon. "I'd like to strengthen that barn, though. I'm not sure wolves couldn't get in, and I know bears could."

He was right. Her group had converted the shed to a barn as best they could, but they hadn't had the proper tools or materials to do it right. The entire front was pretty flimsy. Any old bear could let himself right in and help himself to a goat and chicken feast.

"Okay," Willow said. "Get Josh and Matt to help you."

"Just okay?" He stopped and waited until she halted and looked back. "Not, 'Thank you, Jacob?'"

"Fine." She let the tiniest smile slip through. "Thank you, Jacob."

He grinned and caught up with her. They walked in silence to the creek, and she filled the pail. Just as she was lifting it out of the water, she felt a touch on her shoulder. She glanced up.

Jacob lifted his hand and raised his finger over his lips to silence her. He pointed upstream.

Willow set the pail on the ground and followed his gaze.

Something moved through the trees. Deer? Bear?

Then she saw a flash of royal blue. So it wasn't an animal, it was a person. Very, very close to her group's cabin!

Adrenaline pounded her heart. Who was it? The agents? Some random person out in the forest?

She strained her eyes, but saw nothing more.

Had she and Jacob been spotted? Were they, at the moment, being surrounded? She glanced around wildly.

Oh, God, help us! What should we do?

She wanted to run, to race back home and slam the door. But that would be stupid. It would just bring the danger to her friends and her brother.

No, if this person or people meant to harm or capture her, she'd do her best to lead them away from the cabin.

The birds had silenced, but the creek sang noisily in its rush downhill. The water masked the noise that she listened for – a branch breaking or a voice speaking, or anything, really, that could tell her what that person was doing.

She turned around, looking for danger in all directions. Somebody was out there. Had she been spotted, too? Or had she and Jacob been unnoticed?

Jacob bumped her elbow, and she nearly jumped out of her boots. He gave her a warning stare, then pointed upstream again.

She couldn't see anything. What was he looking at?

A glint, a reflection, drew her eye to a big log. Resting on top of it was a rifle scope. Pointed at her. Or maybe at Jacob.

6

Slowly, <u>Willow</u> raised her hands. No point in getting shot. She could run, and get shot. Or move suddenly, and get shot.

<u>Jacob</u> stood his ground. His hands did not go up.

She turned her head and glanced at him. His rifle still hung over his shoulder.

Finally, he lifted his hands, too.

Mr. Scoped Rifle had the drop on them. If he was any kind of accurate, he wouldn't miss when they were this close. Willow estimated about fifty yards.

"Put your gun down," Mr. Scoped Rifle called over the noise of the creek. "Nice and slow!"

Jacob looped his thumb through his shoulder strap and eased the rifle to the ground. Now they were fully at this guy's mercy. Willow wanted to cry.

Was it an agent?

After all this time running and hiding, and finally feeling somewhat safe... had the agents finally found them? The I.D. Task Force would round them up *now*?

A twig snapped behind her. Willow's head whirled toward

the sound. A woman stepped out of the woods, a handgun trained on Jacob.

"Step away from the gun!" The woman's jeans were torn at the knee, her grey hair fastened away from her face. A thick leather belt kept her loose pants secure above her hips.

There was no way she was an agent.

Jacob took a step back. The woman approached and bent to pick up his rifle.

He pounced toward her, fluidly grasping her wrist with his left hand, knocking her gun out of her grip, and yanking her up in front of him. At the same moment, his right hand flashed behind his back and produced a handgun, which he pointed at her head.

The woman cried out as she tried to find her balance.

Willow took advantage of the changing dynamic, grabbed up Jacob's rifle, and launched herself behind a tree. She trained the gun on Mr. Scoped Rifle.

Her heart thudded as she focused on the man in her gun sight. Jacob had a handgun? She'd never seen it before. And he acted like he knew what he was doing – he took control of that woman like he'd been trained. As a cop? Military?

Why hadn't she found out more about him? He'd been pretty quiet, never volunteering much information about himself. Who was this guy, anyway?

"Set the rifle down and step out where I can see you, or I'll blow her head off," Jacob threatened Mr. Scoped Rifle, whose options were suddenly limited. He could try to shoot Jacob, but might hit the woman. And he couldn't know Willow had no desire to kill him, the way she kept him in her sights.

His gun lowered.

"Don't shoot. I'm coming out."

Willow took a breath and released it slowly, keeping the rifle trained on his center of mass. He raised his hands and stepped into the open.

His wrinkles and grey hair indicated he was about sixty, maybe the same as the woman. His dusty clothing hung a little loose. He wore a royal blue and black flannel shirt, black jeans held up by a plain black leather belt, and hiking boots. He was certainly not an agent.

"Come on over here, nice and slow," Jacob ordered. "No funny business!"

The man kept his hands in the air as he approached.

"How many more are there?" Jacob demanded. He pressed the barrel of his handgun into the woman's cheek when she looked at the man and shook her head.

"I can't say," the man answered.

"What are you doing out here?" Willow asked.

"Camping." The woman's voice trembled.

"How long have you been here?" Willow kept the rifle trained on the man, but glanced quickly at the woman.

"We just got here last night."

"It's an awful long way to hike in from the nearest road," Willow retorted.

"We like hiking."

Willow doubted that. They weren't dressed like typical hikers, with daypacks and sunglasses and non-cotton clothing and hiking poles. No, these people looked homeless. Like her group had been before Tony brought them to the cabin.

Could they be Christians?

"Do you have the mark?" Willow asked.

The woman's glance raced between Willow and the man. She set her lips in a firm line and said nothing.

Keeping the rifle aimed at the man, Willow moved toward the woman and swiftly grabbed her right hand, feeling the soft flesh between the woman's thumb and first finger. It felt totally natural. Probably no I.D. chip.

"Are you Christians?" Willow demanded.

The woman's blue eyes met hers.

"I am." Her voice quaked when she said it, but she held her head up.

"Good! So are we."

The blue eyes filled with tears.

"Oh, thank God!"

Willow and Jacob lowered their weapons, and Jacob released his hold on the woman.

"I'm Willow. Sorry for the scare." She stuck out her hand, and the other woman took it.

"I'm Deborah. This is my husband, Alan."

Alan stepped forward, a grim look on his face. Willow could understand. He'd probably never seen his wife held at gunpoint before, and probably didn't expect that when he'd first confronted Willow and Jacob.

"Hello," Jacob offered. "Sorry about the tension."

The man nodded. "I started it."

Now what? Willow glanced at the new faces. She was uncomfortable about strangers being so close to her cabin, even if they were believers. But there were only two, and they probably wouldn't make more trouble. She could be charitable. And she knew what they probably needed most.

"Do you have enough to eat?" Her eyes studied Deborah, whose gaze shot to her husband. Slowly she shook her head.

"We haven't eaten in two days," she admitted. "And not a lot the week before that."

"Well, I guess we should offer you breakfast, then," Willow said.

Jacob's eyes narrowed, and he shot Willow a questioning look. She mouthed the word "What?" at him.

"We still don't know how many there are," he hissed.

"Right." She glanced at the couple. "I'm sorry. We can't feed a whole tribe. So if there's more than the two of you –"

"Please! We have two grandchildren!" Deborah glanced at her husband. "You don't have to feed us anything. But if you could feed the kids...."

Her words trailed off as she stared imploringly at Willow.

Kids. Oh, great! How could she turn down starving kids? She glanced at Jacob and saw his expression soften just a little.

"So there's four of you then?" Willow asked. They could afford to feed four people breakfast. Especially if some of her group skipped it today.

"Actually..." Deborah glanced at Alan, who cleared his throat and gave her a firm look. She ignored it and plunged on anyway. "Our daughter, and her husband, the kids' parents, are with us, too."

"You shouldn't give so much information to strangers," Jacob said. "What if we were just deceiving you? What if we were the bad guys?"

"But you're not." Deborah looked from Jacob to Willow. "Are you?"

"No." She shot Jacob a reproving look. "We're not."

"Can I talk to you for a minute?" Jacob asked.

"Sure." Willow nodded, and began moving away from the couple. "Why don't you guys gather your things?"

Alan picked up Deborah's handgun, wiped it off and handed it back to her. Jacob and Willow walked just out of hearing range.

"You're going to feed six people? And then what?" Jacob asked. "They obviously can't feed themselves. They're losing weight fast, that's why their clothes are so loose. Are you just going to let them move into the cabin? What's your plan?"

"My plan is to do what's right. And leaving starving Christians in the woods is definitely not right."

"So your plan is to bring them to the cabin." He stared at her.

"Yes. There aren't a lot of options."

"You could just bring a meal out here, to them."

Willow rolled her eyes. "And you don't think they'd sneak behind us, finding the cabin anyway? They know we live somewhere, and we have food. And the cabin is so close, it's surprising they didn't accidentally find it already!"

"I just don't like it." Jacob looked past her at the couple. "And another thing is, I really don't like that you're happy to bring them home and feed them, while you've been so undecided about whether I can stay. And I bring something to the mix!"

"We will pray about what to do about them also. But we'll feed them first, because that's right." She stared him down. "It's important that we hear from God. And you, Jacob, are not in their position. You're able to take care of yourself."

His dark eyes locked with hers. A long silence followed as neither blinked. Finally, he turned away.

"Fine. It's your family and friends at risk. Not mine."

Anger heated her cheeks. He didn't care about her group after living with them for days? He didn't consider them friends yet? Maybe Raven was right. Maybe they should send him away.

Willow gave him a glare and stomped away. She tried to release the tension from her face as she reached Deborah and Alan.

"Okay, you guys. If you'll gather your family, you can come have breakfast with us."

"Thank you." Gratitude shone in Alan's face. "You don't know how much this means."

"You're welcome. Let's get going."

Jacob returned to the cabin to give the group a heads up on

the new arrivals, while Willow went with Deborah and Alan to
meet the rest of the Wilcox family.

She didn't have to walk far. They'd set up camp about a
quarter mile upstream. And "camp" was a generous term.

There were no tents. A white cotton cord suspended a blue
tarp between two trees. The tarp was staked to the ground on
one side, forming a big lean-to in front of the fire ring. Bedding
under the tarp indicated that the family slept there.

A black man sat on a log, warming his hands before the fire. He
appeared a bit older than the brown-haired woman beside him.
She stood up when her parents and Willow walked into the camp.

"Mom? Who's this?" She smiled tentatively at Willow. The
man looked up, but didn't smile.

Deborah introduced Willow to Jaci and Clark Collins. Jaci
glanced at her dad, then shook Willow's hand.

"I guess you've met Dad's approval," Jaci said.

Clark rose to his feet slowly, unfolding a tall, lanky figure
and a long, easy smile. His short, coiled hair indicated African,
but his facial features revealed a mixed race ancestry. He took
Willow's hand in his massive one.

"How do you do?" His formal words were spoken with an
accent she couldn't quite place.

"I'm fine, thanks," she responded, falling into her grandmother's formal greeting pattern. "And you?"

"We are blessed." His hands swept around, indicating the
camp and the fire.

"Well, I'm here to bring you to breakfast," she announced. "I
understand you have children?"

"They are at the creek." Clark turned his dark brown eyes on
her. "You are an angel."

She burst into a laugh. "Hardly!"

"I'll go round up the kids," Alan said. "Be right back."

He disappeared into the woods, returning moments later with two girls. Willow found herself gawking. These weren't kids, they were teenagers. And beautiful ones. Tall and slim like their dad, they were graced with black hair, flawless brown skin and their mom's hazel eyes.

Their grandmother wrapped an arm around each of the girls, and beamed.

"These are our grandchildren, Beth and Delia. Girls, this is Willow."

They both said "Hello" at the same time, then glanced at each other and giggled.

"It's nice to meet you." Willow smiled. "And how old are you?"

"I'm twelve," Beth said. "And she's fourteen."

"Almost fifteen," Delia clarified.

"Okay, then. If you'll follow me, we'll see about getting you some breakfast."

A short hike brought them to the clearing, and the cabin came into view. Smoke curled from the chimney into the cold morning air. Her group assembled in front of the cabin, looking expectantly at the new arrivals. Jacob stood in the back, his arms crossed. Josh elbowed Matt, and the two exchanged a significant look.

Willow introduced everyone. Raven graciously stepped forward.

"Jacob told us you were coming, so we have breakfast ready for you."

"Did you eat already?" Deborah asked.

"No," Raven said. "We've all agreed to skip this morning, so there's enough for you and our little Maria."

Deborah looked like she wanted to protest, but her hunger won out.

"Thank you. Everyone." Her gaze moved from one to another. "That's so kind of you."

Beth's stomach growled. She looked down and covered her stomach with her fingers.

"Well, come in, then," Raven smiled. "The food's getting cold!"

Raven pushed the door open and went inside, followed by the hungry family. Josh and Matt started to follow, but Willow stopped them.

"Let's let them eat in peace. We can visit afterwards," she said. Both boys looked disappointed.

"Did you guys get the goats milked yet?" she asked.

They shook their heads.

"Well, hurry up! You won't want to miss anything."

They took off for the barn in a run.

AFTER THEY FINISHED their venison and egg breakfast, the family joined Willow's group outside. They thanked their hosts profusely.

"Well, let's get to know each other a little," Willow suggested. The sun had finally warmed the ground, so everyone sat on the grass in front of the cabin. Willow jumped in with her questions.

"So, how did you come to be in the forest with nothing... not even a tent?"

Alan coughed.

"It wasn't planned that way," he said. "We thought we had more time. We had gathered some supplies, just in case. But there was a big sweep. We all got caught."

"What? How did you get free?" Raven asked.

Willow's heart skipped a beat. Her mom had been caught in a sweep at a church in Missoula. If these folks escaped, it was possible that her mom might have, too. She shot a look at her brother, who was staring at her, his eyes wide.

"It was the strangest thing," Alan said. "We were on a prisoner transport to Red Lodge. There were twenty Christians on the bus, and six felons. Scary looking guys. Anyway, we were just a couple miles out of Ponderosa, and the bus died.

"The driver got it pulled over to the side of the road, and radioed for help, but nobody responded. My family and I were all in the rear of the bus, and the criminals were in the front. I couldn't see exactly what happened, but next thing I knew, the criminals had jimmied the lock or something and they overpowered the guard and driver and killed them!"

"Crazy!" Matt interjected. "Then what?"

"The criminals ran, and so did we. They headed toward Ponderosa, and we headed for the woods."

"When was this, exactly?" Kristie asked.

"Just over a week ago, I guess," Alan answered.

Clark nodded. "Yeah, a little over a week."

"Where were you when you were rounded up?" Willow asked.

"Kalispell. That's where we live," Beth piped up. "But we know Ponderosa, because Great O'pa Wilcox used to live there."

"That's right," her grandfather said. "My dad lived here in his retirement. So we came to visit pretty often. In fact, that's where we went first. Dad died about a year ago, but his house hasn't sold yet. We had it staged before we put it on the market, so it was pretty cleaned out, but we found a tarp in his barn, along with a few other things we grabbed from the house, like some bedding and kitchen pans. Too bad we didn't leave more useful things there when we listed it for sale."

Clark stretched out his arms. "But we are free. We are together. We are blessed!"

"Amen, that's right," Deborah agreed.

The groups talked a while longer, then went to work. Jacob and Josh went hunting, the older men and Matt went to chop firewood, and the ladies set to work on the garden. Raven beckoned Willow to the far end of the row, where she spoke in a hushed voice.

"How's your spiritual life going?"

Willow sighed. "Not the best. I've been so busy! Just trying to stay alive."

"It's the one thing that matters most," Raven reminded her.

"I know." She turned over a dirt clod and smacked it with her trowel.

"We need to pray about Jacob and the new folks."

"Yeah." Willow glanced toward Deborah and Jaci, who were painstakingly planting tiny carrot seeds one by one. Beth and Delia worked the next row, planting beans. Kristie and Candy led the goats out of the barn and staked them to graze.

"I like their family," Raven whispered. "But I don't see how we can take them in. There's no room in the cabin, and we can barely feed ourselves."

"I like them, too." Willow pulled out a weed. "Let's pray together."

They bowed their heads over their freshly dug row, and asked the Holy Spirit to lead and guide them, and bless their new friends.

JUST BEFORE DINNER, Jacob and Josh returned empty handed.

"We didn't see any deer, and very few tracks," Jacob said. "It's like the game population is just disappearing."

"We heard some gunshots, though," Josh added.

Willow winced. "Were they close?"

"Nah. We were a couple miles out, and they were maybe another half mile. Hard to tell exactly."

"Poachers, probably," Jacob said.

"Like us." Josh glanced at his sister. "Maybe the other Christian group?"

"Could be."

Clark turned his dark eyes on Willow. "There's another Christian group?"

"Yes, and that's what I want to talk about over dinner. Let's go in and get some stew."

"Stew again?" Josh's shoulders slumped.

"Be thankful for it." Willow tousled his hair. "A week ago, you would've danced for joy for stew. Tonight, you can ask the blessing. And give thanks."

The groups gathered, and Josh prayed over the food. Again they ate outside, since there wasn't enough room in the cabin.

Deborah spoke up.

"What's this about another group?"

"We've just met them." Willow set her spoon into her stew. "Actually, only a few of us met one member of their team. We discussed whether we should join together, and agreed to pray about it and meet up again."

"Where do they live?" Clark asked.

"We aren't sure. We've been meeting in a clearing. They don't know our location, either."

"A security measure?" Alan glanced at Willow.

"Exactly. If one of them is caught, they can't reveal our location. And same if one of us is caught. Their retreat won't be compromised."

"Their retreat?" Deborah asked. "Like a house, not just a camp?"

"Yes. Look, I don't want to say too much right now. But I'm going back to meet with their leader, and I'd like to take one of you with me to meet him. I hope they might take you in, since we don't have a lot of room here."

Josh glanced at the girls. His shoulders drooped.

"But we could make room," he offered.

"We wouldn't want to impose." Jaci glanced from her mom to Willow.

"I'm sure you wouldn't," Willow said. "But we can't just leave you out in the woods under a tarp. It's one thing in the summer, quite another in the fall, and deadly in the winter."

Alan finished his stew and set his bowl on the grass.

"When are you going to meet their leader?"

"We'll set out at dawn tomorrow."

"Clark or I will join you." He rose, thanked everyone for dinner, and gathered his tribe. As they headed back to their camp, Jacob joined Willow at the corner of the cabin.

"They have to go live at the retreat. There's no way we can feed them," he said.

Willow turned her gaze to his serious face.

"With God, all things are possible."

She went into the cabin, retrieved her Bible, and walked out to the barn. The boys had just brought in the chickens, and they were talking quietly between themselves as they brought in the goats. A smile, a jab in the ribs... Willow could guess just what – or whom – they were talking about... the pretty Collins girls.

After they corralled the goats in the barn stall, they boys wandered off, and Willow had the place to herself. As a farm girl, she always liked barns. The clucking of hens, the contented noises of the animals, the fragrance of oats and hay. Hay? They'd need to harvest a bunch for winter. They could hand-harvest a lot of the tall grass in the fall, and let it dry in the sun, then store it. It'd be great to have a sickle or scythe, but that was just one more thing they didn't have. Oh, well. They'd find a way to make do.

Willow settled herself on the floor and opened her Bible and read the 24th and 25th chapters of Matthew. She prayed for forgiveness for neglecting spiritual matters, and asked for wisdom about Jacob and the new family.

When she opened her eyes, Raven was shaking her shoulder.

"Hey, were you planning to sleep out here tonight?"

Daylight had faded into the darkest dusk.

"No." Willow held out her hand, and Raven pulled her to her feet. Together, they walked back to the cabin and crawled into their bunks.

7

Willow jerked awake, gasping for air. Her heart pounded and her damp skin chilled as she broke away from her sleeping bag.

The dream had been bad, but she could only remember snippets of it. Running through the trees. Jacob on her heels. Was he chasing her? Or were they both running from someone else?

She took calming breaths and scanned the shadows in the cabin. No movement. No noise.

Still, the hair on the nape of her neck tingled. Something was not right.

She slid silently off the bunk. Her bare feet hit the cold plank floor. No one appeared awake downstairs.

Quietly, she stepped to the ladder and climbed up so she could see into the loft. In the dim moonlight through the window, she saw Jacob's form motionless in his sleeping bag, and the same with the boys.

Her hands shook as she climbed down the ladder. She went to the table and sat down, looking out the window. Eventually, her heart rate slowed to normal. But she had no desire to get back into bed.

Finally, darkness devolved into the opening strains of dawn. When she could make out the deep blue ridges of the eastern mountains, she dressed, then went to Raven's bunk and gently shook her shoulder. Raven's eyes flew open.

"What?"

"Shhhh. Get dressed. I need to talk to you!"

"Okay," Raven whispered.

Willow went to the outhouse, and when she returned, Raven was up, dressed and starting a fire. She shot a questioning gaze at Willow.

Willow beckoned her out the door. Raven slipped out, pulling the door closed behind them.

"What's going on?"

"I'm not sure, but something seems off. I had a bad dream."

"Was it one of your visions?"

"No. I don't remember much about it, just that it was bad." Willow's gaze scanned the horizon before she continued. "I have to go meet John today and I'm taking Alan or Clark with me. Would you stay close to Jacob and keep an eye on him?"

"Sure. But why?"

"You're the one I trust the most. And I don't trust him."

"Neither do I."

"And one more thing... it's weird that Alan and Deborah have guns, don't you think?"

"Everyone has guns. This is Montana!"

"Except that they were prisoners. And they said they ran straight for the forest."

"Good point. But they stopped at his father's house."

"But they said it was staged for sale. I don't think they'd store guns there, do you?"

Raven shook her head. "Probably not."

"If you get a chance with one of the adults alone, ask how

they got the guns. I'll try to ask whoever comes with me today. We can compare notes and make sure the stories match when I get back to the cabin."

At dawn, Willow retrieved her jacket and glanced out the window in time to see <u>Alan</u> walking up to the cabin. He didn't carry his rifle with him. Maybe he had the sidearm his wife had used yesterday?

Willow grabbed her pack, making sure her water filter and bottle were in it, along with some ammo. She handed Alan a big piece of venison jerky, and they began walking. He started to fall behind, so she slowed her pace.

As she walked, she prayed. Life could be such a puzzle sometimes! Even when she tried to do right, she could mess things up. Like when she'd gone searching for her brother and ran into Jacob instead.

And now, she was meeting with John about possibly combining their groups. But she was bringing a new group into the scenario. This could upset the whole applecart.

Lord, please guide and direct us!

She stopped at the creek and filtered water for her bottle. Alan scooped creek water up in his hands and lifted them to his lips.

"Stop! Don't drink that!"

He paused, water dripping between his fingers as he looked at her.

"You don't have a filter." She pointed out the obvious.

"Right. But I'm thirsty."

"You all have been drinking creek water this whole time without filtering or boiling it first?"

"Sometimes we boil it in camp. But out here – " He shrugged.

"Okay, drink mine." She held her bottle out to him. "It's safe."

"You sure?"

She nodded. He accepted it and took a long swig.

"Mmmm, that's good."

It was amazing that they'd been drinking creek water and no one had gotten sick yet. Maybe they happened to stumble across safe water, or maybe God had just protected them. In any case, it was foolish to mess around with the water in these mountains. Giardia was not fun, as she'd unpleasantly discovered on a campout a few years ago. The intestinal distress, the runs, the antibiotics... she'd never forget that experience.

They continued on, and soon reached the clearing. John was waiting in the sun at the far side. He waved them over.

Willow introduced the men and explained to John that they'd happened across this family of believers.

"They don't have supplies, and we don't have extra room in the cabin," she said. "I wonder if your group could take them in."

"Wow. Six more people?" John ran his hand through his greying brown hair. "We'll have to pray about that. It could totally swamp our resources. Sink us all."

Alan's expression went flat. "We wouldn't want to be a burden."

"No, I'm sure you wouldn't. It's just that, well, we've been preparing for a long time. We see our group as the wise virgins in the Matthew 25 parable. The ones who brought extra oil for their lamps."

"And we're the foolish virgins," Alan added.

"I don't know. We don't know you."

"But you were considering taking in Willow's group. You just met them, too."

"That is true. Look, I don't want to argue. We will pray about it. Sincerely." John looked from Alan to Willow. "Her group is different, though. They're young, healthy workers with skills like farming, fishing and hunting."

"I see."

"I hope so. It's not personal."

"Okay."

Willow's shoulders drooped. This was not what she'd hoped for. Now what?

John turned to her. "Did you all pray about possibly joining up?"

It felt awkward to answer that question in front of Alan, whose family had pretty much just been rejected.

"We did."

And suddenly the answer was clear to her.

"For security, I think it's better to remain separate for now, but mutually available for emergencies. If you need sudden help, you could summon us, and vice versa."

"That works for us," John said. "How will we reach you?"

"It would make sense if one member of each of our groups knows the location of the other group. If something comes up, that person could hike over and request assistance."

"Sounds good. Why don't I walk home with you today, and then we can meet here again tomorrow and I'll bring you to our place?"

"Alright. Let's get started, so you can get back home before it gets too hot."

Conversation was sparse on the walk back to the cabin. When they arrived at the clearing, John looked impressed. With help from Raven, Jacob and the boys were building a strong log front on the barn shed, and the others were watering the garden with pails from the creek. Clark chopped logs for the barn, while Delia and Beth babysat Maria and kept an eye on the goats. The hens clucked happily in their portable pen, scratching for bugs and grubs.

"You've got quite a work crew going here." John stretched his arms.

"We've got a lot to do before winter," Willow said.

"And you're making excellent progress."

"We have a good team. Would you like to meet everyone before you return home?"

"Absolutely!" John smiled.

THAT NIGHT AFTER DINNER, Raven pulled Willow aside, and they walked out to the barn. Willow admired the work on the front wall. It was more than half way finished.

"This is definitely going to keep out wolves," Willow said. "You guys are doing a great job!"

"Thanks." Raven ran her hand across a log. They'd left the bark on the logs because they didn't have the tools to remove it. "Did you get a chance to talk to Alan about the guns?"

Willow smacked her forehead.

"Sheesh! I forgot!"

"It's okay. For the best, probably. I talked to Deborah, and she said that her father-in-law, the guy that died last year, was a prepper. When they found the tarp in the barn, they realized it was covering an old freezer that he'd buried in the floor. They found the guns and ammo there, along with two sleeping bags, the belts that they're wearing, and some random other stuff."

"What kind of other stuff?"

"She was vague on that," Raven said. "But it does explain how they got the guns."

"Yeah, that makes sense." Willow took a deep breath, inhaling the fragrance of the freshly cut pine. "Notice anything weird about Jacob?"

"Not really. He's pretty quiet, doesn't talk much."

"Well, please keep an eye on him when I'm not around. I don't trust him yet."

"Are we going to send him away?"

"We probably should. I just haven't figured out how to do that."

"Let's pray about it."

"Yeah, and about the new family."

Together, they bowed their heads and asked for divine help and guidance. Afterwards, Willow looked at her friend.

"I believe we should invite Alan and Deborah's family to join our group. There's not room in the cabin, but together, we can build one for their family."

Raven's eyes shone.

"I agree. They need us."

"We'll talk to them about it tomorrow. After I get back from going to John Anderson's place."

8

The morning's first rays found Willow making her way to the clearing to meet with John Anderson. Her step was light and quick. The trail to the clearing was becoming familiar, in a comfortable sort of way.

She arrived at the clearing just as John stepped out from the trees on the far side. He had a woman with him, trim and fit, average height. John waved to Willow. They met, once again, in the middle of the clearing.

"Willow, this is my wife, Jeannie."

They exchanged greetings, then John led the way back to their home. They crested a hill before descending into a bowl-shaped valley.

"This slope feeds our water system," John said. "We've got a developed spring that flows into a cistern, which gravity feeds to the house."

"So we always have running water," Jeannie explained.

"Nice!" Willow would love to have a plumbed toilet, not to mention a kitchen sink. "How long have you lived here?"

"Oh, not long," Jeannie began, but John cut her off.

"We bought the place twenty years ago, but actually moved in two years ago."

The trees thinned, and Willow spied the back of the house. It was a two-story with cedar siding, a green metal roof, and a daylight basement.

"It's beautiful!" she exclaimed.

Jeannie smiled. "We sure like it. Not a bad spot to ride out the end times."

"The barn is over there," John said, pointing east. It looked like a pole building, with brown metal sides and roof.

"What kind of animals do you have?" Willow asked.

"A couple of Brown Swiss cows, two horses and a flock of chickens," John answered. "C'mon, I'll show you the house and you can meet our crew."

They walked in the back door and Willow caught her breath. It was a mix of modern and rustic, with floor to peak windows on the front, facing south. The light flooded the kitchen, dining room and living room.

"The master suite is on this floor, and the other bedrooms and bathrooms are downstairs, in our daylight basement." John headed for the stairs. "I'll see if I can round everyone up."

Willow surveyed the home. Huge cowboy paintings graced the walls, and a trophy elk antler hung over the fireplace. Brown leather chairs and a sofa welcomed relaxation in the living room, and the dining area provided ample space for a long table with ten chairs. Adjacent to that, the kitchen boasted two ovens and a long island for extra work space.

"This is amazing." Willow turned to Jeannie. "Really."

"Thanks. We love it. We bought it with eighty acres, but sold off forty."

She felt awkward, with her dirty jeans and unwashed hair. This place must have cost a fortune, and Jeannie kept it spotless.

"So you have neighbors?"

"Not really. No one built on the lot we sold off, and we're on a Forest Service road, so there's not a lot of private property up here. There is a house about half a mile down from us, but we don't know who lives there. Then there are more homes further down, closer to the highway."

Willow couldn't imagine not meeting her own neighbors, but she was a Montana native.

"Where are you from?" She asked Jeannie.

"We moved here from Butte." Jeannie lowered her gaze. "I was born in Kalispell, and John was raised in Maryland."

Just then, John came up the stairs with several others behind him. He introduced Willow to Tom, David, Julie, and Jennifer.

"Mike and Sue are sleeping in, because they had the night watch," John said. "So you'll have to meet them another time."

Willow exchanged pleasantries with everyone, then explained that she had to get back, since she needed to help with a work project at the cabin. A disappointed expression crossed Jeannie's face.

"Well, at least take something with you." She hurried into the kitchen and returned with a brown paper bag, which she thrust into Willow's hands. "And if you ever need anything, you know where to find us."

"Thank you. And same to you," she said, slipping out the back door.

She carried the bag carefully home, only opening it when she reached the cabin and was surrounded by her group.

Slowly, slowly, she rolled open the top of the bag and pulled it open. The most delightful fragrance escaped.

"Chocolate!" Candy squealed.

"Brownies!" Kristie exclaimed.

"Brownies it is." Willow lifted them out. "Okay, everybody, let's indulge!"

After the last scrumptious morsel was demolished, Willow

leaned back against the wall of the cabin and sighed content-edly, closing her eyes to let the sun warm her face. The taste of chocolate lingered on her tongue. It was so unbelievably good!

"That's it," Kristie said. "Me and Matt are moving over to their retreat. What the rest of you do, is up to you!"

Her happy moment over, Willow opened her eyes.

"Nobody's moving to the retreat."

"Why not?" Kristie gave her a dark look. "Who made you the boss of everyone? You're just a kid."

Willow pulled herself upright and squared her shoulders.

"If you're not happy with my leadership, you can go home. But you can't go to the retreat."

"Did they dis-invite us? I thought they were open to combining groups," Kristie said.

"They've agreed to a mutual aid pact. If we have an emer-gency, we can reach out to them. And they can do the same."

"I'm sure they'd be happy to have me and Matt," Kristie said. "I'm not staying here when they have flush toilets and chocolate brownies!"

"You don't know how to find them," Willow said. "Now, do you want to be included in our group, or do you want to strike out on your own?"

"It's time that we re-assessed our organizational structure. You being in charge was one thing when it was just you teens and Raven. But there are grownups here now." Kristie looked to the older adults for backup.

"As you know, I am a grownup." Willow leveled her voice. "And I won't be tolerating a mutiny in the ranks. You can leave if you wish. Or you can stay and cooperate. Those are your only options."

Kristie looked from Candy to Raven. They met her gaze but said nothing. Deborah and Alan, along with Clark and Jaci, avoided her eyes.

"Fine," Kristie huffed.

"You want to stay?" Willow asked.

Kristie's shoulders slumped. "Yeah. Of course."

"Don't be stirring up any more trouble."

That afternoon, Alan drew Willow aside.

"Can we talk?"

"Sure. Let's get some pails and get water from the creek for the garden." Willow grabbed the pails and led the way. "What's on your mind?"

"I think you handled Kristie very well."

"Oh." She glanced at him. "Thanks."

"Also, Clark and I have been talking."

Willow stopped and turned to face him. Now he was going to make his point. Whatever that might be. Alan rubbed the whiskers on his chin.

"We know John Anderson's group doesn't want us. And we don't want to burden you."

"You're not a burden. Your family has pitched in to help."

"And eaten your food."

"It's okay." Willow studied Alan's hazel eyes. They were so clear. It was like she actually could see into his soul. And he had a good one, for sure. "Listen. We don't want to leave you out in the cold. It would have been great if John's group could have welcomed you, but since they didn't... you're welcome to join us."

"That's incredibly generous of you."

"We're honored to have you. Christians are supposed to love and take care of each other."

"We'll try to pull our own weight."

"I have no doubts about that." Willow swung her pail, then stopped. "There's a couple of things I want to mention. First, we'll need to get a cabin built for your family as soon as possible. And second, keep this to yourself, but keep an eye on Jacob."

Alan raised an eyebrow and fixed her with his steady gaze. "Why, don't you trust him?"

She shrugged. "I'm not sure. He's new, and... and I'm just not sure."

IN THE LATE AFTERNOON, Jacob approached Willow.

"We're getting low on meat." His gaze swept toward Alan's family, who were working in the garden. "It's going a lot faster now, with the extra people."

"I know," she said. "Why don't you take Matt and go hunting this evening? If you get anything, he can help you field dress it and carry it back."

Jacob nodded and turned toward the cabin. A few minutes later, Jacob and Matt walked into the forest, rifles slung over their shoulders. Willow watched them go, admiring how Matt was growing up. He'd be sixteen soon. A hard worker, he'd proven himself repeatedly over the past few weeks. He was not far from being a man, and he'd be a good one. His faith seemed solid.

Willow's gaze swung toward the cabin, where his mother sat in the shade. Something about that woman bothered her. Partly, it was her defiance earlier. Maybe another part was that she'd played foster mom to Willow and Josh for a few hours. But there was something else, too, and she needed to figure it out.

But at the moment, she needed to help weed the garden.

After dinner, Willow began watching the edges of the clearing for Jacob and Matt's return. She had not heard any gunshots, but if the guys had walked far, she wouldn't have heard any. Dusk was prime hunting time. The deer were moving then, finding water or a place to bed down for the night.

She stood at the corner of the cabin, her eyes scanning the trees and her ears pricked for any approaching sound.

Nothing.

Too soon, maybe.

Turning to the barn, she led the goats inside and shut the door that Clark had fashioned and hung this afternoon. It was made of split logs, and had a crossbar that closed from the outside. She ran her hand over it. Clark, that quiet, dark man with the unusual accent, had some craftsmanship skills. The door was sturdy and solid. It was attached with a couple of rusty old hinges that the guys had found in the back of the shed, but the screws were new. They probably came from the supplies that Raven, Matt and Josh brought back from town.

Too bad they couldn't go back to town for more supplies. There were so many things that were needed or that would come in handy!

But it was too dangerous. With the agents hunting for them, and the volcanic ash betraying their movements, it was too risky.

Willow milked the goats slowly, enjoying the peaceful moment. Her cheek rested on the doe's flank, which rose and fell with her respiration. Willow's hands moved in easy, practiced rhythm, streaming the warm milk into the pail.

Gilligan sat a few feet away, watching intently, his ears perked and eyes keen. No doubt hoping for a little of the fresh milk himself.

The goat's ear flicked back as she cast a wary eye on the dog. Gilligan had made peace with the goats and the chickens, but he would sometimes nip at their heels if he thought they were out of line. They'd usually respond with a swift kick in his direction.

Willow finished milking and carried the pail out the door. The other women were in the cabin, no doubt cleaning up after dinner, but she preferred the barn chores. In so many ways, animals were easier to deal with than people.

She called Gilligan out, then closed the door and swung the crossbar in place, once again admiring the work Clark had done on that door after the wall was finished this morning. It was good that his family would be joining her group. But it would put a strain on the food supply.

Her eyes scanned the trees in the deepening darkness. Still no sign of Jacob and Matt. Soon, it would be dark.

As she approached the cabin, Alan and Deborah and their family walked toward their camp. They saw her and waved, and she smiled and waved back.

Kristie stood from one of the two chairs as Willow entered the cabin.

"Matt and Jacob aren't back, and it's dark."

Willow set the milk pail on the table.

"It's a good sign. If they had no luck hunting, they'd probably be back by now."

"What if they got hurt? There's wolves and bears out there!"

Willow poured the warm milk into smaller containers with lids.

"You should pray for them." She picked up the containers and took them outside to chill in the night air.

A long, lonely howl lifted the hair on the back of her neck. Another howl followed, its long and haunting strains echoing against the mountains.

Goose bumps rose along Willow's bare arms.

She stood and listened as new voices joined in the chorus.

Her breath paused as the eerie, breathtaking sounds filled the wilderness.

The wolves carried on for a few minutes, then one by one, dropped out until a lone voice remained.

Willow rubbed her arms and stepped back into the cabin's safety.

Her brother shot her a concerned look.

"Will the new family be okay? They don't even have a tent."

"They'll build a big fire. Wolves will stay away from them."

"What about Matt? And Jacob?"

"They're well armed. Now get to bed, and be sure to say prayers for them."

Josh cast her a long look, then slowly climbed the ladder to sleep alone in the loft for the first time. At the top, he stopped and looked back.

"Do you think Matt and Jacob will be back tonight?"

She didn't want him to worry, so thought for a moment before she answered.

"I don't think so. They'll probably camp out and come back in the daylight."

She hoped so, anyway.

A glance at Kristie's bunk showed a dark form turned toward the wall. Not likely asleep. And not likely to sleep well.

Had she had many nights like that over the past several weeks? Or had she slept comfortably in her bed at home while her son slept in the woods with bears, wolves, cougars and I.D. task force agents hunting him?

Willow turned off the little solar lamp and pulled off her boots and holster, then climbed into her bunk with her clothes on. Sometimes it just felt better to be prepared for whatever might happen the moment her eyes opened.

9

W illow slid out of her bunk at first light, and silently climbed the ladder to the loft, hoping to find Jacob and Matt's sleeping forms. Perhaps they'd come in quietly during the night and had gone to bed.

But only Josh was there.

Raven stirred, then Kristie. Candy and Maria slumbered like logs, snuggled together in one large sleeping bag.

Kristie rubbed her eyes and sat up.

"Are they back?"

"Not yet," Willow whispered.

Kristie frowned and rolled out of bed.

Willow started a fire, then went out to collect eggs. She watered the goats and the chickens, and poured a little for Gilligan, too.

"You should be drinking from the creek like a good dog, so we don't have to haul water for you." She scratched his ears and was rewarded with a lick on her hand.

Gilligan raised his head and sniffed the wind. His eyes and ears turned toward the far edge of the clearing. Willow followed his alert.

Moments later, Jacob and Matt emerged from the woods. Gilligan bounded toward them, and Willow followed.

They carried nothing besides their rifles. No meat.

Willow's deflated breath left her lungs.

"You didn't get anything," she said as she reached them.

"Oh yeah," Jacob said. "We got something, all right."

She scanned his face for deception.

"What? Where is it?"

"Back in the woods." Jacob jutted his chin over his shoulder.

"We got run off by wolves!" Matt said. "Barely escaped with our lives!"

Raven and Kristie came out of the cabin and hurried toward them. Josh ran out a moment later. Matt's mom wrapped her arms around his shoulders, but he quickly wriggled out of her embrace. She gave him a serious look.

"I was worried sick about you. Why didn't you get home last night?"

"Because there were wolves. So we climbed trees."

"What?" Kristie's lip trembled. "You're kidding, right?"

She glanced at Jacob. He shook his head.

"Nope, that's what happened."

"Tell us the whole story," Willow said. "From the beginning."

"We walked a long time, seeing no deer sign. We'd probably gone four miles or so, and finally came across some fresh tracks in the ash," Jacob said.

"And I shot a deer!" Matt added.

"A young buck." Jacob paused. "So we dressed it out and quartered it, and we were packing it home. Then Matt saw the first wolf."

"Just out of the corner of my eye," Matt said. "I'd turned my head to look over my left shoulder, and there on the hill behind us was this huge grey wolf. It was a monster, and it was following us!"

Kristie shuddered and stared at Willow. Like it was her fault.

"So, I yelled 'Wolf!' at Jacob, and he stopped. We both stopped and yelled at the wolf, and started looking around. And then we saw another one."

"That's right, then a third," Jacob added. "The sun had gone down by this time, so we didn't have much light left. I was hoping to get home by dark, but we saw a fourth wolf, this one in front of us. So we knew they were circling."

"For a kill!" Kristie said. "Why didn't you shoot them?"

"We fired off a few shots, and I think we wounded one." Jacob's gaze moved around the group. "But it was getting too dark to see. The wolves could smell the blood of the deer we shot, and they were hungry. They weren't leaving. So we dropped the deer and tried to get past them, hoping they'd take the bait and leave us alone."

"But they cut off our escape!" Matt said. "And then we climbed the trees."

"They were closing in, and it was looking grim. So I gave Matt a boost up a cedar, and I climbed up the one next to it."

Kristie's face was pale. "Then what?"

"The wolves circled around our trees," Matt said. "It was freaky! Only one went to eat the deer meat. The others kept circling us."

"Then they started howling. One after another. They were right there, and loud," Jacob said.

"But we were safe in the trees." Matt gave his mom a reassuring look. "They couldn't get us. Eventually, they did eat some of the deer meat. But they spent most of the night sitting below the trees, watching us. It's one of the most amazing things I've ever seen."

His mom snorted. "Amazing? You could've been killed!"

"Not in the trees."

"How did you get away?" Raven asked.

"Just before dawn, they disappeared," Jacob said. "It was like, one minute they were down there, and the next, they were gone. Like ghosts."

"How did you know they were really gone?" Kristie asked. "They might have just gone a little way into the forest."

"We waited about ten minutes and didn't see or hear anything," Jacob said. "I came down first, and after a few more minutes, Matt came down. Anyway, we had our rifles, and it was light enough for a decent shot."

"But we didn't see them. We high-tailed it home, looking over our shoulders the whole way." He grinned at Josh, who looked a little sorry to have missed the adventure.

Willow watched their interaction, thinking how glad she was that Josh *had* missed this particular adventure. It would be great if she could protect him from all danger, all the time. But that was beyond her power. She'd have to continue trusting God for that.

Also, she'd have to keep trusting Him to supply all their needs, particularly food, which was running low.

Jacob turned his chocolate eyes on her.

"I'll need some rest, since we couldn't really sleep last night. Then I'll go out hunting again this evening."

"Not with Matthew." Kristie gave her son a firm look. "You'll be sitting this one out."

"I can go," Josh volunteered.

Willow's stomach turned. She didn't want to send her brother out with the wolves. Or with the wolf in sheep's clothing, if that's what Jacob was. But she decided to delay the argument.

"We'll see," she said. "Now, let's get our day started."

When Alan and his family arrived at the cabin, they brought all their belongings with them.

"I thought maybe we'd set up camp next to the barn," Alan said.

"That sounds good." Willow took a roll of bedding from Deborah's arms. "We should pick a site for your cabin, and start building right away."

"Oh, good." Deborah smiled. "I didn't sleep well, listening to those wolves last night."

"You aren't the only one," Willow said. "Jacob and Matt have a fantastic tale to tell you after they get some sleep."

The family stacked their belongings along the south side of the barn and staked out their tarp.

"We'll want our cabin to be nearby for safety's sake, but probably not visible from your clearing," Alan said. "It'd be nice to be close enough to hear a yell, though."

"Let's take a little hike and see if we can find a spot you like," Willow suggested.

She walked with the family into the trees behind the barn, then they veered toward the creek, then up a hill.

"We want to stay close enough to the creek that we do not have to haul water a long distance," Clark said in his soft accent. "But we wish to be far enough from the creek that we don't hear it. So that we can hear if anyone yells from your cabin."

"That makes sense," Willow agreed.

The family wandered a little more, then found a bare spot at the top of a knoll.

"It will be sunny here," Clark said.

Deborah turned in a full circle as she surveyed the spot. "I like it!"

"It's exposed," Willow said. "You'll get some wind."

"That's alright. We'll chink the walls well," Alan said. "Jaci? Girls? What do you think?"

"Looks fine to me," Jaci said, and the girls nodded their approval.

"Alright, then! Home, sweet home!" Alan smiled. "Well, after a lot of work, it will be."

THAT AFTERNOON, Willow approached Clark as he limbed poles for his family's cabin. His skin glistened with exertion as he axed off branches. He looked up as she approached.

"I have a favor to ask," she said.

"Yes?" He lowered the head of the axe to the ground.

"Jacob is going hunting soon. Josh wants to go with him." Willow studied Clark's dark eyes. "I was thinking it'd be good if you went, too."

"Why is that? You think they need three hunters? Or you think I need to learn to hunt?"

That possibility had not occurred to her.

"You don't know how to hunt?"

He smiled, crinkling the skin around his eyes. "Yes, I can hunt. Why exactly do you wish me to go?"

"Last night, Jacob and Matt ran into a pack of wolves. Josh is my brother and I –"

"You worry for him."

"Yes." She glanced at the ground, then back to his face. "Also, I'm not sure that I trust Jacob."

"Because he's new." Clark's features flattened.

Did he think she did not trust Clark and his family because they were new also?

She shook her head.

"It's not that, exactly."

"What is it, then?" His dark eyes pierced her.

"I'm not sure." She sighed. "But would you go?"

Clark picked up the axe and swung a perfect arc, sending a

limb spinning off the tree he'd chopped down. Then he looked at her.

"Yes. If it means so much to you, I will go with them."

ALTHOUGH SHE'D KEPT her son safely at home, Kristie watched for the return of the hunting party that night, and was the first to spot them entering the clearing. They were empty-handed. She sighed loudly. What were they going to eat? How were they going to feed all these people?

"There aren't many deer out there," Josh said. "But there are a lot of people."

"Doing what? Camping? It's too early for picking huckleberries," his sister asked.

He shrugged. "I dunno. We didn't see them, we just saw their tracks. Lots of human tracks."

Kristie didn't have to guess why there were so many people in the woods, or what they were doing. They were hunting for food. The EMP had wiped out grocery deliveries, so those who were healthy and able were turning to the forest to fill their bellies.

Should she tell the group?

Kristie looked from Clark to Jacob to Josh and Willow. They didn't have a clue, obviously. There was no way they would have known about the EMP.

But if she told them now, they would be mad she hadn't told them before. Not that it would make a bit of difference. Knowing or not knowing had zero impact on the state of things.

She could have told them before, of course. She could have told Matt as soon as he showed up at her house and noticed the power was out.

Truth was, she hadn't wanted him or anyone else here to

question her motives for joining the group. They needed to firmly believe she was running from the ID task force, just like they had. If there were any doubts about her motives, they might lead to a discovery of her very biggest secret: the ID chip.

And what would happen if they knew? They'd kick her out. She'd be all alone in the woods, and get eaten by wolves, if she didn't starve first.

Because there was no going back to town. No way, Jose. That place had no water, no power, no food. Just growing desperation and violence.

Nope. She was staying here, with her son in this quiet little cabin. Until she could figure out how to finagle her way into living at the nice retreat that John Anderson and his family had set up. And she would do that. Definitely before winter.

EARLY THE NEXT MORNING, Willow slipped out of the cabin and walked to the barn. She admired its new log front wall. It'd keep out most predators, and once they got it chinked, it would also keep out drafts.

She moved quietly to avoid waking Alan's family, who were still asleep under their tarp. It didn't do much more than keep the dew off them. But soon they'd have a new home. Willow stepped into the barn and pulled the door shut.

The young buckling ran over to her. She held out her hands and he play-butted them. He was just so cute! Willow scratched his neck.

She needed a little time away from everyone. Time alone with her Father in Heaven. She turned her eyes to the rafters and breathed her prayers. Thankfulness for protection of the entire group, and requests for provision and safety. He had gotten them through so many dangers already, and she knew He would get them through more in the future. For that she was grateful.

Her stomach rumbled, and she prayed for food. The garden would only supply so much. They would need meat.

She should go fishing. Maybe the rainbow trout would be hungry this morning, just as she was.

She retrieved the little worm can and a fishing pole, and headed for the creek. Wandering along the banks, she watched for a deep, quiet pool, and found one below a big log that jutted into the water.

The sun's first rays broke through the trees as she approached the pool.

Suddenly, she felt cautious. Something wasn't quite right.

She slid up to a tree trunk and froze, feeling silly, but searching for something out of place.

The birds silenced. The forest fell into a deep quiet.

Something was wrong.

Willow calmed her breathing as her eyes searched each tree, each shadow, each bush. Maybe she was imagining a problem. Maybe she was being ridiculous.

She was just about to step out toward the pool when she heard a voice.

Was it one of her group? One of John Anderson's? Why would they be over here, so near her cabin and so far from their home?

Finally, she saw movement downstream. A man in black tactical gear.

An agent!

The task force was closing in on her and her group!

He hadn't seen her yet.

Could she still slip away, unnoticed?

She turned her head and glanced behind her. There were a few trees. Maybe –

But he was coming closer.

She wanted to run! But then he'd see her for sure.

The tree she'd chosen to hide beside was a good one. A big cedar, at least three feet in diameter at its base. She could scoot around it a little more, and he might never see her.

Willow moved slowly, positioning the tree between herself and the man downstream. He was talking to someone, but Willow couldn't see another person. Maybe they were using radios.

He continued upstream, walking slowly toward her hiding place.

Oh, Lord! Hide me in the shadow of your hand!

She needed to survive, to escape, to warn the others.

He was close enough now that she could make out his conversation.

"I found a good fishing hole here. I'm gonna try it out. You have any luck?"

A pause, then a different voice responded.

"No, man. This place is hunted out. I've run into two other hunting parties."

"Did they get anything?"

"No! Nobody's getting anything. The deer are gone."

The man cursed.

"If it weren't for that EMP – hold on, I think I see something."

Willow stopped breathing. Was it her? Did he see her? She pressed herself into the tree trunk.

10

Willow's pulse thundered in her ears. She froze. And waited.

"It's nothin', just an old pop can," the man said.

Willow's lungs filled with air. How long had she been holding her breath?

She wanted to take a peek around the tree trunk so she could see where the man was. But if she could see him, he could see her. So she stayed still.

"So about that EMP," the other man said. "How come these walkie talkies still work?"

"I had them in a Faraday cage, you fool."

"Don't be calling me a fool!"

"I'm joking, you fool. Anyway, maybe I'll catch something here," he continued. "I'll meet you back at camp in an hour or two."

An hour or two? Willow grimaced. There was no way she could hold this tree-hugging pose for an hour. She was going to have to move eventually, to relax her muscles and joints.

For now, though, she wasn't moving a muscle.

Even though that guy was going to fish in *her* pool.

So what was that about an EMP? Willow knew a little about EMPs, and all of it was bad. They'd take out the electrical grid, they'd fry automobiles, nothing would ever work again. Or not for years or decades.

Had that really happened?

It would explain all the poachers in the woods, and the lack of deer.

Because this guy and his buddy were certainly hunters. They weren't agents tracking down Christians in the forest. And all this meant that there were lots more people in the woods now, besides the Christians who'd escaped the ID task force.

When did the EMP happen? How long had all these people been coming to the woods?

Were Alan and his family in the woods because of the EMP? No, they were believers, escaped from a prisoner transport. Right? Unless they were lying about that, in order to get help from Willow's group or John Anderson's.

Could they be lying?

Did they actually have the mark?

And would they turn Willow's group in later if it helped them?

No. This was ridiculous.

They were Christians. Willow could see it in their eyes. Right? She hoped so.

A branch snapped, and Willow nearly jumped.

It was all she could do to not peek around the edge of the tree trunk and see where that guy was. She didn't dare. It would expose her hiding spot.

And even though he wasn't an agent, she didn't want him to spy her. He needed to go away without any clue that there was a cabin hidden away back in these woods, and a group of people carving out a living there.

Again, she prayed for help.

Finally, she couldn't stand it anymore. Her muscles ached from holding their tense position against the tree trunk.

Slowly, she inched herself into a normal stance, then peeked toward the creek. The man's back was to her as he flung his line into the water.

If she could be silent, she could make her getaway.

ONCE SHE WAS AWAY from the creek, Willow ran toward home, clutching her worm can and fishing pole.

She had to warn everyone.

But could she trust them?

It was probably after the EMP that Alan's family had joined her group. Could she be sure they were who they said they were? What about Jacob? What about John Anderson? What if they were all just trying to survive in the woods because of the EMP, not because they didn't have the mark?

Was she being ridiculous? Not trusting anyone?

Why would they deceive her?

To get her group's trust and help. They had a few assets. A cabin, a bit of food, some animals, a garden. There were a lot of reasons a desperate, starving person would try to deceive them.

Maybe it would help if she knew when the EMP had happened. Then, only the ones they'd met after that time would be suspect.

For now, she could only trust the original group: Raven, Matt and Josh. And Raven's uncle Tony, if they ever ran into him again.

Back at the cabin, she summoned everyone.

"I saw a hunter at the creek this morning."

Murmurs met her announcement, and Raven spoke up.

"Did he see you?"

"No," Willow said. "But here's the thing: the woods are full of people right now. They're hunting, they're fishing, just like us. Deer are getting scarce, and so are fish."

"What are we going to do?" Kristie asked.

"We have to avoid being seen, at all costs. And keep in mind that these folks might get pretty close to our home." Willow's gaze took in each set of eyes. "At some point, they might discover our cabin."

"Maybe we should move," Alan said. "Farther out. Deeper into the wilderness."

Willow shook her head.

"God placed us here. We have a garden planted now, and a barn for the animals. But I understand if your family wishes to relocate. You've only put in one day's work at your cabin site."

Alan looked at his wife, then his daughter and grandchildren.

"We will pray and discuss it," he said. "But there are benefits to remaining close to your cabin, as well."

Willow appreciated that prayer was Alan's first thought. He probably was truly a believer. Either that, or a cunning unbeliever.

And how could she ever know? For sure?

It was mid-afternoon when she finally got a moment to talk alone with Raven.

"I overheard that man at the creek talking on a walkie-talkie. They were talking about an EMP!"

"A what?" Raven gave her a confused look.

"An electromagnetic pulse. An EMP. It can come after a solar flare, or from a nuclear bomb. It fries all the electrical stuff!"

Raven brushed a strand of straight black hair away from her eyes. "So how were they using walkie-talkies?"

"They had them in a Faraday cage. Never mind about that. The point is, all these people are out hunting in the woods because town isn't getting any supplies. No gas, no groceries."

"No scanners!" Raven's eyes lit up. "This raises possibilities!"

"Focus, Raven! This is a huge problem!"

"I know. The fish and game will dwindle."

"Exactly. They already have. But there's more, and it's worse."

"Tell me." Raven lasered her eyes on Willow's.

"All of those people are out in the forest because of the EMP. How do we know the people who joined us recently aren't here because of it?"

Raven turned her gaze toward the mountain. She bit her lip.

"I don't know. I mean, we think they're Christians, out here for the same reason as us. But – I see your point. Maybe they're not. How can we know?"

"Christians don't have the mark."

Raven's dark eyes grew wide.

"You want to line everyone up and inspect them?"

"That would work." Willow didn't like the idea of it, but it would provide definite answers.

Raven shook her head slowly.

"I don't think we should do that. It's incredibly insulting. But beyond that, what if we find someone *does* have the mark? What would we do with them?"

"Send them away?"

"Only to have them come back later, with others, to overrun us and take our home, food and animals?"

Raven was right. Willow needed to think this through better.

"What do you suggest, then?"

"We need to pray that God will drive out any imposters. And we need to keep our discernment up. God gives us the ability to discern. And the Bible says we will know Christians by their love. We can watch for that."

Willow nodded. "And pray for protection. Let's do it now."

The two friends gripped each other's hands, bowed their heads, and earnestly prayed together. After a few minutes, peace filled Willow's heart. She looked up and smiled into Raven's glowing dark eyes.

"Thanks. I don't know what I'd do without you." She gave Raven a hug. "I thank God for you."

A broad smile rippled Raven's brown face.

"And I thank Him for you."

"What was that you were saying before – about possibilities?"

"You said the EMP knocks out the power and fries electrical stuff. So scanners won't work, right?"

"Right." Willow nodded. "I think."

"So... we could go to town, maybe buy stuff. Not worry about getting scanned and caught without the mark."

"But Marcus is looking for you! For us."

"I highly doubt he's even giving us a thought right now. I mean, think about it. After a few days without electricity or grocery deliveries, nobody's going to worry about whether or not anybody has the mark. I'm sure Marcus gave up his search. He's probably dealing with lootings or shootings by now."

"Which brings up the point that town is not safe."

"We'd go armed, obviously." Raven's eyes lit with excitement. "Think about it – all the things that we'd like to get, the things that we need before winter – we could get that stuff now!"

"I don't think we could get any food. And that's what we need most."

"I know, but we could get supplies for Alan's family's cabin. Things we could carry. Tar paper for the roof, nails, screws, hinges, maybe a window."

Willow mulled it over.

"It'd be great if we could get some chicken scratch for winter. Or even more chickens or goats. More hand tools." She paused. "I really wish we could get more food."

"That would be hard to find."

"I know. Maybe ammo and a couple more guns?"

"Who knows?" Raven smiled. "See what I mean? Possibilities!"

"Yeah." Willow's gaze took in the vast forest. "But it would be dangerous. With no guarantees of getting anything in return. The wilderness between here and Ponderosa is filled with desperate, hungry people. Town will be the same, or worse. And then we'll have to run the wilderness gauntlet again, coming back home."

"It could be worth it, though. If it works."

"Maybe. I'll think about it."

"And pray about it?"

"Of course." Willow looked at her friend. "I think I should go tell John Anderson and his group about the EMP. Maybe they will want to send someone to town with us if we go. Or maybe they have some information that we don't know."

"Good idea. When will you go?"

"First thing in the morning."

Kristie rose early the next morning. She'd been awake much of the night, formulating a plan. Last night, Willow had announced that she was going to the Andersons' retreat today. And while Willow had no intention of revealing its location, Kristie needed to know where it was.

Because what if something happened to Willow at some

point? No one else in the group knew how to contact the Andersons. It was stupid, really.

Reckless.

More than one person in their group should have that information, in case of emergencies. And since Willow refused to divulge it, insisting that was the agreement with the Andersons, Kristie had come up with a way to find out for herself.

One day soon, before winter, for sure, she intended to move there with her son.

Matt might not like the idea at first, but he'd get over it. Eventually, he'd be glad he obeyed his mother. Sure, he'd miss his friends, but he'd have a real roof over his head and delicious food to eat.

Kristie knew it'd be hard to get him to go along with her plan. But that was a problem for another day.

Today, she would learn where the retreat was, so at the right time, she could take Matt there.

She dressed and filled a water bottle, then picked up a fishing pole and told Raven she was going fishing.

"Fishing?" Raven's eyebrows rose. "You know how?"

"Of course!" Kristie scoffed. "I'm not half bad, if I do say so myself."

"Good luck, then."

She hustled out the door just as Willow climbed down from her bunk. This was the first time she'd been out of bed before Willow, and that was part of her plan. Be out of sight and out of Willow's mind this morning.

Hurrying toward the creek, she kept an eye open for a good hiding place. She didn't want to go too far, because she wasn't sure which way Willow would go once she got into the forest. Soon, she found a nice grove of cedars. She stashed her fishing pole there, and tucked herself into the trees, peeking back toward the cabin every few minutes.

She didn't have long to wait. That Willow didn't waste much time. Probably hadn't even eaten breakfast.

Willow hurried into the forest, and Kristie moved in behind her, careful to keep plenty of trees between them in case Willow glanced back.

Kristie kept a keen eye on Willow, ready to slip behind a tree if necessary.

It was kind of fun being stealthy. But she also had to pay attention to where they were going. She needed landmarks to guide her way in the future. There was no clearly marked trail to the retreat. Sometimes Willow followed game trails, and sometimes she turned aside, pushing her way through branches.

Kristie tried to be super silent. If Willow heard her snap a twig, it could wreck everything.

Willow hiked quickly, though. She was a young, fit eighteen-year-old. Kristie was her mother's age, and not in the best shape of her life.

Still, she had to keep up.

How far could this retreat be, anyway?

She slowed to pull off her jacket. It was getting too darn hot in the summer sun.

The heat was making her thirsty, too. Good thing she brought a water bottle. She took a swig and lost sight of Willow.

That girl was fast! It was almost like she knew Kristie was behind her, and she was trying to lose her in the forest.

Kristie's heart pounded and she plunged forward through the trees until she could see Willow again. What if she did lose Willow? She wasn't sure she could find her way home.

Which would be worse – losing sight of her, or being seen by her?

Either could have devastating results.

On the one hand, she might starve to death in the mountains. On the other, Willow might be fiercely angry at Kristie's subterfuge. What would she do? Kick her out of the group?

Maybe.

Kristie wiped the perspiration from her brow and tried to keep up. Why was Willow in such a big hurry all the time?

11

Whered Willow returned to the cabin, she called everyone together. Or almost everyone.

"Where's Kristie?"

"She went fishing this morning," Raven said.

"And she's not back yet? It's nearly noon."

Raven shrugged. "Maybe she was really reeling them in."

"There she is now." Matt pointed over Willow's shoulder.

Kristie emerged from the forest with her fishing pole and her jacket.

"Looks like a zero fish day." Raven motioned Kristie toward the group.

Kristie broke into a jog and joined the circle around Willow, huffing and puffing. Her red face glistened in the sunshine.

Willow studied her a moment. She must really be out of shape to be so spent from so little exertion.

"No luck," Kristie said.

"We can see that." Willow glanced at her sweaty face. "You okay?"

Kristie nodded. "Sure. How was your meeting?"

Willow turned so she could see everyone.

"It went well. They weren't too surprised about the EMP, because their radio went down. Also, they had to replace parts on their solar electric system about the same time. They didn't see it as a big deal, as far as it affecting them. I did warn them about all the people in the forest, though."

"Do they want to go to town? Or send someone with us, if we go?" Candy asked.

Willow shook her head.

"They feel like their supplies are adequate, and the risk involved with going into town is too high. Plus, they're older and it's a pretty strenuous hike."

"But didn't you say they're on the road system?" Matt asked.

"Yeah, they are, which makes their hike easier. But it's still about twelve miles to town on the road." Willow's gaze swept the faces assembled before her. "It also makes their retreat more exposed, since people can find it so easily. But they do post lookouts."

"So, are we sending a team to town?" Kristie asked.

"We should pray about it some more, but I think so," Willow said. "The longer we wait, the more dangerous it will be, and the fewer supplies we'll find. Lots of folks will be looking for the same things we need."

"Can I go?" Josh asked.

"Me, too!" Matt volunteered.

"We'll form up a team in the morning, if we feel the Lord's blessing on this." Willow's gaze moved from one person to the next. "Anybody who wants to go should tell me today."

The meeting broke up, but Alan and Clark hung around until they were alone with Willow.

"What's up?" she asked.

Clark spoke first.

"I would be willing to join the team to town, if one is sent. I am in good health and I can carry many supplies that my family needs."

"Thank you, Clark." She turned her gaze to Alan. He fixed her with those deep hazel eyes before he spoke.

"We don't think folks in town will be willing to sell anything for dollars, if this EMP is for real," he said. "They'll want something with intrinsic value."

"Like what?" Willow asked. "We can't trade anything we have here. We need it all."

Alan exchanged a look with Clark, and Clark nodded.

"We have something that might work," Alan said. "Gold."

Willow burst into a laugh.

"Gold? Seriously?"

Alan and Clark's faces were dead serious.

"How?" Willow grew suspicious. "You told me you were prisoners. How could you have smuggled gold all that time past the guards? You would have gone through metal detectors!"

"We did not have it then," Clark said.

"You stole it later?" Willow's stomach knotted. Was she living with thieves?

"No!" Alan looked offended and pointed to his waist. "You see these leather belts? My dad had left them in the refrigerator he buried in the barn. They were with the guns and sleeping bags."

"I've noticed your belts. So what?"

"So, they have a hidden compartment, and Dad put gold coins in them."

Gold coins? Willow broke into a grin.

"Really? How much?"

"Enough for now," Alan answered.

She wanted to hug him. But didn't.

"That is fantastic. Truly fantastic!" She couldn't stop smiling. Gold! Wow! That might be the answer to prayer, right there.

Well, the answer to another prayer, also – Christians would be known by their love, right? And these folks were willing to share their only valuable asset. And it might be very valuable, indeed!

She couldn't wait to start making a list of supplies to pick up in town. This was one of the best things that had happened since they'd run to find refuge in the forest.

She wasn't sure who to thank first – God, or these fine men.

And she just couldn't stop grinning.

KRISTIE WALKED to the creek and splashed water on her face and arms. She'd done it! She'd managed to keep up with Willow, find out where the Andersons' retreat was, and return unnoticed. Plus, she felt pretty confident she could find her way back there when she was ready.

And what a fine retreat it appeared to be!

The house was beautiful, and she saw two horses grazing in the pasture next to the barn. It looked so peaceful and idyllic.

She could easily see herself living there. With her son, of course.

Matt had to come with her. He was her ticket in the door. Young and strong, and a hard worker. It was just what those older folks were hoping for – and needed.

On her own, they might turn her away. She was just another middle-aged woman. But not if she had Matt at her side.

But when should they go? And how could she convince Matt to accompany her? That would take some real cunning.

She was up to it, though. She was his mother, and she was pretty bright.

If she did say so herself.

KRISTIE MULLED it over as she washed dishes after dinner. Matt wanted to go with Willow's team to town in the morning. If she could convince Willow to leave him behind – maybe plead her worries as his mother, after being separated from him for weeks – then maybe she and Matt could go to the Andersons' retreat tomorrow, at the same time as Willow and some of the others went to town.

Then the problem would be convincing Matt to go along with her. He'd be upset about missing out on the town team, and he'd demand to know how she knew about the retreat's location.

Maybe she didn't have to tell him.

Maybe she could trick him a little.

There were lots of options. She just had to come up with the best one.

WILLOW'S EYES flew open as soon as her brain registered consciousness. The cabin's windows revealed the dim light of pre-dawn. Today was the day! She'd lead a group to town for bartering and supplies! She could hardly wait to get started.

She climbed down from her bunk and dressed, double-checking her handgun and ammo, then putting her water filter and bottle in her bag, along with a headlamp and rain jacket.

Clark had volunteered to come, as had Raven, Josh and Matt.

Alan and the rest of his family wanted to work on their cabin, and Jacob had offered to help them. That left Kristie, who didn't want to go, and Candy, who had finally recuperated from her twisted ankle, but wanted to stay home with little Maria.

Willow had to make a decision about Matt. He wanted to go, but late last night, his mom had implored Willow to leave him behind. Kristie didn't want to be separated from him again so soon, and that was understandable.

But he was young and strong, and could carry a good load. Leaving him behind would reduce the amount of supplies the group could bring back from town.

Maybe she should leave Matt, who wanted to go, and bring Jacob, who didn't.

She grimaced. She didn't want to bring Jacob. Still didn't feel one hundred percent sure about him. Besides, it was a long, dangerous trek, and he did not want to participate.

So that was that. Jacob would stay and work on the new cabin.

Matt?

She sighed. He should come.

But Kristie was adamant. And Willow didn't feel like fighting with her again. It was best to pick one's battles, wasn't it?

This one wasn't worth fighting.

Matt would stay home.

Raven joined her at the stove as she started a fire to cook breakfast.

"Would you run out and gather the eggs?"

"Sure thing." Raven headed out the door.

The guys were rustling around in the loft when Raven returned with Clark. He turned those big, dark eyes on her.

"How soon do we leave?"

"Soon as we eat breakfast," Willow said.

The guys came down from the loft and gathered around the warm stove. It was time to make her announcement, as unwelcome as it may be.

"Josh, you're coming with us. Matt, you'll stay here."

His blue eyes lost their twinkle.

"Please let me come. I can pack a lot."

Willow laid her hand on his elbow.

"I know, Matt. But your mom is really worried. It's dangerous, and she just recently got you back after weeks of worrying."

He frowned. "She worries too much."

"Maybe so." Willow regretted her decision as she looked at his disappointed face. "But this time you'll stay home. I'm sorry."

After a quick breakfast, Willow, Raven, Clark and Josh prepared to set out.

"Let's all keep our packs nearly empty, so we'll have room to bring back as much as possible from town," Willow said. "Bring extra ammo, though, just in case."

Clark produced small 1/10 ounce American gold eagle coins, and gave each member two of them.

"This is in case I get caught, or we get separated," he explained. "I think it is best if the gold is already distributed among us. Put it in a place safe!"

Willow considered zipping hers into her backpack, but decided to put them in her front pants pocket instead. Just in case her pack got lost or stolen, or heaven forbid, she had to ditch it to run.

"Let's gather everyone for prayer," she said.

The group formed a circle outside the cabin and joined hands. Alan prayed a solemn blessing and prayer for protection over them.

At "amen," Willow looked up and smiled. The sun had kissed the clearing with its warm, bright rays.

An adventure lay ahead, and an opportunity. She had high hopes for this day. And they were off.

KRISTIE WATCHED THE GROUP LEAVE, and smiled as they entered the forest. They'd be gone all day today, just getting to town. The earliest they would be back was tomorrow night, but more likely, the following evening.

So she had all that time to work on Matt and get him over to the Andersons' retreat.

It didn't look like it'd happen today, though.

Matt was so mad, he could barely stand to look at her.

Well, give him time. He was a kid. He'd get over it.

FOR THE FIRST time in longer than she could remember, Willow felt lighthearted. The sky was blue, the sun was warm, the birds were singing in the pines. She sent up a thankful prayer.

The hike to town took all day. At dusk, the group approached Willow's neighborhood.

"Hey, check it out," Josh pointed south. "Lights!"

The neighborhood was dark, but Josh was right. A big building and its perimeter were illuminated with electric lights. But how was that possible? What about the EMP?

"Isn't that the city's treatment plant?" Josh asked.

"Yeah. I think it is." Willow pulled out her binoculars. "There's a police officer, and I can see a worker going into the building."

She turned to Clark.

"I thought the EMP knocked out the power. And it was going to be out for months or years. This doesn't make sense."

Clark's brows knitted in confusion that matched hers. Finally, he shook his head and shrugged.

"I do not know." He motioned out across the town. "But that appears to be the only building with power."

"You're right." Willow put her binoculars back in her pack. "Let's go to our house. Everybody keep your eyes open, and whistle if you see anything weird."

They crept single file through the darkening night to the

back door of her old home. The door hung ajar. Was someone inside?

What if people had moved in since she and Josh had run to the forest?

She drew her handgun.

Her heart thumped a heavy drumbeat against her chest wall.

She tiptoed up the steps, and the others followed her lead, creeping up behind her. She listened, but only heard her blood pulsing through her ears. Slowly, ever so slowly, she pushed the door open with her foot.

Nothing. No noise. No movement.

Cautiously, she slipped inside, letting her eyes adjust to the darkness.

The place was a wreck. She couldn't make out all the details, but drawers were pulled out, emptied on the floor. Cupboards and cabinets hung open.

She motioned the others inside.

"It's been looted," she whispered, turning on her headlamp. She'd have to be careful to keep the light away from the windows, in case the neighbors were watching.

A broken picture frame on the carpet reflected the light beam. She bent and picked it up. The photo was of her family a few years ago, when Dad was alive. The four of them, Dad, Mom, Josh and herself, were at the lake enjoying a day of swimming.

Willow pulled the photo from the frame. She was about to put it in her pack when she noticed Josh looking at it. Did he have any family photos?

She handed it to him and tousled his hair. He carefully placed it in his backpack.

"Okay, guys – let's see if the thieves left us anything useful," she whispered. Clark and Raven headed to the kitchen, and she and Josh went upstairs.

Willow scowled when she entered her old room. The looters had done a thorough job, even going through her underwear drawer. She picked up a spiral-bound notebook and a couple of pens and pencils – because you just never know when you might need to leave a note in the wilderness – and moved on to her parents' room. Well, Mom's room, since Dad died.

And what if Mom was dead, too? Willow blinked back the moisture that sprung to her eyes. No, Mom was captured, but she'd get free one day. Alan's family had. So Mom might, too.

There was little left of value in her bedroom, though. There were wool socks, so she took those, and Mom's favorite wool sweater. It was nice of the thieves to leave those things. If it'd been autumn or winter, they surely would have taken them.

She pressed the sweater to her face and inhaled. Mom's perfume lingered faintly in the fibers. She drew in another breath. This time, she couldn't stop the tears before they rushed out and slipped down her cheeks. Mom.

A sob escaped as she impatiently brushed away the tears. She didn't have time for this. Shoving the sweater into her pack, she hurried out of the room.

Back downstairs, she stopped at the overturned bookshelf. Mom had a good collection of books. But books would be heavy to tote back to the mountain, and they took up a lot of space in a pack. So she only took one – the Merck Manual. It was kind of an all-around medical manual. She nearly took the Merck Veterinary Manual, too, but couldn't justify the weight and space of the two books.

In the kitchen, Clark and Raven were just finishing up.

"Find anything?" Willow asked.

"It's been picked pretty clean," Raven said. "But I'm taking this manual can opener, because who knows, and this little flexible cutting board. And a bit of honey and some spices."

"Honey?" Willow's mouth watered. "Let's eat it now!"

"I was tempted to do that already," Raven admitted. "But it wouldn't be fair to the others at the cabin."

"Yeah. I know." Willow turned to <u>Clark</u>. "What did you find?"

"I found a box of salt and a tin of pepper." He held them up. "Also, if you do not mind, I'd like to take some silverware and a few dishes for my family."

"Of course!" Willow said. "You're welcome to take anything you want."

"Thank you very much." His accent softened his words. "We will appreciate this."

Josh tromped down the stairs and into the kitchen.

"My room was trashed. I got nothin'." He turned a kitchen chair right side up and plopped into it. "Are we going to Raven's next, or Kristie and Matt's?"

"Let's go to my place," Raven suggested. "We done here?"

"After we double-check the barn. Maybe there's a little more we can scavenge there," Willow said.

The group headed out the back door and walked to the barn. Inside, they switched on their headlamps. Willow swung her light around.

Thieves had looted the barn, too. Nearly everything useful was missing. However, they'd overlooked an old, rusty hammer, so Clark picked it up.

"Alright, moving on, then," Willow clicked off her headlamp and hurried outside. "Let's see if they left anything for us at Raven's place."

As they walked, they marveled again at the electric lights at the treatment plant.

"There's no lights anywhere, except there," Josh said. "I wonder if they'll get all the power up in town?"

"Maybe the EMP wasn't so bad after all," Raven speculated. "Maybe they got the water turned on."

As soon as they reached her house, they went straight to the kitchen and Clark turned the faucet on.

"It works!" Raven marveled. "And I haven't even paid my water bill!"

They stared at the water flowing freely from the tap. It'd been weeks since they'd seen something so simple, yet so convenient.

"Let's fill up!" Josh pulled out his nearly empty water bottle. The others followed suit. Soon, everyone had topped up their bottles.

"Okay, everybody, help yourself to anything the looters left," Raven said.

Willow turned on her headlamp and swung it around the living room. The furniture, except for one old couch, had been taken. Artwork was gone. They'd even taken the wool rug.

They had left the bookshelf alone, though. Apparently the looters weren't big on literature.

POLICE CAPT. MARCUS LARAMIE walked out of the treatment plant. Another officer would arrive in a few minutes to take his place as guard. That's what they'd been reduced to this week – security guards for the city's sewage facility.

But why not? It was the only place in town, probably the only building in the state, and maybe the whole nation, that had functional electricity.

At the front gate, he greeted Officer Marston with a nod, and unlocked the gate to let him into the facility.

"All quiet?" Marston asked.

"Like a cemetery at midnight," Marcus said. "See ya later."

He walked out the gate and headed down the road. No need to bother with his flashlight. The sky was clear, and the moon lit

the street with a pale glow. Most of the homes in the neighborhood were dark, but some windows were lit with candles
or lamps.

A few blocks from home, something caught his peripheral
vision. He stopped, and turned to look.

Had he seen a light in Raven's house? Or had he imagined it?

12

Willow wandered into the kitchen, where Clark and Raven were going through the cabinets.

"More salt!" Clark triumphed, holding up a full salt shaker.

"Anybody want a pizza cutter?" Raven held it aloft like a trophy.

"Guess not," Willow said. "And apparently neither did the thieves."

"They did leave my paring knife, though, so I'm taking it," Raven said. "And these little packages of yeast."

"That's all you found?" Willow's voice revealed her disappointment. This whole trip to town was starting to look like a bust.

"All the food is gone, and almost everything else," Raven said. "Should we head over to Kristie's now?"

"I guess." Willow took another glance around. "Where's Josh?"

She heard a toilet flush.

"Well, that answers that question," Raven said. "I need to use the bathroom, too."

"If there's any toilet paper left, be sure to grab it." Willow went and plunked herself on the lonely sofa. Clark remained in the kitchen, rifling through the drawers. Josh came out and sank down beside her.

"My feet are sore," he said. "I think –"

"SHHH!" Willow sprang to her feet, then glanced at Josh and whispered. "What was that sound?"

"The back screen door?" He whispered, launching to his feet.

Willow grabbed his arm and pulled him toward the front door.

"Clark!" She hissed. "GET OUT!"

She propelled Josh out the door ahead of her, and they jumped off the porch. A shout and a scurry sounded behind them.

"Keep going," she urged her brother as they rounded the corner of the house. "To the trees!"

But he stopped next to the garden shed behind the house.

"We need to help them!"

"I know," Willow whispered.

But how? Who was in the house? How many people had come in? Was Raven still in the bathroom?

She pulled her handgun. Breathed a two-second prayer. Jesus, please help!

"Hold on," Josh hissed. "Look!"

The back screen door creaked, then a white cat jumped off the back porch.

"A cat! It's just a cat." Willow lowered her gun. "Thank God."

MARCUS LET himself in the front door of Raven's house. It wasn't locked, which wasn't surprising, given that it had been looted like so many others that had belonged to Christians.

There might be squatters, though, so he kept his Glock at the ready.

It was dark. Had he imagined that flash of light through the window?

His flashlight beam cut through the blackness.

But wait... what was that sound?

Slowly, he made his way to the bathroom. The door was closed.

Too bad he couldn't radio for backup. If this wasn't Raven's house, he wouldn't even bother. But it was Raven's. His traitor half-sister.

And what if it was her in that room? What if she'd come back to town?

He couldn't remember if there was a window large enough to escape from her bathroom. And he couldn't give her time, if there was.

His hand wrapped the doorknob and turned. Not locked.

Marcus shoved the door open, his flashlight illuminating the sink, toilet, and tub with shower. Nobody.

He sidled up to the shower and yanked open the curtain. Still nobody.

The noise was coming from the toilet.

Someone *had* been here! The toilet was still running. Raven had an old toilet that needed a new flap. Marcus tapped the handle, and water stopped running.

When had it been flushed? Two minutes ago? Ten?

There was no way to be sure, but someone certainly had been here, and had used the toilet. Maybe they were still in the house!

He hurried through the living room, totally ransacked, glanced in the kitchen, then went to Raven's bedroom. Nothing.

Getting on his knees, he checked under her bed. Then in her closet. Nobody.

He sat on her bed, his light playing across the framed art on her wall. It portrayed a stormy ocean beach, with a ray of sun breaking through the clouds. And a verse he'd learned as a child:

Thou wilt keep him in perfect peace, whose mind is stayed on thee: because he trusteth in thee. Isaiah 26:3

Was Raven's mind in perfect peace because she trusted God?

Was his own mind ever at peace?

No. And it wouldn't be, either, until he'd caught her and made her sorry for what she did.

WILLOW'S HEADLAMP beam cut through the darkness in Kristie's kitchen. It hadn't been looted, maybe because it'd been occupied for weeks longer than Raven's and her own. Clark and Raven wrapped kitchen knives in some towels. Willow pulled all the gallon-size plastic bags out of their box and laid them flat in her pack. The box would take up too much space.

She walked past Matt's room, where Josh was rustling around, and went into Kristie's bedroom. Was there anything worth taking here? She'd love to take the pillows and bedding, but they were so bulky. Too bad they didn't have any pack animals, like mules, that they could load stuff up on.

Moving into the bathroom, her light beam fell on the sink. Bar soap, bingo!

She started opening drawers and cabinets. Nail clippers and emery boards, yes! Feminine supplies, yep. Reading glasses? Sure, they'd work as magnifying glasses for splinters and stuff.

Lip balm, pain relievers, toothpaste, two unopened packages of toothbrushes.

Toilet paper! It was bulky, but she was taking it. She squashed it as flat as she could before shoving it into her pack.

This bathroom was a gold mine.

What else was here? Brushes and combs. Jaci and her daughters would love those.

A little magnifying mirror? Shampoo? Why not – if she ran out of room, she could ditch those things later. Same with a hand towel.

Cold medicine? Sure. In it went.

She looked around, adding a few more odds and ends, then went back to the kitchen. Clark and Raven were still there, going through everything.

"Is there anything to eat?"

"Yep. Some of it has to be cooked, like noodles and rice, so that's out of the question tonight. But I found two cans of pork and beans, a half-eaten box of crackers, and dry salami." Raven turned her light toward the counter, where she'd laid those out. "Plus, this little package of cheese and crackers."

"I also found two boxes of jello mix," Clark added. "That's about it. She was almost out of food when your team came back and rescued her."

That was an interesting way to put it. They'd rescued her?

Willow sat on a chair at the table. This was odd – Kristie's place hadn't been looted, yet she was almost out of food. Didn't Matt say Kristie's power was out? So she had been without power, but also hadn't bought any groceries for a while before Matt showed up.

It was possible the EMP took place days before Matt, Josh and Raven had 'rescued' Kristie. Did she know about the EMP? It seemed likely.

If Kristie had known, why hadn't she told them?

On a hunch, Willow got up and looked in the fridge and freezer. Both were empty and cleaned out.

That could mean that Kristie knew the power was out forever, or at least a very long time. If she had been the one that emptied and cleaned the fridge, she must have known about the EMP.

And again, why hadn't she said anything about it?

Why would she keep that a secret from the band of believers?

It would have been incredibly helpful to know as soon as possible. The believers could have been sending teams to town immediately, and possibly gathered a ton more goods earlier. The longer they were delayed, the more dangerous travel became, and the more competition there was for available resources.

Kristie's secret could cost them dearly. Maybe their very survival.

Willow closed the blinds and lit a half-burned candle.

Josh joined them in the kitchen, and they all sat down to pray and eat. The food was tasty, but Willow barely noticed. She continued puzzling over Kristie's secret.

She'd hate to accuse her of withholding important information. Kristie was Matt's mom, after all. But this was weird. When she had a chance, she'd talk to Raven about it and get her opinion. In the meantime, she'd keep it to herself and pray about it.

Clark sprinkled some pepper on his pork and beans.

"Should we spend the night here, or in the forest?"

"Here, I think." Willow glanced at the faces in the candlelight. "Unless anyone has concerns. It's not really safe anywhere, but it's more comfortable here, and we didn't bring a tent."

"Sounds good to me," Raven agreed.

"I'll sleep on the sofa," Clark said. "You all can have the bedrooms."

After dinner, Josh headed off to Matt's room, and Raven and Willow went to Kristie's. Willow kicked off her boots and sank onto the king-sized bed. Her head rested on real down pillows.

"This is amazing." She sighed. "I could totally get used to this!"

"Don't get used to it. Luxury is one thing we'll never get." Raven flopped down beside her. "Oh. My. Yeah, it's amazing."

Willow turned her face toward Raven's voice in the pitch black room.

"Before you fall into dreamland, I need to talk to you."

She could hear Raven propping herself up with the pillows.

"Okay. Shoot."

"Do you think it's possible that Kristie knew about the EMP and never told us?"

Willow waited through a long silence. She was tempted to say more, but shut her mouth. Finally, Raven flopped toward her.

"Yes, it's possible. I was kinda starting to wonder about that, too. While we were going through stuff in the kitchen."

"Her fridge and freezer were cleaned out, Raven! Why would she do that, if she expected the power to come back on like normal?"

"The food would start to spoil in a day or two."

"The freezer food?"

"Maybe three days, if she kept the door closed?"

"Fine. Let's say the power was off for three days, and she cleaned out the fridge and freezer. Why didn't she go to the grocery store for basic stuff like canned goods and bread and bottled water?"

"Maybe she did, but by then the store was closed because they didn't have any power to run their coolers and their chip readers."

"But if the power is out in just one town, you'd still be getting regular grocery and gas deliveries. They'd fuel their generators, and still sell the basics. I don't think she'd been shopping for a week or ten days, or more, before Matt came here."

Raven sighed. "I think you're right. But I hate to think about what this means."

"What do you think it means?"

"Well, that she's intentionally keeping secrets. And this is a big one. And people that keep secrets don't keep just one."

BRILLIANT SUNLIGHT PIERCED Willow's eyes when she finally opened them. She'd slept like a dead woman, but she didn't feel rested. She covered her eyes. Her head hurt.

The rest of her was comfortable, though. This bed was wonderful!

Raven rustled around, putting on her boots.

"Wake up, sleepy head! The day's starting without you."

Willow groaned and rolled away from the sunshine. Slowly, she pushed the comforter off, and sat up. At least she'd found some pain relievers yesterday. Her headache demanded one. She pulled them out of her bag and took two with a gulp of water from her bottle.

After pulling on her boots and gun, she poked her head into Matt's room and told Josh to wake up. He grunted and flopped over. Like he felt as bad as she did, which was unlikely.

Clark was filling his water bottle in the kitchen, and Willow filled hers, too. Raven joined them, and pretty soon, Josh wandered in, his hair all bed-head.

He stretched and yawned.

"What's to eat?"

Typical teenage guy. All about food, all the time. Willow smiled at her brother.

"Not much, I'm afraid. No eggs or fish or venison."

He sent her a pouty look. "No leftovers?"

"We've got some crackers left, and a little salami."

Josh pulled up a chair.

"Let's eat!"

Everyone sat at the table, and they divvied up the remaining food. Clark prayed a blessing over it, and asked for protection for the team and the members at home.

After "amen," he asked, "What's the plan?"

"Should we go to your wife's grandpa's house?"

Clark shook his head. "I don't think there is much left worth looking for there."

"Then today we go shopping," Willow said. "Carefully, though."

"Maybe we should split into teams so we're less obvious as a group," Raven suggested.

"That would be okay, as long as we remain in sight of each other," Willow said. "And close enough to hear, if one of us yells for help."

"So it's me and you?" Josh asked.

"Sure. And Clark and Raven." Willow agreed. "Just keep your eyes peeled, everybody. It's not exactly safe, and we don't know what we'll run into."

Clark turned his dark eyes on her.

"What if we become separated? Should we have meet up locations?"

"Good idea. If we get separated, we can meet in the woods behind Raven's house. If that's not safe, then in the woods here, behind Kristie's," Willow said. "If that's compromised, we will just all return to the cabin, because Clark doesn't know the other locations like our early camps and the cave."

"There is a cave?" Clark asked.

"Yeah, maybe we'll show you sometime," Josh said. "It's pretty cool."

Raven stood up, and pushed in her chair.

"Let's do this!"

Willow retrieved her pack and joined the others at the front door.

"Why don't you two go first," she said to Raven. "Josh and I will wait a minute, then follow you downtown. Be careful, everybody!"

Willow watched them walk down the road about a block, then turned to her brother.

"Ready?"

He gave her a cocky look. "I was born ready!"

They started toward town, keeping an eye on Raven and Clark up ahead, while also scanning their surroundings for threats and danger.

Willow's head still pounded, but she forced herself to ignore it. She needed all her faculties at full performance today.

A few people worked in their gardens, but for the most part, things were looking quiet. Peaceful, even. There were some cars parked in odd locations, and even a few right in the middle of the lane. Other than that, it looked like a normal summer day in Ponderosa.

Hopefully she wouldn't run into anyone she knew. What on earth would they talk about? Would they know that Willow had been hunted because she didn't have the mark? Was there a bounty on Christians – how would she know if there was, unless she was caught?

And on the topic of being caught, where was Mom today? Had she escaped? Been killed?

Josh elbowed her.

"What?"

He pointed, and she followed his gaze. Raven and Clark were getting too far ahead. She needed to step up the pace.

And keep her head in the game!

13

As they reached Main Street, <u>Willow</u> slowed her pace. All the stores were closed. Some were boarded up, and those that weren't, had broken glass. This did not look like her sleepy little hometown!

Still, the geraniums in the hanging baskets were blooming in a riot of yellow, pink and purple. Someone had been watering them. It was odd. Why would they bother doing that, when the town looked like a war zone?

A war zone with beautiful hanging baskets!

Apparently the flowers were of no interest to the thieves.

But despite the closed stores, there were a surprising number of people walking downtown. They seemed headed toward the town square, and <u>Raven and Clark</u> were going that direction as well.

Willow glanced at her brother.

"Looks like something's going on."

His jaw tightened. "Yep."

"Let's start to close the distance to Raven and Clark."

They hurried and joined the group gathering at the square. Tables had been set up, all different kinds and colors. Folding white plastic tables, industrial-type tables, camp tables. And people were setting goods on them, and parking themselves in chairs behind them.

An open-air market! This was new. Perfect!

Willow caught Raven's gaze across the square, and exchanged a smile. This was just what they needed!

Now, to find goods worth buying, and get a good price for them, and get out of here.

"Look, the farm store has a table," Josh said, heading for it. Willow tagged along.

"How much for the chicken scratch?" Josh asked.

They knew the proprietor, Ben Johnson. They'd been buying from him all their lives. Ben smiled.

"What you got?" he asked.

Josh looked at Willow. She shrugged and nodded. They needed that scratch!

He leaned forward and whispered in Ben's ear. Ben's eyes widened, and he looked at Willow. She said nothing.

"Well, I can give you two bags of scratch for that." Ben hefted two 20-pound bags onto the table, and held out his hand.

Josh glanced around, then quickly dropped a $1/10^{th}$ ounce gold eagle coin in Ben's palm. Ben turned it over in the sunlight, looking at both sides, then quickly tucked it into his chest pocket.

"Need anything else?" he asked hopefully.

"Not today," Willow said.

"Well, come back next Saturday. We'll be here every week!"

Willow gave him a smile as she picked up one bag and balanced it on her hip like a baby. Josh picked up the other, and they moved on to the next table.

Nothing of interest there. She looked for Raven and spotted her across the square, watching Clark talk to a vendor.

Something felt off. Willow's gaze swept the square, but she saw nothing disturbing. Still, she listened to her spirit.

"Josh, we need to wrap this up. Get ready to go." Her shoulders tensed. "I'm going to tell Raven we're heading out."

Willow started toward her friend. Raven glanced back over her shoulder, saw Willow, and gave her a thumbs-up.

Willow shook her head and circled her finger in the air, indicating "wrap it up."

Raven's gaze moved away from her, then her expression turned grave. Without speaking to Clark, she moved away from him quickly, then darted for the alley.

What? Willow scanned the crowd. A man cut through the group, running toward the same alley. Was it Raven's brother, Marcus?

He didn't slow as he ran past Clark, but Clark turned and looked as the man went by. Then he looked around, probably for Raven, who was long gone. His gaze found Willow's.

"Get out!" she mouthed, jerking her thumb over her shoulder.

His expression changed from puzzled to panicked, and he scooped up his purchases and walked away quickly.

Willow and Josh exited the way they'd come in, hurrying up the street.

"Should we go find Raven?" Josh asked. "Or wait for Clark?"

"Nope. Keep moving. Look normal." She cast a quick glance behind her, but saw nothing out of the ordinary. Except the boarded up, broken down Main Street.

Even as she controlled her stride, her thoughts raced. Who was chasing Raven? And why? Was it her brother?

Had Clark gotten away? Hopefully he could find his way back to their end of town and the forest meeting locations.

Josh walked beside her, his gaze fixed ahead, gripping his sack of chicken feed.

MARCUS LARAMIE SPRINTED through the alley, looking for the woman. Where did she go? Ahead, he heard a clatter, and as he emerged at the street, he saw a garbage can lid rolling off to his right. He headed that way.

Was it Raven? Or had he imagined it was her?

But if it wasn't, why had she run?

He scanned the street, which was filling with shoppers walking toward the market. Except that one, at the end of the block, running the other way.

He took off after her.

It had to be Raven. Had to be!

WILLOW AND JOSH made their way to the first meet up location, in the forest behind Raven's house. They sat on a log in silence, waiting.

"Are you praying?" Josh asked.

Willow nodded. "You?"

"Yep." Josh fell back into silence again.

Willow's head still ached. Worse, now, probably because she was stressed.

"Someone's coming," Josh whispered. "I hear something."

"Hide!"

They both scrambled behind trees. She peeked out, but didn't see anyone.

Oh, how she hoped it was her friend, Raven. That she was okay and had made it back to the forest.

Moments later, Clark came into view. Alone.

Willow stepped out and waved him over.

"Is Raven here?" he asked.

"No." Willow's gaze fell. "Not yet."

"Should we stay here?" Josh asked. "It's behind her house, so if they're chasing her, maybe this isn't safe. Or she might feel it's not safe to come here."

"Okay, we'll move." Willow hoisted her bag of chicken feed. "Let's go to the other location, behind Kristie's."

They walked in silence. Judging by the sun, it must be high noon. And it was growing warm.

Willow's stomach felt acidic. Where was her friend? Had she escaped? Why did it have to be Raven, her one good friend?

Finally, they arrived at the spot and sat down. It didn't look like anyone wanted to talk, and neither did she, so Willow prayed. Prayed and prayed for her friend.

The sun kept sliding west. Maybe an hour had passed.

She could sense Josh and Clark's eyes on her. She sighed, and looked at them.

"We'll keep waiting. She's in more danger than we are."

A few minutes later, she saw someone coming through the trees. She motioned the others to get up. Just in case they had to run.

But it was Raven, her lanky frame carrying her pack, and her glossy black hair swinging over her shoulders. Like she was out on a casual jaunt!

Willow ran toward her and wrapped her in a bear hug.

"What happened? Are you okay? Who was that guy?"

"Whoa, slow it down, my friend." Raven smiled at her. "I'm fine."

Josh ran up. "What happened to you?"

"Yes, what happened?" Clark asked.

"Just as you were signaling to wrap it up, I saw my brother across the crowd. And he saw me."

"So you ran into the alley," Willow said. "Then what?"

"He gave chase. And he's in pretty good shape," Raven said. "But I'm a marathoner!"

"You just out-ran him?" Josh asked.

"Well, I darted around corners, through parking lots and side streets. Mostly so he wouldn't get a clear shot if he was trying to shoot me."

"Did he shoot at you? Your brother?" Clark's eyes widened.

"No. And he's a half-brother, actually," Raven explained. "Anyway, eventually he tired and fell behind, and I just lost him."

She looked around the forest, then back the way she'd come.

"At least, I think I lost him. But we should move on, just in case."

"I'm all for that." Josh pulled on his pack. "Let's make tracks!"

He took the lead, and Willow fell in behind him. Her head ached like she'd been hit with a bat. And her stomach wasn't too happy, either.

It must have been that salami.

MARCUS PICKED up a bag of groceries from the police department. His paycheck was reduced to a weekly ration of nonperishable food – which was a pretty sweet deal, these days. Most of his neighbors were gardening or hunting, or both. And most of them were losing weight already.

His feet were killing him as he walked home under the hot July sun. Why had he thought he could catch Raven? The girl was a runner. Always had been.

Now she was running from him, and he couldn't keep up. But he could outsmart her. He'd always been able to do that.

Arriving home, he put his groceries in his gun safe. Didn't need to let the neighbors steal them when he was at work.

He pulled off his combat boots and ran the shower. It was cool, but it felt good this scorching afternoon. He was careful not to let any of that water get in his mouth, though. There were already reports of a few residents getting beaver fever.

After his shower, he poured himself a tall glass of sun tea. Too bad there was no sugar to put in it. Or alcohol. A chilled Long Island iced tea would be perfect about now. A chilled anything would be good.

He walked out to the front porch and planted himself on the old swing in the shade.

If it weren't for Raven, life would be pretty good right now, despite everything.

She'd been in town, right under his thumb, and gotten away! After he'd spent weeks combing the forest for her.

He should just let her go. Let it go.

But he couldn't. She'd betrayed his trust, and nearly gotten him fired after he'd helped her. What she'd done was unforgivable.

When he'd first seen her this morning, he couldn't believe his eyes. There she was! Right in front of him.

Had she moved back into town?

Nah, she wasn't that stupid. But she was stupid enough to show herself in town. Maybe she'd do it again. He'd keep a close eye on that new outdoor market. Raven needed supplies, like everyone else.

Montana was beautiful, but no one could eat the scenery.

WILLOW WIPED her brow on her shirt sleeve. The sun was so hot! And she was so thirsty.

"Let's take a quick break." She stopped and lifted her water bottle to her lips, guzzling down the liquid. Her head wasn't hurting so much, but her stomach was still upset.

It'd been pretty stupid to eat that greasy salami. A wave of nausea rose up her throat as she thought about it.

Her stomach gurgled and groaned. She grabbed the toilet paper from her pack and dashed into the bushes.

When she returned, Clark, Josh and Raven were resting in the shade of a cedar.

"You okay?" Raven asked.

Willow shook her head. "I don't feel so good."

"Neither do I." Raven patted the ground beside her. "Come sit down."

Gratefully, Willow sank to the earth. It'd be nice to just sprawl out here and sleep in the shade. But they had a long ways to go. She promised herself five minutes.

Raven's stomach was as noisy as her own.

"I've got toilet paper," Willow offered.

"I'll be taking you up on that." Raven held her stomach and lay back on the ground. It looked like a good idea, so Willow did the same. And closed her eyes.

"Wake up, sleepy head!" Josh nudged her knee with his boot.

"What?" Willow's eyes snapped open. "Was I asleep?"

"You were snoring!" Josh laughed.

Willow sat up. Oh, that tummy ached!

"How long was I out?"

"Half hour, at least. I thought about letting you sleep longer, but figured you'd be mad."

Willow held her hand out to her brother, and he yanked her to her feet.

"We should get moving. Got a long way to go." She hoisted her pack and her chicken feed.

The group pressed on up the mountain, the sun punishing them every time they got out of the shade. Willow felt perspiration beading on her face. Normally, she loved summer. But this was misery.

Her stomach ached continually, and her pack weighed her down and made her feel even hotter. It's not like she could hand off part of her load to someone else. They were all carrying a lot. At least her head wasn't hurting as bad anymore.

She could be thankful for that.

When they finally stopped for the evening, they were about half-way home. The guys built a small campfire, and Raven cooked some of the rice they'd taken from Kristie's kitchen. Willow hoped it would help calm her stomach. But it didn't.

She made several mad dashes into the bushes before finally falling asleep that night. Several times, she woke up with crazy dreams. They were vivid, colorful and intense. Most of them she'd forgotten by morning, except the last one. That one was the one from which she woke up yelling.

In it, she and Josh were walking home to the cabin, when she spotted a gang of men all dressed in black, with rifles and hand-guns, loaded down with lots of filled 30-round ammo maga-zines. Next thing she knew, they were breaking into a rural home and killing the occupants. They partied there and pillaged the house, then moved on to the next home. Willow and Josh ran toward the house, yelling warnings to the inhabitants. Someone came out the back door. He looked familiar. Was it John Anderson? Willow yelled, and woke up yelling.

It was dawn. Josh sat up, staring wide-eyed at her.

Raven jumped up. "What? What's going on?"

Clark rolled over and looked at Willow.

"I had a bad dream."

"I'll say." Raven put a hand on her arm. "Are you alright?"

"No." Willow stood up, her stomach aching. "Something bad is about to happen. We need to get home!"

Raven scurried off to the bushes. She came back holding her stomach.

"I don't think it was bad salami," she said. "I think we caught a bug."

Josh grimaced. "I don't feel that great, either."

"Oh, no." Willow felt his forehead. "Well, you don't have a fever, so that's good."

She looked at Clark and Raven.

"I wish we could stay here today and rest, but we just can't. We have to press on toward home."

Raven picked up her pack. "I'll look forward to crashing on that bunk the minute we walk in the door."

"I hear you, sister." Willow picked up her bag of chicken feed. "Everybody make sure you drink a ton of water. The last thing we need is dehydration."

It was good they were getting an early start. Willow glanced toward the sun, which was just making its way over the mountain. It was so much easier to hike during the cool part of the day. And it wouldn't be very cool for very long.

14

Kristie cooked the eggs that Candy brought in from the barn. It was kind of nice having Willow, Josh and Raven gone for a few days. They weren't horrible to be around, but they *had* convinced Matt to run away with them a few weeks ago. Their religious mindset made that seem okay to them, maybe even the right thing to do, but apparently none of them thought about how it would affect her, the *mother.*

Maybe Willow and Josh, being kids, were too oblivious to think about something like that, but Raven was twenty-four. She had no excuse.

Anyway, it was nice that they were out of her hair for now. She'd enjoyed a couple of quiet days with no one annoying her or telling her what to do.

And why should Willow be the one to tell *her* what to do, anyway? How come she was the leader of the group?

She was too young. That position should fall to a more mature person, like herself. Because Candy was a little too flighty.

Sure, there were other adults in the group now – Deborah and Alan, Jaci and Clark, even Jacob – but they were all newcomers. And while Kristie might be considered a newcomer to the mountains, she wasn't really a newcomer, because she'd known Willow, Josh and Raven, the foundation of the group, for months.

But Willow seemed to have a firm grip on the leadership of the group, and everyone submissively went along with it.

Why? Why didn't anyone else see a problem with this?

Willow was tough and smart, but she was too young. Too naïve. Too inexperienced.

Well, Kristie wasn't going to have to put up with it anymore. Today was the day she and Matt were moving out. She just had to get Matt to go along with that.

It wouldn't be too hard, once he saw the retreat and saw what he was missing. A warm home, a comfortable bed, good food. All the things he didn't have out here in the wilderness.

"Matt! Breakfast!" She hollered up to the loft. She didn't have to yell twice. He scurried down the ladder a minute later.

"I thought we could go hunting today," Kristie suggested.

"You?" Her son looked at her like she was crazy. "You want to go hunting?"

"I need to learn. And it'd be nice to spend some time with you."

"Huh." Matt forked a huge bite of scrambled eggs into his mouth.

"Come on, Matt," she cajoled. "It'll be fun."

He drank a full cup of water.

"Okay."

Ha! Kristie smiled. Her plan was underway. Now, on to success!

"Did you get that campfire all the way out?" Willow asked Clark.

"Yes, I did." He shifted the shoulder straps on his backpack. "I doused it with water."

"Good. Thanks."

It didn't seem like her brain was functioning at 100 percent today. Often when she was sick, she felt that way. Might overlook something important. Like putting out a fire. Good thing Clark was paying attention and taking care of important details like that.

Maybe she was getting dehydrated. She took a swig from her water bottle.

A cramp twisted her stomach. She stopped and bent over, clutching her middle. When would this end?

Raven stepped beside her and rubbed her back.

She wanted to curl up in a ball and sleep. For weeks.

But they had to keep moving. The dream kept playing over and over in her mind. The villains. The victims. Trying to warn people.

Willow straightened up. Heard Raven's stomach gurgle. Saw her face twist in pain.

"Are you okay, Raven?"

She frowned. "I've been better."

"You and me both."

Josh dropped his chicken feed bag on the ground.

"Make that three. My stomach aches!"

KRISTIE LET Matt lead the way into the forest. She'd let him lead as much as possible, as long as he was generally headed in the direction of the Andersons' retreat. They looked for deer tracks, and only found old ones in the volcanic ash.

"When we find fresh tracks, we can follow those," Matt said.

At some point, Kristie would have to take the lead, or she'd be too far from the landmarks she'd memorized. For now, heading in the general direction was okay.

Matt stopped so suddenly she almost ran into him. His hand shot into the air in the universal sign for "stop!"

She froze.

What was it? Deer?

What if they actually killed a deer? They'd have to gut it, dress it and take it back to the cabin. There wouldn't be an excuse to keep walking and eventually "happen" into the Andersons' retreat.

What if it wasn't a deer?

What if it was a bear?

A grizzly?

She'd seen the claw marks on Willow's leg.

Kristie swallowed hard. Reminded herself to keep breathing.

Finally, Matt's shoulder muscles relaxed. He let his hand drop.

"It's Tony," he said quietly. "Raven's uncle."

Oh, no. This wasn't good. She didn't want to run into anybody in the woods, much less someone who knew them.

"Hey, Tony!" Matt yelled, before she could stop him. "Over here!"

Kristie peered around his shoulder. The grizzled old man turned toward them, then raised his hand in a salute. He approached, leaning on his walking stick.

Matt bounded toward him, and Kristie followed. Cursing her luck.

Tony stopped and let them close the distance. He was wearing a Christian band t-shirt from the 1990s. And denim jeans, patched with huge patches over the knees, and a straw hat. His grey hair poked out beneath the hat, looking like it hadn't been trimmed in six months.

Somehow he looked like he'd walked out of the gold rush days. Except for the band t-shirt, of course.

"Howdy! How are you on this fine July day?"

"Fine, Tony," Matt said. "We're looking for deer."

Tony scratched his shaggy beard.

"Well, son, I'm afraid you've got a long look coming. I haven't seen any in days."

Matt's smile faded. "Neither have we."

"But you never know," Kristie said. "Today might be our day."

Tony did not appear optimistic.

"Could be." He took off his hat and ran his dirty fingers through his hair. "How's Raven?"

"She went to town with a few others," Matt said. "Mom wouldn't let me go."

Tony raised his scraggy eyebrows. "Town? When?"

"A couple days ago." Kristie forced a smile. "We expect them back this afternoon."

"That's good. Town isn't safe." Tony looked at her, then Matt. "Neither is the forest."

"We know," Matt said.

"No, I mean there's a new threat. There's a lot of folks in the woods now. With guns."

"Yeah, we've noticed." Matt glanced around, like he was checking for strangers in the trees. "We're being careful."

"That's good." Tony planted his hat back on his head. "I should be on my way. Tell my niece I said hello."

"I will," Matt said. "And stop by sometime. She'd love to see you."

"Perhaps I will," the old man said. "Perhaps I will."

Tony walked away, and Kristie took the opportunity to begin steering Matt in the direction of the retreat. It was probably noon by now, and she wanted to get there before too late in the day. And she wasn't completely sure she knew exactly how to get there.

By NOON, Willow had only hiked half as far as she'd hoped. Between the cramps and bloating and gas and diarrhea, it was all she could do to keep walking. Raven didn't look any better, and Josh was making a lot of pit stops, too. It was time to rest.

"Okay, let's take a break!"

Raven sent a grateful look her way. Josh dramatically collapsed on the ground, and Clark sat down beside him.

Willow set down her chicken feed, then took off her pack. She was unbelievably tired. She lay down in the shade and closed her eyes. Almost wishing she'd never have to open them again.

She didn't know how long she was out, but her intestinal distress woke her up. She made a beeline for the bushes. At least she had real toilet paper!

Walking back to the group, she noticed that both Josh and Raven were sound asleep, but Clark sat with his back against a tree.

Keeping watch?

She sank down beside him.

"Thank you, Clark."

He turned those dark eyes on her. "For what?"

"Watching out for us."

"Always," his deep voice intoned. "We will always watch out for each other."

Josh's stomach rumbled, and he opened his eyes. Slowly, he sat up. Willow handed him the toilet paper. He went off in the woods and came back a few minutes later, looking less pained.

Raven stirred, then sat up. Her beautiful Native face was drawn and pale.

Willow sighed and glanced at Clark. He seemed to be the only one not affected. Yet he'd eaten all the same food, drank all the same water, been around the same people.

"Clark, will you pray for us?"

They huddled in a circle, arms around each other's shoulders, as Clark prayed.

KRISTIE LED the way through the forest. Finally, she found a landmark she recognized from following Willow to the retreat the other day. Two lodgepole pines grew up inches from each other, and now they clung together like lovers, their trunks pressed together and their branches entwined.

She ran her hand over the bark as she walked by. Now she knew where she was, and which way to go. But she had to be careful so Matt wouldn't realize she was purposefully going somewhere.

She'd have to make a point of meandering.

So she did, tracking a bit to the left, then to the right, constantly looking at the ground like she was searching for deer tracks.

It would be so much easier if she didn't have to keep up this charade! If she could just tell Matt she was taking him to the retreat, and they were going to live there.

But he'd never go for that. He'd see it as a betrayal of Willow's agreement with the Andersons, and maybe a betrayal of his friends in general, and an imposition on the Andersons.

So Kristie meandered. But she kept her eye out for landmarks that told her she was going the right direction. The sun's position indicated mid-afternoon when they finally approached the ridge that she was sure led to the back of the Andersons' property.

She started up the ridge, with Matt trailing her.

"Halt!"

She froze.

"Put your guns down, and your hands up!"

Her eyes scanned the area. She didn't see anyone. Where was this person?

"I said, 'Guns down!'" A man with a gun trained on Matt stepped out from behind a bush.

Slowly, she lowered her rifle to the ground. She glanced back and saw Matt doing the same.

"Okay, hands up, and move away from the guns. Slowly!"

Kristie lifted her hands. Surely this must be one of John Anderson's people. They were so close to their retreat now. It had to be them, right? She stepped away from her rifle.

Matt wasn't moving away! What if he got shot?

"Do what they say, Matt!"

"No."

Horror gripped Kristie's throat. What if Matt got killed because of her crazy scheme? Should she tell him the truth, right now? Or was it too late?

15

Willow forced herself to keep marching toward home. As soon as they got there, they could relieve themselves of their burdens and crash into bed. And stay there for days, if they wanted.

Except for the illness, the town trip had been a success. They'd gotten more food, and Clark had gotten some good gear at the market. Plus all the little extras they'd retrieved from their own houses.

She glanced back. Raven trailed just a little behind her, and Josh trudged along, head down like a mule plowing a field. Clark brought up the rear, glancing this way and that, obviously watchful for danger.

He and his family were a good addition to the band of believers. And it was clear Matt and Josh thought so too, but mostly about Clark's pretty daughters.

She almost smiled. Young love. It'd find a way in the midst of any disaster, given a little time.

Not that those kids were old enough to be in love.

But she remembered being fifteen. And a number of crushes before she reached even that age.

What about her – would she ever find love? No, that was doubtful. There was too little time, too little opportunity. And she couldn't waste time pining away over some man. She had a group to lead and look out for. That was her mission now. And she would carry it out faithfully, so help her God.

Or God help her.

KRISTIE DIDN'T KNOW what to say to her son. She had to say something, though, and quick, before he got shot. She turned toward the man with the gun.

"Don't shoot. Please!" What else could she say? If it was one of Anderson's guys – she had an idea. "We're Christians!"

"Who are you? Where are you from?"

"I'm Kristie, and this is my son, Matt. We're from Ponderosa."

His gun remained trained on her boy.

"Move away from the gun, Matt."

He didn't move.

"Do it, Matthew!" Kristie's voice carried an edge of hysteria. He couldn't get shot. Not now. Not in front of her! "Please."

Matt moved one step away from his rifle.

The man pulled a radio from his belt and spoke into it. A moment later, a voice replied, but Kristie couldn't make out the words.

This was not going at all like she'd planned. But what did she think would happen? She'd waltz up to their door and ring the bell and be welcomed in? Maybe this had been a very bad idea, after all.

The man kept Matt in his sights. He said nothing. Asked no questions.

Should she say something? Like what? What could she say?

"Can we leave now? We'll go away, I promise."

"No." That was all he said. No explanation.

"Why not? Are you just going to keep pointing that gun at us forever?"

He didn't answer.

This was such a bad idea! Why hadn't she just complied with Willow and stayed home at the cabin? At least there, she was safe. Had a bed and a little food to eat, and wasn't worried about her son getting shot by some non-communicative idiot who wouldn't let him out of his gun sights.

Tears pressed at her eyes and began to spill.

Oh, why had she done this? She was so stupid! She wiped her eyes with the back of her hand. Sniffled a little.

Kristie looked at her son. He stood erect, hands at shoulder height, glaring at the gunman. Strong and defiant. Maybe not the best choice, but he was no coward. He was becoming a good man. If only he could survive this crazy world.

Another man, dressed in camo fatigues and carrying a big rifle, crested the hill and approached the gunman.

"Who are they?"

"Kristie and her son Matt. Say they're Christians from Ponderosa."

The second man approached a little closer.

"Are you alone, or are there others?"

She wasn't sure how to answer that. Wasn't sure about anything anymore. Finally, decided to lean toward the truth.

"We are here alone, but we've been living with others."

"Who?"

"A group from Ponderosa, mostly."

"Names?"

"Raven, Willow, Josh, Candy –"

"Shut up, Mom!" Matt's tone was fierce. "Don't tell them anything!"

She glanced at him. He glared at her.

"But, Matt –"

"Don't say anything!"

She looked back at the men.

"Please, we don't mean any trouble. We'll go away."

"You mentioned some names we're familiar with," the first man said.

"Please, just let us go."

"Not yet."

The two spoke between themselves, and again Kristie couldn't make out what they were saying. The first one got on the radio again. Moments later, a third man approached. She recognized him, because he'd come to the cabin once. It was John Anderson!

What a relief! These were the Andersons' people. They were Christians. They wouldn't hurt her and Matt. She hoped.

John spoke quietly with his guys, then approached Kristie and Matt. His jaw was set, his eyes hard.

"What are you doing here?"

"We're hunting," Kristie said.

"The middle of the afternoon is a weird time to be hunting. And you're a long way from your cabin."

"We've been out since this morning. We've had to go farther and farther from the cabin, because it's getting hard to find deer."

He stared her down.

"Did Willow tell you how to get here?"

"What?" Kristie's voice trembled. "No!"

"It's pretty strange that you'd be here, of all the places in the wilderness, if she didn't tell you."

Matt finally spoke up.

"She didn't. She'd never do that."

John's eyes turned toward Matt.

"So." John studied Matt's face. "You just wandered over here, totally by accident?"

"Yeah. We've been walking around all day."

John took a long breath and expelled it slowly. He turned toward his men.

"You guys can get back to your posts. I'll take care of this."

A shot rang out.

WILLOW BROKE out of the trees, into the cabin's clearing. Home never looked so good! Alan hollered a greeting, and soon the entire group hurried toward her, Josh, Clark and Raven. Jaci and the girls launched themselves at Clark, who managed to wrap all three in his big arms.

"I'm going to bed," Willow announced. "Clark can tell you guys all about it."

Raven and Josh followed her into the cabin. Willow didn't even bother to take off her boots. She just climbed into the bunk and closed her eyes.

Made. It. Home.

But sleep, so desperately desired, eluded her. Instead, she remembered the nightmare that woke her up this morning. The bad guys in the woods, attacking people's homes. Attacking the Andersons' retreat. It was still so real.

She opened her eyes. Across from her, Raven snored lightly in her bunk. Josh was probably napping in the loft.

If only she could sleep, too. But what if that dream was real? What if the Andersons needed help, or needed to be warned of danger?

She was too exhausted and too sick to go. But she couldn't send anyone. No one else knew how to get there.

It was all on her, even if she was wrong.

She climbed down from the bunk. There was still time to get to the retreat and be home again by dark. But she should take someone with her... if nothing else, to help her back to the cabin if she got too weak.

Maybe Clark? Or Matt? If Andersons needed help, they might need guys with guns. Alan? Jacob?

She eased open the cabin door and stepped out into the sun. Clark was wrapping up his story, and the rest of the group hung on each word.

Willow's gaze flitted from one face to the next. But where was Matt? And where was his mom?

"Hey, guys." Her voiced sounded a little weak. "I had a dream."

All eyes turned to her.

"I think the Andersons and their group might be in danger. I want to take a team over to give them a heads up."

"I'll go." Jacob's voice was clear and sure.

"Me, too," Alan offered.

"Where's Matt?" Willow asked. "And Kristie?"

"They went hunting this morning," Deborah said. "I guess they'll be back by dinner?"

Willow scowled. Something didn't seem right. But what was it?

"Alright... Jacob and Alan will come with me. Bring guns and lots of ammo. Deborah, would you keep an eye on Josh and Raven? We all picked up a bug in town."

"I will." Her blue eyes registered concern. "Are you okay?"

"Not really." She shrugged. But what were her choices? Stay here and hope nothing happened? Or go warn the Andersons that she had a dream.

She wanted to climb back in her bunk and forget about it. But the consequences for the other believers could be dire. So she retrieved her rifle and put extra ammo in her bag.

"Okay, guys. Let's move out."

Alan and Jacob swung in beside her. Together, they entered the woods. She had to make a decision: take them clear to the retreat, or have them wait a distance away?

If she took them to the house, she'd be breaking her deal with John Anderson. So maybe having them wait a quarter mile or so away would be better. It wasn't like they couldn't find the retreat on their own in the future, though.

Maybe the Lord would tell her what to do as she got closer. In the meantime, it was a good long hike.

The trio stopped to filter water into their bottles at the creek. Willow's stomach seemed less upset. Maybe she was getting over that bug. Or Clark's prayers for her had worked. Whatever, she thanked the Lord, and asked for guidance as they drew nearer the retreat.

They were still about a mile away when they heard it.

"Was that a shot?" Jacob asked.

Everyone froze.

Another shot rang out, and then several more. Willow's heart thumped.

"C'mon, guys, let's go!"

All three ran toward the sound of the gunfire.

16

Kristie huddled behind a tree about eighty feet from the back of the house. Every time she moved, someone shot at her. She tried to raise her hunting rifle, but another bullet sprayed her face with tree bark.

Where was Matthew?

Without moving, she tried to look around, but everything was out of focus. She blinked her eyes hard, and the forest reappeared.

But she couldn't see Matt. Couldn't see anybody.

She hated herself for coming here. It was supposed to be such a good idea, a wonderful place for her and Matt to live. But instead, she was getting shot at. And who knew what had happened to Matt?

Maybe he was one of the ones still shooting back.

The shooting had been getting more sporadic the last few minutes. But she couldn't tell if the attackers were getting driven off, or the retreat residents were getting killed.

If only she could get in the house! But she was pinned down. There was nothing she could do, but get shot.

A wail filled her throat and shook her shoulders.

Why? Why? WHY?

JACOB CRESTED the hill behind the retreat first. He dropped to his belly. Willow and Alan joined him there, concealing themselves behind huckleberry bushes with small green berries.

Below them, several shooters exchanged fire behind the house.

"Which ones are the bad guys?" Jacob whispered.

Willow squinted, then raised her rifle scope. She studied the impromptu battlefield. John Anderson's guys were in camo and tan and green. The other guys looked like special ops ninjas.

"The ones in all black!"

Jacob's rifle boomed, deafening her.

"Let's split up! Cover me!" Without waiting for a reply, Jacob took off in a crouched run to the left.

Alan fired off several shots as Jacob ran. Then, as Jacob took aim, Alan jumped to his feet and sprinted off to the right.

Willow sighted one of the black ninja guys, paused her breath, and squeezed the trigger. Her aim was a little lower than she intended, nailing his left hip. He fell, dropping his rifle.

She kept him in her sights. If he went for the gun, she'd nail him again.

Jacob fired off two more shots, then started running.

Alan's rifle roared three times. Willow couldn't see him. He must have found some good cover or concealment.

She focused again on the guy she'd hit. He was pretty still. Then Jacob approached him. Willow closed her eyes as Jacob's rifle resounded.

Oh, Lord. Oh, Lord.

Minutes later, the forest fell silent.

Willow wiggled forward on her elbows so she could see

more of the area surrounding the retreat. There were two motionless bodies in black, and several in various colors.

Where was Jacob? Alan?

Finally, she saw John Anderson pressed against a bull pine. Staying low, she hollered at him.

"Hey! It's me, Willow! Don't shoot my guys!"

"Stay down!" He yelled back.

She did, but scoped the area looking for survivors and danger. Other than the dead ones, the ninja guys seemed to have evaporated into the forest.

After what seemed to be a very long time, John Anderson yelled out to her again.

"I think it's safe. You can come out."

Slowly, she pushed herself off the ground, keeping her eyes peeled and her rifle ready. She made her way down to him.

His blue eyes were steely, his jaw tight.

"I brought two guys with me," she said.

"That saved us. We were outnumbered and surrounded."

Willow looked around her.

"Alan? Jacob? You can come out."

Alan emerged from a cluster of boulders not twenty feet from her. He held his left arm, and blood ran down his sleeve.

She hurried toward him.

"How bad is it?"

"Just a flesh wound. I'm fine."

"Let's get a bandage on that. You're losing blood."

He waved her off. "Take care of the others first."

John took a look at Alan's wound. "Go down to the house. My wife, Jeannie, will fix you up."

Alan nodded and headed toward the house. Willow watched him for a moment to make sure he was steady on his feet. Then she turned to John.

"I've got another guy. Jacob. Did you see which way he went?"

John shook his head. "You've got a couple others here, too. Kristie and Matt."

"What? When?"

"They showed up this afternoon." John walked over to one of the attackers and felt for a pulse. "Gone."

"How? I never told them where to find your retreat."

"They said they were out hunting, and just stumbled on us." He stood up and looked around. Spotted one of his guys.

"Tom!" He ran to the fallen figure. Willow hurried to catch up.

Tom lay on his side, holding his bloodied stomach.

"Let's get you to the house." John turned to Willow. "Help me carry him."

Tom shook his head.

"Too late for me," he wheezed. "Go help the others."

Willow gripped his arm and felt his pulse. It was weak and irregular.

Tom coughed and looked at John. "I'm going to Jesus. I'll see you up there."

He closed his eyes. Took a deep breath and sighed it out. Willow lost his pulse. Tears sparked in her eyes as she turned to John and shook her head.

His adam's apple bobbed as he turned away from her. Then, swiftly, he knelt by his friend and put his hand on Tom's forehead.

"I'll see you soon, brother. Before you know it."

Willow pressed her lips together and gulped hard. She blinked out tears and stood up. There were others. Maybe some still alive.

"Jacob?" She called out. "Jacob!"

Where could he be? Shot?

A moan came from the trees west of her. She lifted her rifle. It might be Jacob, or it might be an attacker. John fell in beside her as she moved toward the sound.

Another moan. A woman's legs stretched from behind a tree. Willow hurried forward.

It was Kristie!

She sat at the base of the tree, legs splayed out in front, gripping her lower right side. Blood stained her shirt and the top of her jeans.

"Help." Her voice was weak, barely above a whisper.

Willow dropped to her knees beside her.

"Let me look." She pulled Kristie's hands away and peeled back the wet material. Blood oozed from a bullet wound above her hip. At least it wasn't gushing.

"We need to get you to the house. Can you stand up?"

"I don't know." Her blue eyes reflected a wild terror. "Am I dying?"

John knelt beside her.

"Put your arm around my shoulders, and your other arm around Willow's." He glanced at Willow. "Count of three... one, two, three!"

They pulled her upright between them. Now, to get her down to the house. She was able to carry some of her weight, but she leaned heavily on John and Willow. Her breath came in gasps as they carry-dragged her up the steps to the back door. Willow shoved it open, and they took her into the house.

"Where?" Willow asked.

"Here, for now." John eased her to the tile floor outside the kitchen. "Jeannie?"

"Coming!" Her voice floated from the living room. "Be right there!"

Alan emerged with her, his wounded arm bandaged in white. "Can I help?"

"Yeah," John said. "You and Jeannie can work on Kristie, while Willow and I go back out."

"Are there more wounded?" Alan asked.

"My son's out there," Kristie sobbed.

"Lots of people are still out there." John gave Willow a sad look, and the two of them hurried out the back door.

Twenty minutes later, they'd located three dead attackers, and three more dead from John's group: David, Jennifer and Sue. They couldn't find Jacob or Matt.

"It's so weird! Where could they be?" Willow scanned the forest around her.

"Wounded? Dead? Maybe they ran away," John suggested.

She stared at him. "I saw Jacob kill a guy I'd wounded. He wouldn't run away."

"What about Matt? He's pretty young."

"He's no coward. He's got to be here somewhere." She turned and yelled into the trees. "JACOB! MATT!"

John cupped his hands to his mouth and shouted their names.

They stood still and listened. Nothing.

A cold tingle slid up Willow's spine. They must be dead. But where did they fall?

"We have to find them!" Her eyes searched John's face.

He nodded. "But it'll be dark soon."

That was true. Willow watched the sun slink behind the western mountain range.

"We should gather the bodies."

"Let's get our guys first." John's face hardened. "We'll put them in the basement for now, and bury them tomorrow."

It was fully dark by the time the last believer was carried through the door of the daylight basement. Jeannie met them downstairs.

"Julie and Mike are at the lookouts." Her eyes were lined with red. "We lost half our group today."

Willow put an arm around her shoulder.

"I'm so sorry. This was just horrible."

Jeannie nodded but didn't speak. John's face was ashen in the LED light. Finally, he looked at Willow.

"You'll stay here tonight, right?"

She nodded. "I'll check on Kristie and Alan, then I'm going back out for Matt and Jacob."

Jeannie led the way upstairs, and Willow followed. In the living room, she found Alan seated in a chair beside the sofa that Kristie lay on. She clutched his hand, her face as pale as the sliver moon that rose in the window behind her. Her eyes searched Willow's face.

"Matt?" She coughed his name.

"We haven't found him yet." Willow went to stand by Kristie's feet. "Did you see which way he went?"

Kristie slowly shook her head and closed her eyes. Tears dripped down her cheeks.

"It's all my fault," she whispered.

"What do you mean?"

Instead of answering, she pinched her eyes tighter, sending new tears onto her face.

"I'm dying." She sobbed. "Please find my son!"

Alan stood. "I'll help you search."

"Are you sure?" Willow looked at his bandaged arm. "You're okay?"

"Jeannie fixed me up. I'll be fine."

"Stay with me!" Kristie's hand shot out and grabbed his good arm. Her eyes were deep wells of panic. "I'm afraid to die alone."

"Jeannie is here. You aren't alone," Willow said. "But Matt is."

"Yes, I'm right here." Jeannie hustled to Kristie's side, then glanced at Willow. "There are flashlights and radios on the kitchen counter. Let our lookouts, Julie and Mike, know where you are."

Willow picked up her rifle, then she and Alan headed for the back door, grabbing the radios and flashlights on their way out. The cool night air swept down from the hills, chilling her arms. She'd been dressed for a hot July afternoon, and had expected to be home hours ago.

She flicked on the radio and announced that she and Alan were searching the woods for survivors. Mike responded an acknowledgement and thanks.

"Let's split up but stay in sight," Willow suggested.

"What about the dead attackers? Should we pick them up?"

"Later. Let's find the living, first."

She strode up the hill, calling for Matt and Jacob, and swinging her flashlight across the ground. Where could they be?

In the distance, an owl hooted its haunting call. Further away, another answered. Goosebumps prickled Willow's skin.

She stopped to listen for noise or movement. Heard nothing. Saw Alan's flashlight off to her left. She yelled out Jacob's name, then Matt's.

There was no reply. What on earth had happened to them? Where could they have gone?

The sense of death lingered on the hill behind the house, where the worst fighting had created a battlefield. Dead men still lay where they fell.

What about their cohorts? If three of the attackers had been killed, how many escaped? Would they return? With rein-forcements?

How soon? Were they, even now, creeping toward her in the dark?

17

Terror gripped Kristie in its cold clutches. What if she was dying? Would she go to Hell? She had that horrible chip in her hand, the one Matt believed was the devil's mark that damned its wearers to Hell.

Was the place even real? She shivered. Heaven might be real, but Hell?

She was probably going to find out. Maybe tonight.

Her gunshot wound was bad. It'd bled a lot. And torn up who knows which internal organs and was causing who knew how much infection.

She couldn't die. Not now. She wasn't ready! And she was too young, far too young. Only forty-three years old, and still raising a teenager.

As far as she knew... but where was he, anyway?

He'd been there with her, he'd exchanged gunfire, and then she was pinned down and couldn't see him. And then he was gone.

Maybe it was good that they hadn't found him. At least they hadn't found a body. So he might still be alive. But why didn't he come in? Or answer their calls?

Tears broke free and cascaded down her damp face.

He must be seriously injured. Or dead.

Like she would be, soon. And all of this was her own stupid fault! If not for her, they'd be home safe, tucked into the cabin for the night.

She pressed a hand over her mouth to suppress a sob. Her stupidity was killing her, and probably killing Matthew. If only – if only she could go back, just a few hours, and return to the cabin where life was better. Hungry, sure, but safer than here!

WILLOW WASN'T sure how long she'd searched in the dark, but it felt like hours when she and Alan returned to the house. The moon had made a big arc through the night sky, brightening the forest. But the search was in vain.

Jacob was missing. And so was Matt.

Surely they'd find them – or their bodies – in the morning.

John was still awake when she and Alan slipped in the back door, locking it behind them. He took them to the loft, where he'd set up cots.

Willow yanked off her boots and fell into bed, pulling the blanket over her body. She'd never been so exhausted. At least she'd gotten over that intestinal bug, thanks to Clark's prayers earlier. Was that today? It seemed like ages ago.

Her eyes closed, and the next thing she knew, it was daylight.

Probably not very early, either, given the angle of the sunlight through the windows.

She pushed herself up on her elbows. Alan was gone, his bedding folded neatly at the foot of his cot.

It would be easy to flop back, close her eyes, and sink again into the blissful unconsciousness of sleep. She certainly needed the rest.

But Matt. He was out there, somewhere, maybe with Jacob. She had to find them.

She swung her legs over the edge of the cot and pulled on her boots. As she laced them, she prayed. For her friends. For their safety. For her own.

Then she went down to the living room. Kristie was asleep on the couch, her face flushed. Jeannie came into the room with a bowl of water and small towels as Willow put her hand on Kristie's forehead.

"She's burning up!" Willow yanked her hand back.

"I know. She needs antibiotics, but I haven't been able to wake her." Jeannie dipped a hand towel into the water, twisted it out, and patted Kristie's face.

"You have antibiotics?"

"Yes, some oral ones. No good if you can't wake up and swallow them."

"How's her wound?"

Jeannie turned sad eyes on Willow. "Not good. If there had been a hospital, maybe...."

"She's not going to make it, is she?"

Kristie let out a long groan, but didn't open her eyes.

Jeannie frowned. Then sighed.

Willow took a step back. "I'm going looking for Matt and Jacob."

"Be careful." Jeannie swabbed Kristie's face. "Your friend Alan went back to your cabin this morning. He said he was going to get a dog. To help with the search."

Gilligan. Why hadn't she thought of that? The border collie wasn't a trained search dog, but his sense of smell could be a huge help. Not to mention his hearing and vision.

"Good. Hopefully he'll bring some help, too. We have bodies to bury."

Jeannie said nothing, but wiped her cheeks with the back of her hand. Willow put an arm around her shoulder.

"I'm sorry about your friends."

Jeannie smiled the saddest smile Willow had ever seen.

"They're the lucky ones. They're with the Lord now. I hope we can find *your* friends." She pressed her lips together and turned back to Kristie.

Willow went out and found John digging a grave on the far side of the barn. It was close to six feet deep already. Sweat shone on his red face as he looked up at her.

"I'm going to drag all three of the attackers and dump 'em in here," he said.

"I'll help, when you're ready."

He climbed out of the hole. "I guess I'm ready now."

Together, they dragged the three dead men to the grave. Willow checked their pockets for identifying information or anything valuable, but found little worthwhile. She did pull off their ammo pouches, holsters, pocket knives and flashlights, and set those aside with their rifles and handguns.

"They sure have impressive gear," she said. "These are expensive guns."

John nodded, kicking one of their boots.

"There were some preppers who only prepped with guns and ammo, not food or equipment. They just figured that when the time came, they'd take what they wanted."

"That didn't work out so well for them." Willow picked up the first guy's feet, and John gripped under his arms, and they swung him into the hole.

"It didn't work out so well for us, either." John kicked a dirt clod into the hole. "We lost half our team last night. Might have lost the whole group, if you and your friends hadn't shown up."

He stopped, then turned to study her.

"How'd you know, anyway?"

"That you needed help?"

He nodded.

Ugh. She hated explaining this stuff. But he was a Christian, too, so....

"I had a dream." There. It was out. She met his gaze.

"A dream." He didn't believe her.

"Yeah. Like Joseph in the Bible. I have those kinds of dreams."

"Prophetic dreams."

"Mhmm."

"Tell me about it." He grabbed the next guy under his arms.

Willow picked up his feet. "Should we keep his boots? They're pretty nice."

"Take 'em, if you want."

It was weird, pulling boots off a dead man, but they were nice black leather, and Josh's feet were still growing. Or someone else might need a pair of good boots. Willow set them aside, then grabbed the bottom of the man's pants legs.

"Ready."

Together, they hefted his body in on top of his friend.

One more. Willow took his boots, too. Then she and John threw him into the hole.

"I dreamed that there were gunmen attacking people's homes. We went to warn the next house, and it was yours."

"That's pretty clear." John shoveled dirt on the men. "Why didn't you come sooner? You got here late in the day. Maybe if you'd been here in the morning...."

"We were coming back from Ponderosa. And we were really sick. After we got back to the cabin, I came as soon as I could."

"You were sick?" He stopped shoveling and stared at her.

"Yeah. Me, and Raven and Josh. Clark prayed for us, and I started getting better on the way here."

"Huh." He shoveled in more dirt, covering their faces. "Thank you for coming. We wouldn't have made it."

"Of course." She kicked some dirt into the hole. "How did it start?"

John leaned on his shovel.

"Your friend Matt and his mom showed up at the back of the property, and the two guys who were on lookout both ended up back there, and I did, too. So we never saw them coming. We were distracted."

Willow's stomach felt queasy. If Kristie and Matt hadn't been here, John's lookout guys might have seen the danger approaching and been in a better position to run them off. Why did she feel like that was her fault? She had nothing to do with it.

"Think they'll come back?"

He leaned on the top of the shovel. "You tell me."

"I think they might. For revenge, if nothing else."

"There's lots of reasons to come back. They wanted what we have, that's why they were here in the first place."

"But they took losses. Maybe they'll decide it's not worth it."

"Maybe." He shoveled more dirt.

A dog bark sounded through the forest behind her. She turned to look for the black and white dog. He bounded toward her, tail wagging. Alan trailed far behind him, with Clark.

"This is Gilligan. He's going to help us search."

Gilligan nuzzled her hand, then sniffed the dead men's boots. Alan and Clark caught up.

"Here, let me help with that." Clark held out his hand for the shovel. John handed it over.

Clark made quick work of the dirt pile, filling the hole and mounding up the remaining dirt.

"Those were the bad guys," Willow said. "We also have four retreat members to bury."

Clark looked at John. "Where do you want to lay them to rest?"

"There, I think." John pointed at a slope. "It's a nice shady spot."

"Very well. I'll get started."

"I'm going to look for Matt and Jacob," Willow said. "You want to come with me, Alan?"

"Yep." He bent and picked up one of the attacker's rifles. "This has a nice scope. I'll carry it this morning."

Willow picked up one of the others.

"Take all that ammo, too," John said.

As they walked away from the burial site, Willow scanned the forest and the hills. She prayed for direction and help. Gilligan trotted beside her, sniffing the ground. After a minute, they came to the road.

"Which way?" Alan asked.

She looked left, then right. Downhill.

"Let's go down."

They'd gone about eighty yards when they spotted boot tracks in the dusty volcanic ash. Headed toward the retreat.

"They definitely came from below, which makes sense if they were working their way through all the homes on the road, and started at the highway," Alan said.

"Yeah. Keep your eyes peeled. They might be holed up at a neighbor's house." Willow felt exposed on the open road. "Let's move into the trees. Easier to hide if we have to."

They climbed the slope above the road and continued following it down toward the next home. Eventually Willow spotted it through the trees. She went into a crouch, and Alan followed her example.

"Gilligan, down!" The dog dropped to his belly.

The house looked quiet. Maybe it was vacant.

They watched the surrounding area for a few minutes.

Seeing nothing unusual, Willow lifted her rifle and scoped the house. She tried to look in the windows, but there was too much glare. Someone had kept them clean and shiny.

A shrill scream shattered the silence.

Willow nearly dropped her gun. Gilligan growled. The sound came again, from the hill above them. It sounded like a woman. The cry was creepy. Hair-raising.

"Gilligan, heel!" She whispered. The dog moved to her left side. She and Alan rose and began making their way up the hill, cautiously moving from tree to tree.

The scream sounded again, quieter this time, and hoarser.

Disregarding her safety, Willow broke into a jog. Gilligan loped beside her, his hackles raised.

His low growl turned into a menacing bark.

"Hush, Gilligan!"

But it was too late. The bark had surely given them away. Willow slipped in behind a tree and saw Alan doing the same.

The screaming stopped.

Silence gripped the forest.

Willow's heart thudded in her ears as she strained to listen. Glancing at Alan, she signaled that she was moving forward. He nodded.

They stepped out in a stealthy crouch, slinking between trees and bushes.

She listened between steps, but heard nothing. She didn't think the woman had been terribly far away. But her attackers surely heard Gilligan's barking. Had they moved? Or were they prepping an ambush for her and Alan?

They continued up the slope. Gilligan growled. She shushed him.

Alan paused behind a tree about twenty feet away. She glanced at him. He sent her a confused look, shrugged, and started moving again.

Soon, she could see the top of the hill. It must be the same ridge that ran behind the Andersons' home. But no one was there, and no sign of anyone that she could see.

Maybe the attackers had seen her and Alan approaching the house, and had sent a woman out to lead them away. Or into an ambush.

She moved toward Alan, finally stopping at a tree just a few feet from his. Gilligan plastered himself against her left leg and let out another soft growl. Clearly he thought there were bad guys around.

"Anything?" She whispered.

Alan shook his head. He lifted and dropped his shoulders, a confused look on his face.

"Ambush?" She mouthed the word.

"Maybe," he mouthed back.

She looked down toward the house. It was out of sight now. Were the attackers there?

Studying the forest around her, she watched for any movement, listened for any unusual sound. The only unusual sound was silence.

It was quiet.

Way too quiet.

18

Kristie opened her eyes. It was bright, so bright here. Where was she?

Heaven? Hell?

She blinked. Felt so hot, and sick.

Not heaven. Maybe hell.

Groaning, she pushed off a blanket. A coffee table came into focus. Not heaven or hell. She was at the Andersons' retreat.

"Hello?" Her voice rasped. "Anybody?"

No one answered. She was alone. Had to go to the bathroom. She wiped her forehead with her hand. It was beyond clammy. She was drenched in her own sweat.

Where was everyone?

"Hello!"

Her demand was met with silence. Had they left her here? Decided it was safer at the cabin, and went there without her? Left her here to live or die on her own?

A cough rattled her chest. Her lungs felt heavy.

She really had to find the bathroom. Could she make it on her own? She was tired. Her eyelids drooped. So very tired.

WILLOW STEPPED out from behind her tree. She motioned Alan to continue uphill. If they could crest the hill, maybe they'd find the woman on the other side. If they didn't get shot.

Cautiously, she moved from tree to tree. She reached the ridge and looked down the other side. A long hill sloped away from her. No sign of a woman. Or anyone.

If this was an ambush, she should be getting out of here, rather than hanging around. Anyway, whoever had been here appeared to be long gone. She moved closer to Alan.

"I think we should make our way back to the Andersons' place," she whispered. "I can't tell if this was an ambush."

"Sounds good to me." His eyes scanned the trees behind Willow's back. "Let's go."

It might be safer to be on the opposite side of the hill from the house, so she moved down the north slope, then followed the ridge east toward the retreat. This would keep them out of view from anyone on the road or at the neighbor's place. And it should eventually put them behind the Andersons' retreat.

Soon, she saw familiar trees and shrubs. She motioned Alan south, crossed the ridge again, and entered yesterday's forest battlefield.

If one didn't look carefully, they might not even notice. But Willow saw fresh chips cut from tree trunks by bullets, drops of dried blood on last year's pine needles, and ammo shells ejected from hot firearms. Her stomach flopped at the memory. The noise, the losses, the fear.

Most of the kills were pretty clean. They'd died within a few minutes. But not Kristie.

She'd suffered.

Was she still suffering?

Or had she died this morning?

And the real mystery was, what happened to Jacob and Matt?

Through the trees, she spotted the Andersons and Clark. They stood somberly at the site John had pointed out for his friends' graves. She headed that direction, Alan at her side. Gilligan seemed relaxed now, and trotted happily behind her.

Clark looked her way and raised his hand in a slow wave.

She returned the wave and closed the distance between them.

"We are just getting ready to begin," Clark said. "Did you see any sign of Jacob or Matthew?"

"No. Not yet."

The Andersons held hands, looking into the hole. The bodies of their friends, wrapped in sheets, lay together in the bottom.

Clark's brow was damp, no doubt from exertion. He looked to his father-in-law.

"Perhaps you could start with a prayer?"

Alan cleared his throat. John gave him a nod. Willow hated funerals. But she couldn't escape this one. Four in the ground, and five gathered to honor their memory. Plus two friends who couldn't join them, because they were standing guard as look-outs over the retreat.

After Alan's prayer, they all sang "Amazing Grace," then the Andersons shared a few memories and Clark read some scriptures about hope in heaven. They closed with the Lord's Prayer. And that was it. The shortest funeral she'd ever seen. But it didn't seem like anything was missing.

John shook the men's hands, and Jeannie gave Willow a hug, and they walked slowly toward the house.

Willow didn't want to seem rude, but she needed to know how Kristie was doing. And if she might have remembered anything more about what had happened to Matt.

As soon as she entered the house, she smelled death. Or sickness, at least. She hurried toward the living room and found Kristie on the sofa. A blanket had been tossed to the floor.

She knelt beside her and placed her hand on the woman's forehead. Warm. Too warm.

"Kristie?"

Her eyelids fluttered, then opened. Her tongue flicked out and dampened dry lips.

"I thought – thought you'd left."

"No, we're still here. I was looking for Matt."

"Matthew." Kristie groaned. "Did you find him?"

"Not yet." Willow made a point to breathe through her mouth, because Kristie stank. "I need you to think. To remember. Was there anything that you saw that might help us find him?"

"No." Kristie closed her eyes. "Nothing."

"You didn't see him move, didn't see him go anywhere?"

"No. He was there, then... gone." Kristie coughed.

She smelled so bad! Willow tried not to gag. Kristie closed her eyes. When she spoke, her voice rasped.

"He was here because of me. It's my fault!" Her eyes flashed open. "I brought him here!"

Willow's brows tightened. "How?"

"I followed you last time you came." She sobbed and gulped. "And now I'm dying, and Matt is gone."

Willow wanted to shake her. "Why? Why would you do that?"

Kristie just snuffled.

"Why, Kristie? Why?" Her voice was hard and cold, and she didn't care.

"I wanted to live here. In a nice house." Her blue eyes flitted around the living room. "With good food!"

Willow shook her head. "And now, maybe you've killed your son. Did he know? That you were bringing him here?"

"No! No, he never would have come." She closed her eyes. "I tricked him."

Heat flared in Willow's chest. This *was* Kristie's fault. If only she'd followed Willow's rules, Matt would be home safe at the cabin.

Safe. At the cabin. What if he *was?*

Willow stood up so fast the room spun. What if Matt and Jacob had somehow made it back to the cabin after the attack last night? Sure, it made more sense that they'd gather with the others when it ended, but what if the fight had taken them farther away, and they got turned around and didn't know how to get back to the retreat?

Or maybe they'd gotten lost in the dark, but found their way home today?

She hoped they were together. Wherever they were.

"I have to go."

Kristie's glassy eyes panicked. "No! Stay with me."

"I can't. I have to find your son."

"I'm dying...." Her words gave way to a sob.

Jeannie came in from the kitchen.

"Whew!" She wrinkled her nose. "I'm right here, Kristie. I'm going to bring you some antibiotics."

It sounded like she was holding her breath.

Willow took the opportunity to bolt for the back door.

Outside, she sucked in a deep breath of fresh mountain air. John stood talking to Clark and Alan at the corner of the house. He gestured toward the forest, the barn and the house as he spoke.

"I need some more folks to help out here, since we lost so many yesterday." He turned toward Willow as she approached, and offered her a sad smile. "Hey. I was just inviting Clark and Alan to move their family over here."

"Oh."

Willow mulled that over. It was only a little surprising. On the one hand, John had turned them down a few days ago. But things can change so much in a few days. Or even a single day. For John, yesterday had brought devastating change. He lost half of his group. His remaining group was certainly in danger of the attackers coming back. While he might have plenty of food, water and livestock, he no longer had the people needed to guard and protect those assets.

"We will pray about it," Clark said.

Willow took the opportunity to change the subject.

"I'm going to head over to the cabin. Maybe Jacob and Matt have found their way back there by now."

"They weren't there this morning when I was there," Alan said.

"I know. But that was pretty early. Maybe they were lost, and have found their way home."

"That is possible," Clark said.

"Besides, I want to check on Raven and Josh. They were sick when I left yesterday."

"They were still sick this morning." Alan gave her a sympathetic look. "Do you want one of us to walk back with you?"

"You don't need to. If you and Clark could keep looking for Jacob and Matt, that'd be great." She shifted the weight of her backpack. "If things are okay at home, I'll probably be back here before dark. To keep searching."

She glanced at Alan. "Did you tell them about the screaming lady?"

"Yeah, I sure did. We'll go take another look up there in a few minutes. See if the three of us can turn anything up."

"Why don't you take Gilligan with you?"

The dog, lying in the shade beside the house, lifted his head and pricked his ears at the sound of his name.

"We will. Thanks."

As Willow hiked to the cabin, she stopped often to call out Jacob and Matt's names. No one responded. The sun warmed the air and toasted her head and shoulders as she walked. Finally, she reached the clearing.

Candy, Deborah and the older girls were weeding the garden. Maria played under a tree nearby. Raven, Josh and Jaci were nowhere to be seen. Neither were Matt and Jacob. Deborah looked up and smiled.

"Hey! You're home!" She rose and gave Willow a quick hug, then pulled back and studied her with bright blue eyes. "Are you okay?"

"Fine. Tired and hungry. Any sign of Jacob and Matt?"

Deborah's gaze fell. "Not yet."

"Where's Josh?"

Deborah took her arm and steered her toward the cabin, her grey hair shining in the sun like silver tinsel.

"He and Raven are still sick. Got that bug bad. You look like you got over it."

"I did. God healed me after Clark prayed."

"When Alan came by this morning, he told us what happened over there. So sad! Is there anything we can do?"

"Keep praying. I was hoping Matt and Jacob would have made their way here by now. And Kristie is in bad shape."

Jaci met them at the cabin door, concern in her hazel eyes. She held the door open for them.

"They're both asleep," she whispered. "Rest is the best thing right now."

"How bad is it?" Willow asked.

"No fever, but we're fighting dehydration. They're just exhausted."

"Is anyone else getting sick?"

Jaci's brown hair swirled around her cheeks as she shook her head. "Nope. Thank God."

"So maybe it's not contagious."

"Or it has a long incubation period," Deborah suggested.

"I don't think so." Willow peered at Raven's sleeping form. "We got it pretty soon after we got to town. Maybe a day or two?"

"Let's go out, so we don't disturb them," Jaci said.

Outside, they found some shade on the north side of the cabin. Willow lowered herself into the grass. It was good to have dependable people around. She'd worried less about the group when she was gone. She had full confidence in Raven, of course, but she was out sick. And Candy – well, it'd be a long time before Willow trusted her.

She looked at the new ladies. Deborah and Jaci were becoming valuable friends.

"I'm glad you're here," she blurted. "Thanks for taking care of – of everything."

Deborah smiled.

"Of course! Thank you for taking us all in."

"We're all happy to have you," Willow said. "But I'm not sure how long you're staying."

"What? Why?" Jaci stared at her. "We're building a home!"

"John was talking to your husbands about moving to the retreat."

Deborah pressed her lips together but said nothing.

"But it just got shot up! People got killed," Jaci protested. "I can't take my girls there."

"I agree, it's dangerous." Willow plucked a daisy and began pulling off the white petals, one by one. "On the other hand, it's a nice home, much better than a cabin. With food and equipment and running water and everything."

"But is it defensible?" Deborah asked.

"I think it could be." Willow tossed the torn flower, feeling a little bad for destroying it. "And if God defends it, it's a fortress."

They fell silent. Willow pinched off a blade of grass. Why hadn't God defended it yesterday? Did He not love that group? Of course He did. It was the age-old question of why do bad things happen to good people... and yet, she couldn't dismiss the idea that the believers who died yesterday had been spared all kinds of trouble in the future. They went straight to Heaven. As Jeannie put it, they were the lucky ones. Wasn't that what she said? Something like that.

Deborah sighed.

"We'll all have to pray about it."

"For sure." Willow rose and offered a hand to Deborah, pulling her onto her feet. "Is there anything to eat? I want to get back to the retreat and keep looking for Jacob and Matt."

Jaci stood up and dusted off her jeans. "There's leftover rice from lunch. I've been feeding that to your brother and Raven because they have the runs."

"And we can send some venison jerky with you, too."

"Sounds good." Willow walked around the cabin and opened the front door. "I'll go up to the loft and check on Josh before I go."

The cabin was warm, and the loft was hot as she climbed the ladder. Josh's cheeks were flushed, but he'd already thrown off his sleeping bag. His eyes opened as she approached.

"Hey." He turned and propped himself on an elbow. "I'm glad you're back."

She squatted next to him. "Actually, I have to leave again. Matt is missing."

"What?" He sat up. "I'm going with you."

"No, you're not. You're staying right here until you're well."

"But –"

"No buts. That's an order."

He gripped his stomach and lay back. She touched his forehead. Warm, but not bad.

"Are you feeling any better? Since yesterday?"

"No." He groaned. "I wish you could stay. But you can't."

She wished she could stay, too.

"Jacob is also missing." She moved a lock of hair away from his eyes, and he swatted at her hand. "Pray for both of them."

"Okay. Come back soon." He closed his eyes.

"I will." She patted his arm, then hurried down the ladder. She glanced at Jaci.

"Keep the door and windows open so he gets some air circulation up there."

"Will do."

Willow checked on Raven, but she was still asleep.

"When she wakes up, fill her in on everything, okay?"

"We will." Deborah handed her a bowl of rice.

She ate quickly.

"I'll just eat the jerky on the way." She pulled on her pack and headed out the open door. "I don't expect to be back today."

"We'll hold down the fort," Jaci said.

"Thank you." Willow took a moment to give her new friends a meaningful look. "Really. Thanks."

KRISTIE STARED at the fire racing through the forest, headed straight for Matthew. She yelled for him to get out of there. Her hollering woke her up.

Her wild eyes scanned the room. The living room. She was still on the sofa at the retreat.

A crazy beat drummed in her chest. Her lips were hot and dry. She tried to moisten them, but her tongue was dry, too.

Jeannie came into her line of sight.

"Water," she wheezed.

From the coffee table, Jeannie picked up a glass with a metal straw in it and held it to Kristie's lips. She took a short sip, then a long one.

"Drink more," Jeannie encouraged. "You need to drink as much as you can."

She took another long sip, then waved the glass away. Pain burned through her midsection as she laid her head back on the pillow.

"Matthew?" There was a hopeful note in her question.

"Not yet. I'm sorry."

Tears filled her eyes and trickled onto her cheeks. Her lips twisted into a frown and then released a sob.

"It's my fault. All my fault."

"You just rest. They'll find him." Jeannie's tone sounded a lot less sure than her words.

"What if they don't? He'll die, alone out there, because of me." The last word came out as a wail.

"Then he will be in Heaven. A whole lot better place to be than here."

Kristie grabbed her hand. "I'm dying."

"You might make it," Jeannie said. "But again, if you don't –"

"No. You don't know. I might go to Hell."

Jeannie pulled her hand away. "Why would you say that? Aren't you a Christian?"

"Sure. I think so." Her voice trembled. "But – but I got the I.D. chip."

19

Hot and tired, Willow let herself in the back door of the retreat. It didn't smell so bad now. Jeannie must have bathed Kristie or something. She could hear conversation in the living room, so she made her way there.

"What?" Jeannie's voice sounded shocked. "You got the mark?"

Willow's breath stalled out. She froze in the hall just outside the living room. Did she hear that right?

Kristie coughed, a rattling, wheezing cough, like she was dying.

"The chip," she rasped. "I got the chip."

"The I.D. chip," Jeannie clarified. "What we call the Mark of the Beast."

"Matthew thought so."

"He knew you had the mark?" Jeannie sounded incredulous. "Does he have it, too?"

Kristie didn't respond. Willow peered around the corner. Kristie lay on the sofa, her face and hands pale as paper. Her eyelids drooped.

No! She couldn't fall asleep. Not now!

Willow raced into the room and shook Kristie's shoulder.

"Does Matt have the mark?" She shook her again. "Wake up!"

Kristie took a deep breath and expelled it. Her eyes were half closed.

"Wake up!" She slapped Kristie's face gently. "You have to wake up!"

Kristie didn't look up. She didn't even blink.

"Tell me! Kristie, you have to tell us!" She shook her shoulder.

Had she stopped breathing? Her half-open eyes were fixed on some distant point.

"Kristie! Kristie?" Willow stared at her chest. It wasn't moving.

Frantic, she grabbed Kristie's wrist. Pressed her fingers into the soft flesh and held her breath. She swung around to look at Jeannie.

"I can't feel a pulse!"

"Let me try." Jeannie took Kristie's wrist.

"I don't think she's breathing!" Willow studied Kristie's chest. "Did you find a pulse?"

"No. I think she's gone."

"She can't go! Not now. We have to do something!"

Willow shoved the coffee table out of the way, and pulled Kristie to the floor. She tried to remember the CPR she'd learned in her sophomore year of high school.

A-B-C... what did it mean? Airway, Breathing, Chest? Whatever!

She tilted the woman's head back, pinched her nose, and expelled two deep breaths into Kristie's lungs. Felt for a pulse.

Nothing.

Linked her fingers and began chest compressions. Looked wildly at Jeannie.

"Help me!"

Jeannie knelt beside her and prepared to give her air. When Willow got to fifteen compressions, she nodded at Jeannie.

"Now!"

After a couple minutes, she stopped and checked for a pulse. Still nothing. She continued with the CPR. Jeannie worked alongside her, saying nothing as Willow counted out her compressions.

A few minutes later, Willow stopped again and checked for breathing and pulse. Nada.

"We've lost her." Jeannie sounded sure.

Willow slumped over the woman's body as a wail clawed its way out of her soul.

"Nooooooo!"

She pounded her fists once on the floor.

"Oh, God, no!"

Tears blurred everything as Jeannie's arm wrapped around her shoulders and pulled her close. Willow let herself go and sobbed into Jeannie's hair. Grief and exhaustion and agony and frustration mingled in her tears.

After a minute, she pulled back.

"I'm sorry." She wiped her cheeks with her hands. "I don't usually do that."

"Cry? It's fine if you do."

"Lose it." Willow blubbered and sniffled.

Jeannie patted her back. "You've been through a lot the last couple days. It's good to let it out."

Willow looked at Kristie's body. Blonde hair in disarray, eyes half open, mouth agape. She smoothed her hair and tried to close her eyes. They didn't stay closed. Why? They did in the movies. She tried again. No luck.

Slowly, she reached for Kristie's right hand. Felt the flesh web between her thumb and first finger.

There! Willow almost dropped her hand. A tiny hard lump! Her gaze turned to Jeannie.

"She does have the mark." Her voice was hoarse. She stretched Kristie's arm toward Jeannie. "Here, feel."

"No." Jeannie pulled away. "I believe you."

Willow set Kristie's hand down on her abdomen.

"We have to dig another grave," she whispered, staring at the dead woman's face. "Poor Matt."

"I wonder if he knew...."

Willow sighed. "I wonder if he's alive."

It was so crazy that Kristie had gotten the mark. Then she'd come to live with them in the wilderness. And they'd never known. Probably never would have known, if she hadn't confessed it on her deathbed. It's not like they would have examined her hand before they buried her body.

"Why did she tell you, Jeannie?"

"I think she was scared."

"She had every reason to be!" Willow frowned.

"Do you think she's damned?"

"Yeah." Willow stared at her. "The Bible's pretty clear about that."

"Such a shame." Jeannie gazed at Kristie's face.

Willow moved away and sat on the floor.

"And you know the really sad thing? She thought she was a Christian. If she'd died before she got that chip – just a few weeks ago – maybe she'd be in Heaven right now."

"You think she was a Christian and she went to Hell?"

"I think she got the mark and went to Hell. I can't say whether she was a Christian or not." Willow stood up. "I can help you move her, if you want. Then I need to go look for her son and Jacob."

Jeannie waved her off. "You go on. She's too heavy. We'll get the men to move her."

OUTSIDE, Willow found the men coming back toward the house.

"Find anything? Any sign of that screaming woman?" Willow asked.

John shook his head. "Not a thing. Your dog sniffed around a lot, but we didn't even see any tracks."

"Strange." Willow scuffed her boot in the dirt, then blurted, "Kristie died."

"I'm sorry," Alan said. "Were you with her?"

"Yeah. We tried CPR, but...." She dropped her gaze. "She was gone."

"What can we do?" Clark asked, his dark eyes earnest. "Do you want us to prepare a grave here?"

"That would be good, thanks." She straightened her spine. "I'm going to go look for the guys again."

"One of us should go with you," Alan said. "I'd be happy to go."

"No, I'll be fine. If I find anything and need help, I know where to find you." She glanced at John. "If Julie and Mike are still on lookout, would you radio and let them know I'm wandering around?"

"Sure thing." He studied her. "I'm really sorry about Kristie."

"Thank you." She gave him a sad smile and turned away.

Willow moved through the forest slowly, looking and listening. Her brain felt foggy. So much grief and craziness lately. First, her Dad died. Then she discovered he'd had an affair with Candy. Then her mom was taken by the I.D. task force.

Where was Mom now? Was she even alive? She'd never take the mark. Would she?

Kristie had.

But Kristie was nothing like Willow's mom.

Her toe caught a root and she tumbled forward, scraping her knee and scratching her hands.

Man! She had to pay attention to where she was going!

She sat and brushed the dirt from her palms, then looked up and saw movement. What was it?

She strained to see through the foliage. Nothing. Had she imagined it?

A twig snapped. Not real close, but close enough to make her jump. Someone, or something, was out there!

She peered through the bushes. Saw nothing. But something was definitely out there.

Attackers? A bear?

It was hard to see from this position. Maybe she should stand up. But that might draw attention to her and expose her location. If they didn't already know where she was.

Actually, it was probably a lucky thing that she'd fallen here. She'd been wandering around in her brain fog, and might have wandered right into them.

Maybe it was better to stay low and let them wander off. She couldn't hear them anyway, so maybe they'd already moved along. But who was it? What if it was Matt? Or Jacob? She had to know.

Slowly, she got to her feet, scanning the area all around her.

To her left, something moved behind a tree!

She froze. It must be a person, and they must have spotted her.

And she was exposed, in the open, no trees within twenty feet.

She ran.

Made it to the nearest tree and flung herself behind it. Well, if they hadn't noticed her before, they surely had now.

"Willow!" A deep voice called her name.

"Willow?" It was closer this time.

She peeked around the tree. Jacob strode toward her.

"Jacob!" She squeaked and raced toward him.

"You're okay!" She was so happy, she flung her arms around his neck.

"Whoa, Missy." He pulled out of her embrace.

"Where's Matt?" She looked past him. "Is he with you?"

"No. And that's the problem. I escaped, and he didn't."

"What? Escaped what?"

"We were captured the other night, during the gunfight at the retreat."

"Why didn't they kill you? Why did they take you? Where are they?" As the questions spilled out, she noticed the red marks on his wrists. "You were tied up?"

He leaned against her tree and studied her.

"It's good to see you, Missy."

"WHERE'S MATT?" Her emotions reached a boil and she yelled.

His hand snaked out and covered her mouth.

"SHHH! Keep quiet, you fool." Slowly, he released her.

She nearly slapped his face, but thought better of it.

"They're close?" she whispered.

He nodded. "Let's get out of here. I'll tell you everything when we get someplace safe."

"Let's go to the retreat."

"Lead the way."

Willow started back the way she'd come. But nothing looked right. On the way here, she'd been wandering pretty much aimlessly, and she hadn't taken note of landmarks. Now, walking the opposite direction, she didn't recognize anything.

Eventually she would, though, so she kept walking.

Should she tell Jacob she was lost? But she wasn't lost. Yet. Was she?

Soon she'd find something familiar, and then she'd know the way back.

How long had it taken her to get here from the retreat, anyway? An hour? Half?

Man! If only she'd been paying attention. It was such a rookie mistake.

And in the forest, mistakes could be fatal.

Finally, she stopped. Turned back to Jacob.

"I'm not sure where we are."

"What?" He stepped closer and grabbed her shoulders. "You're lost?"

"Maybe." She wiggled free and turned in a full circle, trying to find something familiar. But she couldn't see any hills. Only trees and shrubs. "I thought it was this way."

"If we can find the road, we can get there." Jacob scanned the area past her shoulder. "It can't be far. Anyway, the sun's going down. We don't have much time."

"We can't just rush off before we figure out where we are. We might go the wrong way."

He stared at her. "Isn't that what you've been doing?"

She glared back. Why'd he have to be so antagonistic all the time?

"I'm doing my best."

He was right, though. The sun was setting. Then they'd have dusk, and soon it'd be dark.

"Let's pray." She didn't feel like praying with him at that moment, but knew it was the best thing they could do.

He coughed to cover a laugh. "You think God's going to get us out of this?"

"Yeah. You got a better idea?"

The attitude drained from his face. "No."

"Alright then." She held out her hand. He took it. She drew a deep breath, let it out, and closed her eyes. "Dear Lord, please help us to find our way back. In Jesus' name, amen."

She released his warm, tough hand. Looked around. Still saw nothing familiar. But felt a sense of direction.

"I think we should go that way." She pointed uphill.

"Lead on, then, Missy."

Dusk fell as they climbed the slope. She really didn't remember coming down a long hill earlier, but continued anyway. After about half an hour, darkness was settling over the forest. They were nearly at the crest of the hill.

Still, she recognized nothing. They were lost. Really, truly, in the middle of the wilderness lost. With no idea of where they were, or where to go. And it was her fault.

Where was that road, anyway?

Why couldn't she find it?

She plunked down on a stump.

"We'd better spend the night here. It's stupid to wander around in the dark."

20

J acob squatted on the ground beside Willow.

"Are you okay, Missy?"

Why did he still call her that? It was so annoying. But his tone was kind, so she decided not to lash out.

"I'm lost. But we'll find our way out in the morning." She could just make out his features in the deepening darkness. "Tell me everything. Is Matt okay? How did you escape?"

"Matt is okay for now, I think." He stretched out on the pine needles. "It was weird. I got on the outskirts of the firefight, and some guy got the jump on me. I think he snuck up behind me and hit my head with a rock or something."

He rubbed the back of his head.

"It's still pretty sore. I went down like a sack of potatoes. Next thing I knew, I was tied up on the floor of a dark room. No light at all."

A cool breeze blew up from the valley. Willow shivered.

"Keep going. Then what?"

"I could hear movement in that room, so I knew there were other people in there with me. But there was a guard, too. If anyone started talking, the guard would shut them up."

"How?"

"Not gently." Jacob's deep voice paused. "But in the morning, the sunlight cut through between the boards of the walls, and it turns out that we were in a barn or shed – some kind of outbuilding. And Matt was there."

"Is he wounded?"

"Not too bad. He had some cuts and scratches, and an egg on his head where they'd whacked him."

"I don't get it. I thought those attackers wanted to steal the retreat and take all the food and stuff. Why did they take prisoners alive?"

"At first, I thought for a prisoner exchange. You know, if the Andersons had some of their guys alive, they could exchange for me and Matt. And if not, then maybe ransom – get you guys to pay big time to get us back." Jacob snorted. "But I wouldn't expect you to pay much for me."

"So you never overheard them talking? Maybe something that would indicate what they really planned for you?"

"I'm getting to that. Like I said, there were other people in the shed that night. In the morning, they came and got all of them except the two of us. There were three others. A young guy, and two middle-aged guys."

"What happened to them?"

"They put them to work. Chopping and splitting firewood. When I escaped, I saw them hauling water in buckets. One guard with a gun kept them in line."

Willow's mind was exploding with questions. She didn't know what to ask first. Good thing they had all night to talk about it.

"How many bad guys are there? And where is this place? How did you escape?"

Jacob laughed dryly.

"Hold on there, Missy. I'm getting to all that." He stretched out on the ground, then turned on his side so he was facing the stump she was sitting on. "I counted nine of them, but there might be more. They're in a little farm with a white house and a big grey barn."

"How'd you get away? And why didn't you break Matt out with you?"

"After they took the others out to work, they locked the door but didn't guard it. I found some tools and wire in that old shed, and picked the lock."

"Wait." Willow's eyes narrowed. "I thought you were tied up."

"I was. It took over an hour to get loose."

"And you just left Matt there?"

"It's not like I planned it that way! What do you think I am, a coward?"

"I don't really know you."

"Thanks a lot."

Jacob stretched out on his back. Not saying another word. Willow needed him to talk, to spill everything. There was so much she still needed to know! But she'd irritated him, and now he was being a baby about it. So annoyingly frustrating! And she'd have to play his game to get her questions answered. She curled her lip. Jerk.

"I don't think you're a coward."

"Hmmph."

"What happened to Matt?" She could feel Jacob's eyes staring at her in the star light.

"Just as I got the door open, I could see the guard bringing the prisoners back. It was now or never, I had to go."

"Why didn't Matt come with you?"

Jacob was silent for a moment before he answered.

"He was still tied up."

"WHAT?" She could kill him. "Why? Why didn't you get him free?"

"I was going to. That was next."

"But you'd already opened the door. Sounds like you planned to run off by yourself."

"I did not!" Anger flared in his voice. "Man, you really think I'm a coward."

"You're the one who keeps bringing that up."

"You're – you're – I don't even have a word for you!"

"Whatever. Just tell me about Matt." She tried to bring down the fury in her tone, but it rose to the surface.

"My plan was, to get free, get the door unlocked, check the surroundings so I could get the layout of the place, and figure out the best plan as I untied Matt."

"But you saw the guard and ran."

"It was the only thing to do. If he'd come back and found the door unlocked, that'd be the end of it. I'd be dead, and Matt would still be there and you still wouldn't know if he was alive or where to find him. This way, I was able to bring the intel out. So we can mount a rescue operation."

Willow wanted to argue, but what he said made some sense. If he wasn't lying to her.

What if he was? What if he was working with the bad guys to bring down the believers? What if he was actually part of the attackers' group? He might have gotten separated from them some time ago, and then ran into her that day they met.

He could lead her and her friends into an ambush, because they believed Matt was alive at that farm. Maybe he was, but maybe he wasn't. Jacob might be lying.

Even as she thought it, she knew it was crazy. But was it too crazy to be true?

She didn't really know Jacob. Didn't yet trust him. She decided to play along for now.

"So, have you thought about how we'd do this rescue?"

"Yeah. Like I said, there's nine of them, at least. How many do we have?"

"The Andersons lost four in the battle. So they're down to four now." Willow winced a little. She probably shouldn't have told him how vulnerable they were, if she didn't trust him.

"And our group?"

He'd find out soon enough anyway, if they ever found their way back to the retreat.

"Kristie was killed, and Matt's gone. The rest are still with us."

"Okay, so two men, three including me, and a teen boy. Plus the Anderson guys."

"Hello? There's me and Raven and the other women."

"I don't want to send you in against those guys. They're ruthless."

"It's not up to you."

"Missy." He paused, then started again. "Willow. We have to be smart about this. We can't put everyone in the line of fire to save one guy."

"Says who?"

"Me."

"As I just pointed out, you're not in charge."

He had a point, though. She shouldn't risk everyone to save Matt. As much as she wanted him back.

If Josh found out where Matt was, he'd be ready to charge in like a yahoo. For the first time, she was thankful that he and Raven were home sick. She would try to run the rescue operation before they even knew about it. No sense dragging ill people into battle.

What if they could do it without a battle?

That'd be best, of course. A stealth operation in the middle of the night. Avoid a direct confrontation if possible.

So... who could she count on? John might not want to risk his whole group, since they'd just lost half their number to these guys. Maybe two from his retreat? Plus Clark and Alan. That was four, plus herself. Five. Jacob? Six.

Maybe she shouldn't bring Jacob, since she didn't trust him. Could she leave Jacob to help guard the retreat?

On the other hand, she needed his knowledge of the place. So they had six. That would be plenty, if they didn't run into too much trouble.

Willow put her backpack on the ground and used it as a pillow. Jacob lay a few feet away, his back turned to her. She closed her eyes and willed sleep to come.

The cold air chilled her skin and crept toward her bones. She wrapped her arms around herself.

A scream ripped through the woods and raised the hair on her neck. She scrambled to her feet. Jacob jumped up.

"What was that?" His form was barely discernable in the light from the stars.

"A woman." Willow grabbed her pack and gripped her rifle. "I think."

Another eerie wail pierced the night.

"We've got to help her!" Jacob moved closer. "Give me one of your guns."

Reluctantly, she pulled out her handgun and handed it to him.

"I think it came from over there," she pointed east. "Let's go."

They crept slowly through the trees, avoiding making noises that would give away their approach. As they neared a clearing, Jacob grabbed her elbow. He pointed up the hill to their left. A rock outcropping dominated the skyline at the crest of the hill. The light was so dim, Willow couldn't see any detail.

"What?" she whispered.

"Cougar!" he hissed.

She stared at the outcropping but saw nothing. The sky was clear tonight, but the moon was new, so it didn't help illuminate anything. The stars put out only the dimmest light.

"Top," Jacob whispered.

It moved, and she saw it then. A cougar, bigger than she'd imagined, crept along the ledge at the top of the outcropping.

Willow caught her breath. He was magnificent! Stealthy and muscular, he moved along the ledge, then leapt down to a lower ledge. It had to be fifteen feet if it was an inch! His legs acted like shock absorbers when he landed, perfectly poised on the narrow ledge.

Then she saw what he was after.

She elbowed Jacob and pointed just below the outcropping. A smaller cougar strutted out from behind some brush, watching the big cat above her. She opened her mouth and caterwauled a creepy wail.

"There's our screaming lady," Jacob whispered, his mouth just behind her ear.

Willow knew they should get out of there. One big cat was dangerous enough, but two? Her heart hammered.

But the cats, busy searching for a mate, hadn't noticed them yet. If they ran, the cats would see them as prey.

Her feet felt like lead blocks. Transfixed, she watched the male leap down to the female's level. They were such amazing creatures! Powerful, muscular but lithe, with perfect balance and incredible speed.

She couldn't move. Couldn't take her eyes off them. They were so big! The male had to be 140 pounds, the female maybe 110. All muscle. All beauty. All lethal.

The cats were amazing hunters. They generally hunted alone, and they'd take down deer, elk, even a moose sometimes.

She shivered.

Jacob touched her elbow and leaned toward her ear. "Let's go."

He was right. They needed to get away from here before the predators smelled, heard, or saw them.

The cats might not turn down a nice dinner, just because they were looking for a mate.

Slowly, she turned back the way she'd come. Quietly, one step at a time. She couldn't risk any noise. Jacob followed. She sensed him, more that heard him. Which was good.

It was just so dark! If only she had a flashlight – but of course the cougars would notice that. She risked a glance back, and saw Jacob. Couldn't see past him to the cats.

Her boot slipped on a mossy rock, and she felt herself scrambling for balance. Her legs went one way, her arms the other. Jacob's big hand gripped her forearm and pulled her up just as she started falling. Her feet struggled and found solid ground.

She looked back toward the cats. Couldn't see them.

"Where are they?" she whispered.

He stared into the darkness with her, head turning left, then right, then back again.

"They must have heard us and moved out," he whispered. "Keep going."

"They might be stalking us!"

"Keep going!"

She started forward then, moving quicker and making more noise. It didn't matter now, if the cougars were already aware of them. She wanted to get into a clearing where she could see them coming.

Pausing to glance back, she saw nothing moving except Jacob. She hurried toward the crest of the hill, where rocks reduced the available soil for trees and shrubs. If they could get to a high point and have a clearing around them, they might see predators approaching. And have time to react.

21

Willow scrambled onto a low boulder at the crest of the hill. Wind whipped across the mountains, cutting through her t-shirt and raising goose bumps on her arms. Jacob climbed up beside her.

"Let's face opposite directions, so we can see anything coming." He sat behind her, blocking the breeze. "You can lean against my back if you get tired."

Not likely. She was so wired, she didn't feel like she'd ever get sleepy. Still, it was nice to have him there, watching her back and creating a windbreak.

"I'm fine. Thanks."

She strained her eyes at every dark shadow in her periphery. Was something there? Did it move? No. It was just her imagination. Right?

Taking a deep breath, she tried to relax.

But who knew where those big cats were? Even now, they might be creeping up for the fatal pounce.

She'd heard that their incisors were both huge and sensitive enough that when the cats bit their prey's neck, they could manipulate their incisors into the spaces between the vertebrae, then power down to force the vertebrae apart, breaking the prey's neck. Or they'd attack from the front, biting the neck and closing the victim's airway with a crushing bite until they suffocated, while gripping the doomed creature with their muscular legs and sharp claws.

Their kills were quick and usually unexpected, since the cats liked to sneak up on their prey, rather than chase it. She remembered hearing an elk hunter's story of getting a creepy feeling, turning around while raising his gun, and seeing a cougar leap at him from a big tree. He was able to fire a round in that split second. Otherwise, he'd be a fatality.

She shuddered.

"You okay?" Jacob asked.

"Yeah. It's just creepy."

"I don't think they'll come after both of us, especially out here in the open."

"Hope not." She finally realized she should pray about it. "Lord, please keep those cougars far away from us. And help us to figure out where we are in the morning. In Jesus' name, amen."

"Amen," Jacob echoed.

After a few minutes, he broke the silence again.

"Maybe the time will go faster if we talk. Tell me about Kristie and how you came to find me yesterday."

She yawned, then began telling him all about it. Before long, she felt relaxed. And tired. She scooted back and leaned against him, spilling her tale and willing the night to be over.

At some point, she nodded off, and then startled herself awake. The sky had turned from black to darkest blue. Morning was coming. They were still alive, and unscathed. Soon, dawn would bring daylight. And hopefully they could find their way back to the cabin or the retreat.

She stood up and stretched. Her neck instantly reminded

her that she'd slept in a bad position. Rubbing the tender muscles, she glanced back at Jacob. He sat hunched on the rock, her handgun beside him.

"You awake?" she whispered. No response. She walked back to the rock and reached for her gun. Instantly, his hand shot out and latched onto her wrist.

She yelped. "What are you doing?"

He stared at her for a moment, then let go.

"Sorry. I was half asleep. Didn't realize it was you."

She rubbed her wrist, then stuck her pistol in her holster and picked up her rifle.

"Well, you've got an impressive reflex response."

He turned his head, taking in his surroundings. Maybe getting his bearings.

"Did you sleep?" He stood and stretched his arms.

"A little. You?"

"You just caught me catnapping." He grinned. "Anything look familiar now that it's getting light?"

She took her time to turn in a complete circle. Something did seem vaguely familiar. But what was it? She turned again, even slower.

"There," she pointed east. "I wonder if that ridge is the one that runs behind the retreat. It kind of looks like it."

"Time's wasting. I'll follow you."

The sky grew lighter as Willow walked, thinking about last night's events. They'd climbed the wrong hill, but this morning that elevation put them high enough to see the ridge they needed to find. And the cougars had left them alone.

She breathed a thankful prayer for the guidance and the protection, although she couldn't have recognized God's help last night. She'd felt completely lost. And she had been.

But those cougars! The creepy caterwaul of the female made her shudder. What an eerie sound! Especially after dark.

Even in the starlight, they were magnificent creatures. All muscle and power.

Sunlight touched down on the top of the ridge just as she crested it.

"Hold on." She slung her rifle over her shoulder and stopped for a moment, letting the very first rays of the morning wash over her, flooding her in light. She closed her eyes, and the sun burned red behind her eyelids. If she stood perfectly still, she could feel its warmth, even though the air was still quite cold.

She raised her arms and held her hands out to the sun. A smile curved her lips. A deep breath in and out.

"Ahhhhh..."

"You are one goofy girl, Missy."

"A new day." She grinned at him. "Glorious!"

He shook his head, then turned to look at the sunrise.

The sun's radiant heat warmed Willow's face and arms. The sky lit into a brilliant blue. Not a single cloud to be seen. It was going to be a hot July day, but at this moment, it was perfect.

And she recognized this ridge. It was the right one.

"C'mon, we're almost to the retreat!"

They reached the house in less than five minutes. Willow knocked lightly on the back door. No one answered.

"Maybe they're still asleep." She tried the knob, and it turned, so she let herself and Jacob in. No one was in the kitchen or living room. She picked up a walkie talkie from the counter and keyed the mic.

"Hello. This is Willow."

No response.

"Anyone there?"

Nothing.

"Hello? Anybody?"

She looked at Jacob. His face was a blank mask.

Her stomach turned sour.

"No one's at the lookout posts. What's going on?" She ran to the bedroom door and knocked, lightly at first, then harder.

"John? Jeannie? Hello!"

Jacob walked up beside her. She felt sick. What had happened? Were they still alive? She couldn't bear to look.

"Would you go in and check?"

He nodded, a quick, solemn movement. "Stay close."

She waited by the door as he entered the bedroom. Moments later, he emerged.

"Not here. Let's look downstairs."

They stormed down the steps to the daylight basement. Checked every room. They were all vacant.

"Now what?" Willow sank onto a chair. "Where could they be?"

"They might be out looking for you."

"All of them?" She shook her head. "No. They'd want to keep lookouts here, at least. To guard the place."

"Maybe they felt threatened and went to the cabin."

"Possibly." Willow's hands trembled. Exhaustion from a poor night's sleep mixed with weakness from missing too many meals was giving her the shakes.

If only she could lie down and sleep, and wake up to find everything back to normal!

But that wouldn't happen.

"Let's go upstairs." Jacob offered her a hand, which she numbly took and stood to her feet. "We should eat something and figure out what's next."

She nodded, and followed him up to the kitchen. He pulled open the fridge door.

"Wow!" He stared into the appliance like he'd never seen one before. "They have eggs, milk and meat."

He pulled out the eggs and milk, then looked in the cupboard. Grabbing a can, he let out a low whistle.

"Bacon!"

"Canned bacon?"

"Yeah, check it out." He handed the can to her.

"Put it back, Jacob. You can't open and eat all that."

"Wanna bet?"

"Can you please be serious? We've got a big problem."

"And we'll figure it out as soon as we eat." He grabbed a fry pan from a hanging hook, and plunked it on the stove. "The miracles of propane. Cook on the stove, cool the fridge... I can see why those guys attacked this place. It's decked out like a castle!"

"Jacob!" Her tone carried her full rebuke.

"What? It is." He opened the canned bacon, rolled out four pieces, and dropped them in the pan. "They're pre-cooked, but we'll warm them up. We should have pancakes, too."

The aroma of the bacon almost made her swoon. She settled onto a stool at the bar and took a long, appreciative inhalation. Instantly, her mouth watered.

Jacob pulled a box of pancake mix from the cupboard, mixed it up, flipped the bacon and pushed them aside. He cracked eggs in the middle of the pan, and they sizzled in the bacon grease.

The sight, the sound, the smells – Willow could barely stand it. When was the last time she'd had a real breakfast? She swallowed.

Jacob started the pancakes in a separate pan. He flipped the eggs, turned off that pan's element, flipped the pancakes, then stared at her.

"What, you're not going to do anything but drool? Find some plates and stuff!"

She slid off her stool, found plates and glasses in the cabinets, and grabbed utensils from a drawer. Jacob took the plates and piled the food onto them as Willow poured milk into the glasses.

They sat down at the kitchen bar. Jacob dove into his eggs.

"Hold on! What about a blessing?"

He set down his fork and bowed his head as she prayed over the food. At the first syllable of "Amen," his fork dove back into the eggs.

They ate in silence. Willow varied between wolfing it down and savoring each bite. It was all so amazingly good. And the milk was fresh from the Brown Swiss cow out in the barn. So creamy!

When she only had a quarter of a pancake left, her stomach tightened and turned. It wasn't as thrilled about the culinary deluge as her mouth had been. But she polished off the pancake anyway. She'd need the calories and nutrition for whatever lay ahead.

She rose and took her dishes to the sink. Running hot water into it, she marveled again. The retreat had a propane water heater, obviously. They had all the conveniences of the modern world, almost – until they ran out of propane. Then they'd be cooking and heating their water over a fire like everyone else.

Splashing dish soap into the sink, she grabbed a sponge and went to work. Jacob had cooked, so she cleaned. She didn't mind, either. There was something about having one's hands in warm soapy water that gave one clarity. And she needed clarity. She needed a plan. She prayed silently as she scrubbed.

Jacob brought his dishes over and splashed them in the sink. He grabbed the pans and set them beside the sink, then put the milk and eggs back in the fridge. He picked up the canned bacon and paused.

"This was really good."

"Put it in the fridge, Jacob."

"Spoil sport." He opened the fridge and set it on the top shelf. "Who made you boss, anyway?"

"God."

He scoffed, then broke into a laugh. "You're a funny chick, you know that?"

"Sometimes." She began rinsing the dishes. The clean hot water felt like heaven. Maybe someday she could take a bath here, or a hot shower.

What was she thinking?

She needed to focus on finding everyone. It was not likely they were out looking for her, at least not all of them. John was too compulsive about having lookouts guarding the property. So there were two likely possibilities: either they'd abandoned the retreat, or they'd been killed or captured.

Hopefully, they'd abandoned the place for some reason, and headed off to the cabin. But that seemed doubtful. The other possibility was far worse.

What if the ninjas that captured Matt and Jacob had captured John's group, along with Alan and Clark? But if that had happened, why weren't some of those bad guys here, at the retreat? Why would they just take the residents, and leave the residence vacant?

It didn't make sense.

And the Andersons abandoning the retreat didn't make sense, either. Just yesterday, she'd heard John talking to Alan and Clark about moving here. If they agreed to do that, John should feel pretty confident about having enough team members to live here in relative safety.

She shook her head, willing the cobwebs to fly out. Wishing things would make sense.

"Missy?"

She glanced at him.

"You okay?" His eyes held concern.

She shook her head. "I just can't figure it out. It doesn't make sense."

"Why they're gone?"

"Why they're gone, where they're gone – any of it."

"What do you want to do?"

She placed the last pan in the drying rack and wiped her hands on a white kitchen towel.

"I don't know. Maybe go back to the cabin and see if they're there." She turned to face him. "What do you think?"

"We could either do that, or –" he paused, his deep eyes studying her. "Or, we could find the place that held me hostage, and see if they are there."

"And if they are, then what? It's just me and you. We're going to storm the place with two people?"

"I was thinking more like reconnaissance."

"If they are there, we'll have to go back to the cabin to get more help. So we'd waste time by going to that farm first, because we'd have to make two trips: first, to check it out, and second, after we go to the cabin for backup." She filled her water bottle at the sink. "Besides, if they were taken prisoner, why would the attackers leave this place vacant? It makes no sense."

"So we'll go to the cabin first."

"Right."

"Why didn't you just say so?"

She glanced at him. His eyes sparkled and he winked. Since he was teasing, she ignored it.

"Okay, let's go." They went out the back door, leaving it unlocked. "Let's check around the barn and grounds first, see if we find anything."

It took less than ten minutes to make a cursory check of the property and outbuildings. No one was around. The animals were still there, though, so Willow watered and fed them.

"I'm tempted to take some of these guys home for now," she said. "Just in case the worst happened, and the bad guys are coming back."

Jacob's eyebrows flew up. "You want to lead livestock through the woods, *just in case?*"

"It might be a good idea." She ran her hand over the milk cow's flank. "She's going to need to be milked in a few hours. We can't just leave her with no one to take care of that."

"What about the other cow?"

"She's a heifer. We'll give her extra water, and she'll be fine here for now."

Jacob looked at the mature cow. "I'm not leading a cow across the mountains.'

"Fine. Can you ride a horse?"

22

W illow saddled the gelding and haltered the milk cow. She also saddled the mare, but put her halter on instead of her bridle. She put the mare's bridle into a saddle bag, so they'd have it later if they needed to ride her.

"You'll pony the mare," she told Jacob.

"Pony her?"

"Yeah. You'll ride the gelding and lead the mare."

"What are you gonna do – ride the cow?"

She burst out laughing.

"I'll lead Bossy."

She gave Jacob a leg up into the saddle. The gelding took a few steps and Jacob jerked awkwardly in the saddle.

"Don't grip with your heels unless you want to go on a wild ride. Sit up straight. Grip with your thighs."

"I don't know about this." Anxiety etched Jacob's brow. "Maybe I should just lead him."

"Just relax. Then he will. You'll be fine." She handed him the mare's lead rope. "Don't tie this to anything. If things get crazy, you don't want her attached to you. If you need to slow down, pull back – gently – on the reins. Say 'Whoa,' and pull back to stop."

She took the cow's lead rope and started away from the barn. Glancing back, she snickered as Jacob lurched with the gelding's steps.

"It's not funny!" He shot a glare her direction.

"Yes, it is. A little." She chuckled. "Keep your hands low. Relax your shoulders."

She started up toward the ridge behind the house, the cow trudging beside her. At least this beast was halter trained. Most cows weren't.

Willow made a point of picking a wide path through the trees to allow extra room for the cow beside her and the ponied mare. It'd be no good to get pinned against a tree, or stepped on if the animal scrambled for footing.

The volcanic ash was barely noticeable at the ridge now. Wind and rain, along with wild summer foliage, had effectively reduced its grip on the mountains.

Still, she and her menagerie were leaving a deep trail for anyone who might follow them. She stopped at the crest of the ridge. Was it a bad idea to take the animals to the cabin?

Was she leading the bad guys straight to her home?

Perhaps she could stash them somewhere – not too far from the cabin, but not too close, either.

No, that wouldn't work. Cougars or bears or wolves could make quick work of them.

She had to just stick to the plan.

The day grew warm as they made their way toward the cabin. They stopped at the creeks along the way so the horses and cow could drink. The cow's plodding pace slowed their progress to what felt like one mile an hour.

Finally, after the longest time, the clearing and cabin came into view. In the garden beyond, Raven and the girls worked in the midday sun. The missing men were nowhere to be seen.

Willow yelled a greeting, and Raven jumped up and ran to meet her, wrapping her in a hug.

"A cow? Horses? What's going on?" Raven took the mare's lead rope from Jacob.

"I'm not sure. It's a long story." Willow looked toward the cabin. "Has anyone else come back from the retreat?"

Deborah, Jaci and Candy hurried out of the cabin and came over.

"No." Her gaze latched on Willow's eyes. "Were they supposed to?"

"I don't know. They just disappeared!"

"Who disappeared?" Deborah demanded. "My husband?"

"And mine?" Jaci choked on her words.

Raven gripped Willow's shoulders. "Tell us what's going on!"

"Where's Josh?" Her eyes flitted toward the garden and the barn. She only saw the girls.

"He's still recuperating," Raven said. "Focus!"

"Okay, I'll start at the beginning. I went looking for Matt and Jacob yesterday –"

"And found one of them." Deborah jutted her chin toward Jacob, who struggled to dismount from his saddle.

"Yes. But we got lost on the way back to the retreat, and had to spend the night in the woods. This morning, we found our way to the retreat, but no one was there."

"They didn't leave a note?" Jaci asked.

Willow shook her head. She hadn't thought about that, but it was another indication that something bad might have happened. Otherwise, why wouldn't they have left a note for her?

"Were they out looking for you? Maybe they got lost," Deborah suggested.

"Or they're just still out looking." Jaci's hazel eyes brightened with hope.

"But they always post lookouts." Willow rubbed the cow's lead rope between her fingers. "We tried to radio them, and got no response. We looked around and couldn't find anyone."

"So what's the deal with the animals?" Raven scratched the top of the cow's head.

"There's no one there to milk her, which she needs right now," Willow answered. "And there are some real bad people around. If they found the retreat and took over, I'd hate to have left the animals all there when we could have used them ourselves."

It sounded callous, maybe. But life was dire these days, and hung by the thinnest thread. Livestock could mean the difference between survival and starvation.

"Where's Gilligan?" Raven's voice scratched out the words, and she didn't meet Willow's eyes.

"I left him with Alan and Clark."

Wordlessly, Raven took the mare and led her toward the barn.

"It's just a dog," Jacob said, watching her go.

"Spoken by someone who obviously never had one." Willow stepped on his foot, driving her heel down hard.

"Ow!" He gave her a sideways glare. "I just meant, we're missing *people*. The dog is less important."

"Moving on." Willow's glance took in Deborah, Jaci and the girls. "If they are not out looking for us, I have a good idea where they are."

Deborah's eyes darkened. "Go on."

"During the gunfight the other night, Jacob was captured with Matt. They were taken to a neighboring residence. There were a few other prisoners there, as well."

"So you think our husbands were captured?" Panic edged

into Jaci's voice.

"Maybe. And the Andersons' group, too."

"What about Kristie? Did she make it?" Deborah asked.

Willow shook her head. "She died yesterday morning."

"Oh, dear. Poor Matt." Deborah's eyes grew misty. Then she glanced up quickly. "But what happened to Matt? You said he was taken with Jacob. And you brought Jacob back."

"Matt wasn't able to get free. We have to rescue him."

"And everyone else." Jaci wiped at her eyes. "If they were captured."

"Why do they take prisoners, anyway?" Deborah asked. "That's just more people they have to feed."

"I guess they were making some of them work."

"Like slaves?" Jaci's eyes grew round.

Willow nodded. "Or maybe they were hoping to do a prisoner exchange if any of their guys that they left behind after the gun fight survived. Or maybe they were hoping for ransom for the safe return of our guys. Who knows?"

The conversation stalled, and Willow looked at the gelding.

"We need to get the cow milked and the horses rubbed down. Then we can figure out our plan of attack."

After lunch, Willow gathered the group in the shade behind the house. Josh came out and joined them.

"You're still sick." Willow gave him a stern look. "Get back in the cabin and rest."

"Not a chance! Matt needs me. You do, too. Me and Jacob are the only guys left around here."

"You can stay for the discussion. Then you and I will talk."

He scowled. "Fine. But I'm going!"

She turned to the rest of the group. The teen girls played

with little Maria on the grass. Raven, Candy, Deborah, Jaci and Jacob stood around in a loose circle, all eyes on her.

"I think we should scout out the location where Matt is held hostage. Hopefully, we'll be able to tell if the others are there, as well. If not, we'll form a plan to rescue Matt, at least."

"And free the other prisoners, if we can," Jacob added.

"Of course. We'll try to free anyone we can." She looked toward the sun. "It's early afternoon now. It'll be late afternoon or early evening by the time we find the place. We can watch it until dark, then get some rest. I think we should go in during the middle of the night, maybe around 2 or 3 a.m."

"Why wait so long?" Jaci asked. "Why not as soon as it's fully dark?"

"More people might be awake. Or not sleeping deeply."

"This is going to be a risky mission." Jacob squared his shoulders. "We might not all come home. That said, we need as many volunteers as possible, while still leaving some capable folks here. Just in case."

"Jacob's right. It's dangerous. But we've got to do it." Willow looked from one face to another, seeing courage, doubt, fear and hope all mixed together. "So who's in?"

"I'm in," Raven said.

"Me too," Josh added.

"I'll go, but I think Jaci should stay here with the girls," Deborah said, looking from her daughter to her granddaughters. Jaci's head nodded slowly.

"I'll stay," she said.

"I'll stay with you," Candy said.

"Jacob?" Willow turned her gaze his direction.

"What? Of course I'm in. Sheesh!" His offended look said as much as his words.

"Okay, so we've got four. Five if Josh comes," she said.

"I'm definitely in." Josh jutted out his chin.

"We'll talk in a minute." She turned to the others. "Those who are remaining are in charge of everything here – milking, tending the garden, taking care of the cabin and livestock, running off predators and protecting the place."

"We can handle it." Jaci exchanged a glance with Candy, who nodded. "Just bring back our family."

"Good. Now, those who are going, get your things together. Pack extra water, some food, flashlights, guns and ammo... Jacob, why don't you see if you can find some tools we might need to break locks or chains?"

"Sure." He headed off toward the barn, while the rest scattered to begin their preparations. Josh stepped in front of her.

"You can't make me stay here."

"Josh. You're sick. You need to get well." Her tone softened. "Besides, what if we don't make it back? Everyone here will need your help to get through the winter."

Josh's gaze slid toward the pretty teens walking to the barn with Maria. It took a moment for him to return to the conversation.

"It's just – if I don't go, and anything happens to Matt – I won't forgive myself." His eyes sparked. "Matt would absolutely come rescue me."

"Greater love hath no man than this, that a man lay down his life for his friends," Willow quoted, not recalling where the verse was located in scripture. "But are you well enough? If you slow us down, or can't handle this because you're too sick, you'll be more of a burden than a help."

"I'm feeling a lot better." He met her eyes. "Really."

"Okay."

Josh grinned and started to turn away.

"But if you get sicker or have any trouble, I'm sending you back home. Got it?"

He smiled, shrugged and jogged around the corner of

the cabin.

FATIGUE DRAINED Willow's mind and muscles as her tiny team finally approached the property where Jacob believed he had been held prisoner. They'd returned to the retreat, found it still vacant, then slowly made their way down the road, checking each home until Jacob recognized the third one.

The sun dipped low in the sky, falling into the valley between two craggy mountains, as they crept through the forest near the property. They took their time making a wide arc to circle in behind the home and outbuildings. Finding some boulders, they hunkered down.

"That's definitely it." Jacob pointed to a small, unpainted wood structure between the barn and the house. "That's where they kept us."

Josh pulled out his binoculars.

"Wait!" Willow grabbed his hand. "The sun could glint off the lenses, and they might see a reflection. Hold off until the sun finishes setting."

Willow crawled to the edge of a boulder and peered down at the homestead. A tidy white house perched near a little stream at the curve of a circular driveway. It was flanked by an abundant garden and a fenced yard with a large doghouse. She didn't see a dog, though. Perhaps it'd been killed by the invaders. Had the same fate taken Gilligan?

It would be a big loss if they lost him. He was a good watch dog. Alert, obedient, energetic and just plain endearing. Somehow, she felt responsible for his absence now, even though it wasn't necessarily her fault. Hopefully, she could find him and return him to Raven.

But first things first.

A man dressed in all black sauntered out the back door of the home. He swaggered toward the wooden shack, a rifle slung over his shoulder.

Willow held her breath. Binoculars would help immensely right now. Her gaze shot toward the western horizon. The sun was half down.

And she and her team were directly east of the house, so they were in the worst location as far as reflections. What was she thinking? If they'd circled a little more, they'd be south of the home, and probably could use the field glasses. Plus, the sun wouldn't be in their eyes as they surveyed the property. Another stupid mistake.

The man walked past the shack to the barn. The sunset behind the barn painted its front in deep shadows, and Willow shielded her eyes with her hand.

"We gotta move," Jacob hissed. "No point in surveillance if you can't see."

"You're right." She motioned to the others as she backed away from the boulders. They made a swing to the left, placing them south of the buildings as the sun made its final hurrah.

"Now we can use the binoculars." Cozying up to an old ponderosa, Willow surveyed the buildings below.

Two men stood outside the barn, both dressed like the ninjas that attacked the retreat the other night. All black, ballistic vests, nice rifles, radios, ammo pouches, the whole bit. It looked like they were guarding the barn.

No one hung around the shack where Jacob said he'd been detained. Maybe they'd abandoned that, and moved the prisoners to the barn?

Another guy exited the barn, made a comment to the two guys in front, and continued on to the house. As Jacob had said, there were quite a few men here. The only thing she could do was stage a sneak attack, and it was going to be risky.

23

As darkness fell, Willow gathered the group for dinner and whispered prayers. Silently, they chewed on their thoughts and their venison jerky.

"We should get some sleep. Even three or four hours will help," Willow said. "But we need to take turns on watch. Who wants to go first?"

Raven volunteered. As the others settled in and tried to get comfortable, Willow pulled Raven away from the group.

"When this goes down, watch my back and keep an eye on Jacob. Don't let him get behind you."

"Why?" Anxiety colored Raven's tone. "You still don't trust him?"

"I only half trust him."

"Then why'd you bring him?"

"He's the only one with any knowledge of this place. And he's a good shot."

"Have you been praying about what to do about him?"

"Yeah. I've been praying that God would remove anyone that doesn't belong with us." She sighed. "And look what happened to Kristie."

"That's not your fault. It was hers."

"I know... but still." Willow paused and shivered. "Anyway, keep an eye on him."

"Alright. I'll do my best." Raven squeezed Willow's arm. "Now get some rest."

WILLOW TOOK the final watch at about 1 a.m. Her band of believers slept restlessly under the big pines. A single light flickered from a window in the white farmhouse. Most likely a candle. Other than that, the place was dark.

The sky was dark, too. The moon's new phase last night left the tiniest sliver of a crescent tonight. And frequent clouds covered up the bit of light it reflected to earth.

She took the peaceful hour to prepare her mind and soul for the battle to come. It felt a little – no, maybe a lot – like Gideon, who had to trust God to grant him the victory over armies of Midianites with his tiny band of 300 men. God had said Gideon's 22,000-man army was too large. So God had whittled it down. Way down.

Willow prayed for a success like Gideon's.

Then she woke her team and assembled them together.

"Okay, guys, here's the plan. Josh and Deborah and I will check the shack first, to make sure no one's there. Then we'll move on to the barn." She tried to see Jacob's face, but it was obscured in darkness. "Jacob and Raven will hang back a little, to alert us of any approaching danger, and engage the bad guys if necessary."

Slowly, they crept down the hill toward the buildings.

Willow's boots splashed as she stepped through the little stream. She reached the back corner of the shack and waited as Deborah and Josh caught up. Both carried a handgun and a tool – Deborah, a bolt cutter, and Josh, a crowbar.

Willow raised her rifle to the ready position.

"Let's do this!" she whispered, sidling around the corner. She was now in view of the barn, but couldn't see anything over there other than blackness. Hopefully, that was all they could see her direction, as well.

Slowly, she felt her way along the side of the shack until she felt the door frame.

The clouds moved away from the sliver moon, and she was able to make out the door's handle. She gripped it and pushed against the door. It gave easily, with a loud, yawning creak.

"Anybody here?" She stepped in and risked turning on her flashlight. Josh and Deborah followed her inside.

Her light flitted across rough board walls, a tool bench, a window, an old bicycle, some tools and not much else. Maybe Jacob had been held here, but there was no evidence of people. She turned off the light.

"Okay," she whispered. "To the barn!"

Her pulse filled her ears as she darted outside. The moon cast enough light that she could see the front of the barn. Two guys sat on either side of the door, leaning up against it. Their heads were bowed toward their chests.

Were they asleep?

She tiptoed forward, hearing only the slightest rustle from Josh and Deborah behind her.

Her heart thudded as she stepped to the door. She rested her hand on the handle and it moved easily. Not locked.

And why should it be, when it was guarded by two men?

She pushed, and it swung silently open. Taking a deep breath, the scent of hay and rabbits filled her senses. But she couldn't see a thing. Only pitch blackness.

Did she dare use her light? It would destroy her stealth approach.

But without it, she'd know nothing.

She flicked it on.

To her left, a row of rabbit hutches ran along the wall. Her light illuminated the rabbits' soft white coats, and reflected pink in their eyes.

To her right, there were some feed bags, three garbage cans, a few bales of straw and two pitchforks.

Dead ahead, large animal stalls lined both sides of a central walk way. If there were any people in this building, they must be up there. She glanced back. Josh and Deborah were almost on her heels.

"Stay here and watch the door," she whispered.

Hurrying forward, she shone her light through the old wood planks of the first stall. Nothing but old hay and manure. Same with the next stall. She crossed the aisle and checked the first two stalls. Nothing there, either.

That left the two stalls in the back corners. Her light illuminated the left stall.

Bingo!

Three men and two teen boys slept on the floor. They were all chained together, and the guy at the end of the chain was also chained to the wall. Willow didn't recognize any of them.

As her light flitted over the older teen's face, his eyes blinked open. His hand shot up to cover his eyes from the blinding light, yanking on the chain that tethered him to a middle-aged man.

"Knock it off!" The man growled. His eyes opened, and he sat up. "What's going on?"

"Quiet!" Willow hissed.

"Who're you?" The man stared toward her.

"I'm here to help. But you have to be quiet."

Where were her friends? Maybe in the other stall?

"I'll be right back," she whispered.

By now, the other guys were waking up.

"Don't leave us," the first teen pleaded.

"If you don't shut up, I won't be able to help you!" Willow hissed. She dashed across the aisle and flashed her light over the gate.

They were here! Matt, Alan, Clark, John, Jeannie. And Julie and Mike, whom she didn't know as well but recognized instantly as John's friends.

She unlatched the gate and let herself in, shining her light on their faces.

"Wake up!" She shook Matt's shoulders. He groaned and turned over. Dark bruises ringed his eyes. His wrist was chained to Alan's, but they weren't chained to the wall. Her flashlight flicked over the group as they began waking. All of them were chained in pairs, but no one was chained to the wall as far as she could see.

She scrambled back into the aisle.

"Josh!" She hissed. "Bring those bolt cutters!"

He raced toward her.

"Cut Clark and John free, then give the cutters to Clark to free the others!"

The guys across the aisle were getting noisy.

"Hey, get us out of here!"

"Yeah, c'mon, man!"

Willow leapt across the aisle to reassure and shush them.

A shot rang out.

Then another.

Well, that would wake up the whole neighborhood. No point in shushing anybody now.

"Hurry, Josh!"

"Got it!"

"Clark, take those cutters across to the other stall," Willow ordered. "One of those guys is chained to the wall. Just cut them free from that wall. We gotta get out of here!"

She lit the way for Clark and shined the light on the chain for him.

Gunshots filled the air. Raven and Jacob must be engaging the guys outside the barn, or other guys from the house.

"Can we get out the back?" Willow asked.

"Yes. There is a big door in the center." Clark cut cleanly through the metal.

"Okay, you guys, we don't have time to cut everyone apart. So you'll have to run together," she said, shining her light toward the back of the barn, illuminating the door Clark mentioned. "Hurry!"

The five-man chain gang needed no urging. They scrambled toward the door, got it open and ran into the night.

Willow's friends came out of the other stall, chained in pairs except John and Clark, now. Willow shoved her rifle toward John, who took it with a quick nod. She grabbed her handgun.

"Deborah, let's go!"

Deborah left her post near the front of the barn and rushed toward them. She planted a kiss on Alan's cheek. He was still chained to Matt, who leaned heavily against him.

"Josh, maybe you can help Matt, too." She glanced around quickly. "Let's go!"

A full-blown gunfight raged behind them as they raced out the back of the barn. It sounded like Raven and Jacob were putting up a spectacular fight. But they only had so much ammo. When it was gone, they were doomed.

Willow turned off the flashlight to avoid painting targets on her group. She led the way, straight for the woods and the hills behind. Gunshots pummeled her ears. She didn't dare look back. They had to reach the safety of the trees!

Her legs stretched out in slow motion, grabbing the ground and thrusting it behind her.

BOOM! BOOM! BOOM!

The shots rang out in time with her heartbeat.

Slowly, the trees grew larger, then loomed in front of her.

A few more steps, and she'd be there.

Pain tore through her leg. Felt like the grizzly claw, raking her flesh again. She lurched forward, grabbing a tree trunk and pulling herself behind it. Bullets blasted the tree, slicing bark bits into shrapnel.

Where were her friends? Had they made it? Some had gotten ahead of her in the run from the barn.

What about Josh?

She didn't dare look, yet she had to.

When bark quit hitting her skin and the shots slowed, she took the chance. A quick peek around the trunk of the tree told her nothing. She couldn't see anybody. She pulled back just as another volley of bullets blasted her tree.

Until that guy stopped shooting at her, she couldn't move. She was pinned down.

24

Willow plastered herself against the tree trunk, waiting for a break in the shooting. Her left calf oozed warm blood into her boot. It was painful, but not as bad as she'd feared – maybe because of adrenalin, or maybe it wasn't that bad of a wound.

A moment of silence gave her an opportunity, and she seized it, racing deeper into the forest. Limbs and brush reached out and clawed at her as she pressed forward into the blackness. She kept running, arms held out in front of her so she wouldn't run straight into a tree.

Tripping, she fell forward, breaking her fall with her outstretched hands.

Shooting blasted all around. She stayed low, crawling toward safety.

Her hands found the rough, cold face of a big boulder, and she scrambled behind it and hunkered down, pressing her back against the stone.

A break in the gunfight gave her a chance to peek around the rock.

Light emanated from the lower windows of the house, and

from the barn. Flashlights blazed randomly around the barn-yard; their users would flick them on for a moment, sweeping an area, then flick them off. That made it harder for their enemies to pinpoint their location and shoot them.

She couldn't tell if they were her friends or her enemies.

More importantly, she couldn't see Josh or anyone else. Foot-falls, snaps and crashes sounded in the forest around her, but it was too dark to tell who was who.

The shooting pause grew longer. Had the gunfight ended?

Maybe her team ran out of ammo. That was certainly likely. Or maybe they'd been killed.

A shiver rocked her whole torso.

She got to her feet slowly, then started deeper into the forest, feeling her way as she moved forward in a crouch. After a few minutes, she stopped behind a tree and pulled out her flashlight.

Illuminating her left leg revealed torn jeans and oozing blood from the outside of her calf. She sat down and pulled up her pant leg. The bullet had just nicked her leg, leaving a hori-zontal cut about an inch long. It needed to be cleaned and covered, but she was lucky.

Or protected.

She lifted her eyes to the starry skies and thanked the Lord for that. And prayed for her friends and brother.

Then she waited. Morning could not come soon enough.

THUNK!

The sound startled her awake. A pine cone bounced off her boot.

"Psssttt!"

She turned to the sound and gathered her feet under her at the same time.

Raven crouched against a tree trunk about twenty feet away. She held another pine cone, and looked ready to launch it.

Willow looked around quickly. Dawn was well underway, and the early birds were chirping already. It wouldn't be long before sunrise.

She scrambled across the ground between her and Raven.

"Where is everyone? Have you seen Josh?"

Raven shook her head. "You're the first one I found."

"How long have you been looking?"

"Just a few minutes. But we should hurry. It's getting light fast."

"Okay, but tell me what you know. You can talk as we search." Willow started stealthily forward, Raven falling in beside her.

"When you went into the barn, Jacob and I moved off toward the side, so we could shoot the guys in front if necessary, without hitting anybody inside the barn. When the clouds parted and the moon lit up for a minute, we had the guys at the front of the barn in our sights. But then it got so dark. Without night vision, it was hard to keep our targets."

Willow paused under a larch tree, searching for a sign of anyone.

"Yeah? Then what?"

"Something woke them. They both jumped up."

"That was some other prisoners in the barn. They were making a bunch of noise."

"So Jacob fired, and I did, too."

"Did you hit them?"

"I have no idea. It was so dark!"

"Then the gunfight started."

"Yeah. But we don't have night scopes. We were totally blind."

"So what'd you shoot at?"

"We fired a couple more shots at those guys, then we stopped. We couldn't see anything, and couldn't afford to waste ammo on worthless shots."

"But the gunfight..." Willow stopped and turned to her friend. "It kept going. It was intense. For quite a while."

"Crazy, right?" A slow smile crossed Raven's face. "I thought it was you guys, fighting back. Maybe it was the bad guys, all fighting each other because they couldn't see anything, either."

"Some of them could see. Probably with night vision scopes. One of them could see me, for sure."

"And yet, here you are!" Raven thumped Willow's back. "Big as life, and twice as lovely!"

"Josh!" The word rushed from her mouth as Willow's gaze landed on her brother. She ran to him, wrapping him in a choking hug. "And Matt!"

Josh looked unscathed, but Matt looked rough. Black and purple bruises ringed his eyes and stained his cheekbones.

"Are you alright?" Willow stared into his eyes.

"I'll survive." He frowned and turned his gaze to the ground. "Josh told me about Mom."

"I'm so sorry." She wrapped her arms around him. "So sorry."

"Has she been buried?" The words choked out of his tight throat.

"I think our friends did that. Before all this craziness was going on."

He nodded, turning his head away and wiping it with his shirt sleeve.

"I'll take some flowers to her grave."

"Of course." Willow glanced from him to her brother and Raven. "We all will."

"We need to keep moving," Raven urged. "Find our friends and get out of here."

"You're right." Willow started forward. "Let's go."

Her leg burned and her stomach rumbled as she walked, stepping over fallen logs and around bushes. The day grew lighter and brighter by the minute. She glanced east. The sky blazed with a sun that was about to break over the mountains.

She crossed into a dip with a little creek running through it.

"Hey! Over here!"

The hushed call came from her right. She stopped and looked, but didn't see anyone. A cedar branch wiggled, then shook as John stepped out from the tree's cloak. He held her rifle in one hand, and Jeannie's hand in the other.

Willow grinned at the couple.

"Anybody else with you?"

"You bet!" He turned and motioned to others.

A lump formed in Willow's throat as Deborah, Alan, Clark, Julie and Mike all emerged from the cedar grove.

"What? This is everyone! Except Jacob." Willow's eyes asked a question her mouth wasn't willing to. Had they seen Jacob? Was he alive?

"We haven't seen him yet," Jeannie said.

"What about those other guys – the prisoners all chained together?" A quick glance told Willow that her friends had all gotten their chains off.

"We gave them the bolt cutter," John said. "So I'm pretty sure they're all loose now."

"Do you know who they were?"

John nodded. "Two were from town, and the others live down the road, by the highway."

"Any idea why they kept you all prisoner? Alive?"

"I overheard two of them talking," Deborah said. "They think there's going to be a market for slaves soon. They figured they'd sell us and get rich. Also, they were going to move their operation to our retreat."

Willow's eyes narrowed. Scum! The ninjas might be right, though – slavery had been around for thousands of years, and was lucrative for the human traffickers. With the government weakening or collapsing, it might come into vogue again in America. Apparently these guys were making a double-pronged business effort – capture slaves and take over their homes and supplies.

She picked up a branch and broke it in two.

"I think we'll need to do something about those guys. Otherwise, they'll be back."

"Absolutely." John nodded. "Let's take a peek at things now, in the light. Then maybe go home, eat and clean up our wounds, get some rest and lots more ammo."

"Sounds good to me." Willow glanced at her friends. Solemn nods met her gaze. "Maybe we'll find Jacob, too. Which way back to that place?"

"I believe it is that way." Clark pointed down into a draw. "It is not far."

"Lead on, then." Willow fell in beside him as he walked.

"Have you thought about moving to the retreat?"

"Yes. Alan and I have discussed it."

She studied his face, but was unable to find any revelations there.

"And? What will you do?"

"We will continue praying, and discuss with our wives."

"Jaci doesn't want to go."

Clark stopped for a moment, looking at her, then continued walking. He didn't reply, so Willow continued.

"I mentioned it when I was home at the cabin. Was it just yesterday?"

"It was." He stopped again, holding up his hand. The entire group behind him came to a quick halt.

"I believe the house is right over this hill," he whispered.

Willow motioned for the group to get down. As they squatted or knelt, she and Clark moved forward cautiously.

Her eyes searched out every movement, her ears strained for any sound. She and Clark hunched down as they neared the top of the hill. Then they dropped to their stomachs and crawled. A vulture circled overhead.

The house appeared below, the barn just beyond it. She saw no movement on the ground, but there were bodies. She began counting, and got to five.

Was Jacob among them? It was too far to tell.

She glanced over her shoulder and motioned the others to come forward and join them.

Josh and Raven caught up first.

"I see five bodies," she whispered.

Josh pulled out his binoculars. He glanced at Willow, and she nodded. The sun was to their backs. She didn't worry about a reflection at this angle. He looked for a minute.

"I count seven," Josh said, handing her the binoculars.

She took them and slowly swept the scene. He was right. Five were down out in the open, one was in the shadow of the house, and one guy lay half in and half out of the barn.

Was Jacob among them?

She held her breath as she slowly moved the binoculars, searching each body. She couldn't clearly see each face, but they were all dressed in black. Jacob had been wearing a black t-shirt and camo pants.

Handing the field glasses to Raven, she turned to John.

"We can see seven down. Jacob told us there were at least nine. So there are at least two that might still be alive."

Raven looked, then passed the binoculars to John. As he studied the property, Willow continued.

"I think we should go down now and clear the place out. We've got at least five guns, all with ammo. And we can grab more guns off the ground down there before we enter the house."

"Hmmm." John handed the field glasses to his wife. "Maybe you're right. We're tired, but if we wait, they might leave and regroup."

"Exactly." Willow looked from one person to the next. "Let's sort through our guns and ammo, say a prayer, make a plan, and get down there before the sun hits the house. Maybe we can catch them sleeping."

Ten minutes later, the group crept toward the house as two more vultures began circling. Exhaustion and hunger nagged at Willow, but she tried to ignore them. She pressed herself to focus. Get this done and stay alive, and then she could eat and sleep.

She held the group up at the edge of the forest. Taking the binoculars, she again swept the grounds. Saw no movement from any of the presumed dead guys. No movement through the windows of the house. It looked good. The sunlight had already hit the hilltop and was rapidly descending toward the house.

Willow glanced at John. He nodded. They were ready.

According to their plan, the five armed members – Willow, John, Clark, Alan and Raven – hurried toward the house. Those without guns – Josh, Deborah, Jeannie, Julie and Mike – raced toward the battlefield and scooped up weapons and as much ammo as they could find. Their job was to clear the barn and then provide backup as needed. Matt was posted at the edge of the clearing as a lookout, because he wasn't in fighting shape.

Willow and Raven ran around to the front door while John, Clark and Alan headed toward the back door.

She stared at Raven as they posted themselves on each side of the door. When she heard the sound of the back door being breached, she grabbed the handle and shoved.

It was locked.

She stepped up and tried kicking it open. Her wounded leg protested the effort, and the door didn't open.

"Let me," Raven said, stepping up. She tried kicking it in, but it didn't budge. Maybe it had a crossbar inside.

Shouts filled the house, then it grew quiet.

"Get ready!" Willow took a few steps away from the door and trained her handgun on it. Raven took a position opposite her.

When the bad guys came out that door, they'd be ready for them.

Instead, someone knocked from the inside.

"Willow?" It was John's voice. "Don't shoot. I'm opening the door."

She kept her gun ready, but drifted the sights toward the doorpost, ready to put them back on target if anybody besides John appeared in that doorway. There was a shuffling noise inside, then the sound of a deadbolt being unlocked.

The handle turned. The door eased open. John appeared.

Willow was about to breathe a sigh of relief, when a big mass of black and white fur blasted through the door and hurled itself at Raven.

"Gilligan!" Raven set her gun down and the dog bounded into her arms. "What were you doing here? I thought you were dead!"

Moisture sparkled in her eyes as she ran her fingers through the glossy coat and tousled his ears. He responded with a happy lick on her chin. She laughed and hugged the dog.

Willow turned toward the doorway, looking past John into the house.

"Any bad guys in there? What happened?"

He opened the door wide and held it open for her.

"There was a dead one in the kitchen, and one dying in the living room. We didn't find anyone else. Except Gilligan, obviously."

"Is the dying one still alive? We should question him. See if there are others. And if he knows what happened to Jacob."

"He's alive, but he won't be answering questions. He's unconscious."

"Maybe we can wake him up." She moved past him, through a basic farm kitchen with a dead man on the floor, and saw the living room off to the left. Two grey sofas, a fireplace, a TV, and an easy chair.

The bad guy was in the easy chair, and he wasn't resting easy. Jeannie and Deborah had already arrived and stationed themselves on each side. His head lolled at an awkward angle toward his right shoulder, and his breath came in long, shallow rasps. Blood soaked through his shirt over his engorged stomach. He did not appear long for this world. Jeannie gripped his wrist, taking his pulse.

"Let me know if he wakes up."

"Okay." Jeannie nodded, but gave a sad shrug. "I doubt he will."

Willow walked out to the barnyard. She scanned the edge of the forest, saw Matt, and waved him down. Josh came out of the barn.

"Nothing?" She asked.

"Nothing but dead bad guys."

Alan walked around the side of the barn.

"I found something." He swung the bolt cutter. "It was just a little ways into the woods. Guess those other captives cut themselves free and took off. All I found of them was a few footprints."

"Well, they were local guys." Willow shaded the bright sun out of her eyes. "I'm sure they headed straight for home. Glad you found the bolt cutters, though. We can't afford to lose our tools."

Willow's gaze took in the faces around her. "Still no sign of Jacob? No clues at all?"

Matt and Josh shook their heads.

Alan frowned. "Not a thing. It's like he vanished."

"Well, let's all keep our eyes and ears open. He's got to be somewhere."

She looked around the property.

"Let's gather up all the guns, gear and ammo, then dig a pit for these ninjas. Then we'll go to the retreat for something to eat."

Deborah approached from the house. "There's food here."

"But I don't know whose house this is. The owners, if they're alive, will need it."

"Seems unlikely they're alive, with this bunch living here." Deborah gestured at the dead men in the yard. "Also, the one in the living room just died."

"So we won't get any info from him. Still...." Willow glanced toward the tidy house. "We don't know. Maybe the owners will come home."

25

A s the sun reached its zenith, the believers straggled back to the retreat. Willow's arms and shoulders ached from helping dig the mass grave for the ninjas. Her stomach had stopped growling from hunger.

Still, her heart grew lighter with every step. Her friends were rescued mostly unharmed. They'd neutralized the threat of the attackers, so the Andersons' retreat should be safer for now. God had been her help when her team was vastly outnumbered.

Just like Gideon.

In the dark of night, the bad guys heard threatening weapons, and in their fear and panic, they'd killed most of their own men. Maybe one or two had escaped and run off, as had a few Midianites in Gideon's battle. But the modern attackers were far from a fearsome force now, if there were any still alive.

She lifted her tired eyes and arms to the sky and thanked God.

~

JACOB WASN'T at the retreat. Willow even checked in the barn, but there was no sign of him.

Where could he have gone? All the way back to the cabin? That was possible, if not likely. Had he just left? Why would he do that?

She was too tired to worry about that now. She walked back to the house.

John and Jeannie offered everyone showers at their home, and no one declined. Willow's leg wound stung as the warm water rushed over it. After she dried off, she dressed the wound with a first aid kit the Andersons provided.

The smell of baked chicken met her as she stepped out of the bathroom. She hurried to the kitchen. Jeannie mixed a green salad with fresh vegetables from the garden, while Deborah mashed potatoes. Raven stirred gravy, bringing it to a simmer.

Soon, the group was seated for lunch. Willow's mouth watered as John blessed the food and thanked the Lord for all He had done.

She was pretty sure it was the most delicious meal she'd even eaten. Or at least the one she'd most savored and appreciated. Mom's meals were always delicious.

A wave of sadness washed over her. Where was Mom? Was she alive? Okay? Willow sighed.

Wherever Mom was, she was in God's care. And one day, they would meet again. Either here on earth, or in Heaven. Of that one thing, she was very sure.

She took a bite of mashed potatoes smothered in chicken gravy, and nearly swooned. Josh put into words what she was feeling.

"This is so amazing! I could eat this every day for the rest of my life, and die happy."

Jeannie laughed, and passed him the platter of chicken.

"Eat up. You're still a growing young man."

Josh grinned and pulled a drumstick onto his plate, then passed the platter to Matt, who was looking a little better this afternoon.

"After lunch, maybe we can rest a bit before we head home," Willow said. "We need to go soon, though, since the gals there are waiting anxiously, I imagine."

She glanced at John, then Alan.

"Still no sign of Jacob?"

Alan shook his head. "Nope. I'd thought he might have made his way back here, but there's no sign he did. Just up and disappeared."

"Maybe he found his way back to the cabin."

"We'll know soon enough," Alan said. "Would someone pass the salad?"

IT WAS late afternoon as Willow and her friends arrived back at the cabin. Jaci ran toward them, her daughters on her heels. They wrapped themselves around Clark, then hugged Alan and Deborah.

"You're back!" Jaci grinned. "All of you!"

"All except Jacob," Willow pointed out. "Have you seen him?"

"No. You're the first we've seen of anyone since you left yesterday."

Willow frowned. Where could he be? There wasn't any indication he'd been injured. Or that there were enough bad guys remaining alive to capture him, especially in the dark.

And yet, he was missing. Again.

But he was a big boy and could take care of himself.

Candy emerged from the cabin, Maria on her hip. The girl wiggled free and made a beeline for her best furry buddy.

"Gig-gan!" She squealed, wrapping her arms around Gilligan. The dog rewarded her with a wagging tail and a lick on her ear.

Willow smiled. Except for Jacob, everyone was home. And safe, for the moment. Tomorrow, they'd take the horses and the cow back to the Andersons' retreat. Deborah and Alan's family would have to decide soon whether they'd move to the retreat or not.

For now, life was good. As always, God was good. Very good, indeed.

THE END.

EPILOGUE

As the memorial service ended, Willow followed Matt in placing wildflowers on his mom's grave. Raven came behind her with another bouquet. Their friends said quiet words to Matt, then everyone slowly walked toward the Andersons' home, where Jeannie had prepared lunch.

Willow touched Raven's elbow and led her aside.

"I don't think he knew about Kristie's mark," Willow whispered, then watched her friend's face as she mulled it over.

"I don't think so, either."

"Should we tell him?"

"No!" Raven shook her head vehemently. "What good could possibly come from that?"

"I don't know." Willow paused and thought about it. "None, I guess."

"So we'll let Kristie take her secret to the grave."

"Why not?" Willow looked back at the flower-strewn mound of earth. "She can't take it anywhere else."

Raven started toward the house, but Willow reached out and grabbed her sleeve.

"Hold on. There's another thing I want to talk to you about."

Raven stopped and glanced back. "What?"

"Jacob." Willow looked around at the retreat and the forest, as if he might pop out from behind a tree. "You were with him the last time he was seen. He wasn't shot, as far as you knew. And yet – he's missing. Again. Where could he have gone?"

"I have no idea."

"Well, I don't like it. He knows everything – where the retreat is, where our cabin is, what our assets are – everything. I've never really trusted him. What if he betrays us?"

Raven's smooth forehead rippled into furrows.

"Do you remember what you prayed for?"

Willow knitted her brows. "About what? Jacob?"

"You prayed – we prayed – that God would remove anybody who didn't belong with our group." Raven gave her a pointed look. "So. Jacob's gone. Maybe it's an answer to prayer."

"Maybe...." But Willow didn't feel good about it. "I'd be a lot happier if I knew where he was. If he'd said goodbye or something."

"Sure. We all would." Raven shrugged. "But that's Jacob. He's weird."

JACOB MYERS POUNDED on his uncle's buddy's front door. It'd been a while since he'd seen the guy. Maybe he didn't even live here anymore.

Nah, he'd still be here. He'd had career aspirations in little old Ponderosa.

Jacob pounded again, then went around to the side of the house to look in a window. Just then, the front door banged open. He hurried back.

"Marcus!"

"Jacob?" Disbelief registered on his face. "What in the world are you doing here?"

"Just kicking around. Thought I'd come over for a beer and a steak."

Marcus punched him playfully on the shoulder. "You're about two weeks late for that."

"Maybe I'll borrow your shower, then."

"You could sure use it!" Marcus wrinkled his nose, then swung the door open. "C'mon in!"

Jacob bounded through the door and into a small foyer. To his left, a living room sprawled out with big south-facing windows. The kitchen was to his right. The house looked reasonably well kept, for a bachelor pad.

"How about some sun tea?" Marcus asked.

"Sounds good." Jacob followed him into the kitchen. "Are you still working?"

"Sure. Minus the squad car, obviously." Marcus poured tea into a tall glass, then turned a critical eye on him. "I haven't seen you in what, three years? Tell me what you're doing in Ponderosa. And how long you've been here."

EXCERPT FROM BOOK 3, DESTRUCTION

Something moved in the darkening Montana sky, and eighteen-year-old Willow Archer cast an anxious glance upward, hoping to see an owl or a bat winging its way through the deepening twilight. Could the government agents have gotten their drones working? Were they, even now, peering at her as she walked back from the outhouse to the little one-room cabin? Was her group in danger again? So soon?

She froze, straining to find the source of the movement.

The brightest stars twinkled in the sky's blue velvet canvas. The moon had not yet risen. Willow scanned the celestial space slowly, then finally spotted it – one star was moving across the sky. But was it a star? Or a satellite?

Could it be an airplane? Was someone flying a jet in the United States? Maybe they were coming from a region that hadn't been hit by the EMP?

No, it wasn't a plane. Too high, too far away, wrong speed.

She exhaled slowly. Well, nothing to fear from a satellite. Not yet, anyway. Even if the government wanted to find Christians by satellite surveillance, they'd have to have functioning electronics on the ground in order to see any of the data from the satellites. And that wasn't too likely, given the recent EMP.

Although maybe satellite surveillance wasn't too far off, either, given that the City of Ponderosa obviously had gotten some electricity back online. And some running water, as well. Who knew how the rest of the country was faring?

She started back toward the cabin, the breeze blowing her long auburn locks across her face. Satellites and drones might be worries for a future day. For now, she just needed to keep her group safe, alive and fed.

Someone had propped open the cabin door with a large rock. She couldn't blame them. July was turning hot and muggy. All those bodies in the cabin made it feel like a slow cooker. The ancient window only opened about an inch before it got stuck against its warped wooden frame. Matt and Josh were up in the loft, while Raven snored like a baby bear on one of the top bunks at the rear of the cabin. Candy and little Maria appeared to be sleeping soundly on the lower bunk beds.

The breeze blew, fanning fresh air across Willow's skin as she paused in the doorway. They'd all sleep better with the ventilation. But an open door was an invitation to bears.

She shuddered. The scars on her leg from the grizzly attack were still bright and fresh. The sow's roar thundered through her memory. The beady eyes, the snapping jaws, the agony of those huge claws shredding her flesh... she winced.

Her hand trembled as she pulled the door shut and latched it. She took off her boots, then climbed into the bunk above Maria. Except for the toddler, most of the group had given up the luxury of removing clothing before going to bed. One never knew when the next crisis would strike, and if it struck in the middle of the night, nobody wanted to waste time pulling on their pants.

She wadded up Mom's sweater under her head and once

again wished for a real pillow. That was another luxury that had been given up when they'd fled civilization. If she ever had another chance though, she'd get one... a nice, big, fluffy white pillow with a cool cotton pillowcase.

Lying on top of her sleeping bag, she closed her eyes. She was tired, so very tired. But she was also hot. The air was stifling, even with the window cracked open.

She flopped onto her side. The odds of a bear coming to the cabin were slim, she knew. The odds of a second attack seemed minuscule.

Her discomfort fought with her fear and finally won out. She slipped to the floor, padded to the door in her stocking feet, and opened it.

A blessed blast of fresh mountain air cooled her sweaty face. She was just turning around to return to her bunk when her peripheral vision caught motion in the night sky. She scurried outside.

A blazing star streaked across the dark sky, then burned out.

A meteor! Willow smiled. A wishing star.

What should she wish for? Mom. She wished that somehow, she could find Mom. Or even get news of her. Since she'd been detained in the church roundup in Missoula, there had been no news. And that had been before the EMP. Was she still captive? Was she still alive?

A second star blazed across the sky, this one brighter than the last one. So she could make a second wish.

What about Jacob? She frowned. Since he'd disappeared after the gunfight, they'd found no trace of him. She truly did not believe he'd been injured. Had he abandoned them? Betrayed them?

Should she wish that he'd be found alive? Or that he'd be found dead?

A third star flashed a blazing trail, then flickered out.

This was a regular meteor shower! She should awaken the others, so they could watch. She hurried inside, shook Raven awake, then left her to tell Candy while Willow climbed the ladder to the loft. Grabbing Josh's ankle, she gave a good tug.

"Wha –" Josh yanked his foot away.

"Wake up! There's a meteor shower!" Willow shook Matt's ankle the same way. "Wake up! Shooting stars!"

Matt sat up. Willow climbed down the ladder and walked outside. Raven and Candy had already come out, and were gawking at a meteor. Then two blazed off at once.

"Look at that!" Candy enthused. "This is great!"

The boys stumbled out the door. They stared at the heavens.

"Did we miss it all?" Matt asked.

"I doubt it," Raven said. "Just give it a minute."

Josh flopped to the ground, then settled on his back, eyes to the sky. "I see one!"

Matt gave a low whistle as the meteor flashed to its death. "Awesome!"

Suddenly, the sky began to brighten.

"What on earth?" Candy's tone mixed amazement and fear.

A ball of brilliant light blazed overhead, illuminating the cabin, the clearing and the mountains beyond as if it were mid-day. It was like looking at the sun. As it grew nearer and brighter, Willow covered her eyes. And then it was gone.

She opened her eyes, but couldn't see a thing. Slowly, they started to adjust.

"Whoa." Josh sat up. "That was crazy."

BOOM! BOOM! BOOM!

The shockwave felt like an earthquake but sounded like a bomb explosion.

Willow clapped her hands to her ears. The cabin shook, its windows rattling precariously in their frames.

Inside the cabin, Maria screamed. Candy rushed through the door to her daughter. Gilligan rushed out, barking.

For several moments, booms like thunder continued filling the air. Finally, the noise tapered off.

Ears ringing, Willow struggled to refocus in the dark night.

Candy carried her wailing toddler outside. "What should we do?"

Willow laughed. "You mean to hide from meteorites?"

"We should pray," Raven suggested.

She was right. As more meteors ripped open the sky, the group held an impromptu prayer vigil. Everyone kept their eyes open.

Only one more meteor came as close as the first one. This one appeared much smaller, though, and they actually saw where it landed.

THE HOUSE SHOOK and threw Jacob Myers out of bed. He scrambled in the darkness, untangling his feet from the blankets. Glass shattered and tinkled on the hard floor.

What in the world? Where was he?

Concussive bombs were going off. It sounded like a war zone.

He leapt up, cutting his bare foot on the broken glass.

Yelping, he loosed an expletive and grabbed his foot. Then he remembered. He was at Marcus Laramie's house in Ponderosa, Montana. There had been an EMP. How could the country be at war? Maybe they were under attack, but they couldn't be fighting back. They weren't able to.

The explosions and thunderings died down. Their noise was replaced by the barking of about a dozen dogs. Little yappy yelps, big ferocious woofs, and a cacophony of canine voices in between.

He'd been sleeping on the sofa. And he remembered putting a flashlight on the coffee table, within reach.

Feeling around on the floor, he found several shards of glass, and finally, the flashlight. He flicked it on.

The window had been blown out by the blast, shattering and throwing huge shards of glass down on the sofa where he'd been sleeping moments before. It might have killed him, if he hadn't been thrown off the sofa at the same time

His pants were where he'd left them, on a chair across the room, and his boots were on the floor beside the chair. He hobbled over to them, watching for glass as he took each step.

"Marcus?" He yelled. "You okay?"

"I'm outside." The answer drifted through the broken window. "C'mon out!"

The cut on his foot didn't look too terrible, so Jacob shook out his clothes and boots, dressed, grabbed his handgun, and hurried out the front door.

"What's going on?"

He flashed the light on Marcus, who sat on a lawn chair in the middle of the yard. The guy turned, then shielded his eyes from the light.

"Get that out of my eyes!"

Jacob lowered the flashlight.

"What are you doing out here?"

Marcus spat in the grass. "Watching the meteors, obviously. Just had a real fine one."

"That? It wasn't an earthquake?"

"Nah. Impressive, wasn't it? I almost fell out of my chair."

"It busted your window."

The next door neighbor, about the age of Jacob's grandmother, came screaming out of her house in her bathrobe and slippers.

"War! We're at war!" Her shrill voice reached a high-pitched shriek. She looked toward Marcus. "Do you have a bomb shelter?"

"We're not at war, Mrs. Dennison," Marcus assured her. "Calm down, now. It's a meteor shower."

"Are you crazy? Meteor showers don't explode like bombs!"

"We had a close one. If you go back inside, stay away from your windows." His voice was calm, maybe from his years of working crises as a police officer. He seemed unflappable. Jacob had to give the guy credit for that. He lowered himself to the grass beside Marcus' chair.

"I cut my foot."

"How bad is it?"

"Not too bad, I guess. About an inch long, but superficial."

"When this show blows over, we'll have to clean it up. Don't want an infection getting started there."

Jacob stretched out on the lawn. The barking and yapping wound down as the neighbors gathered their dogs and spoke excitedly over their fences. Overhead, a distant meteor streaked, then faded away.

Eventually, the neighborhood quieted. Jacob yawned. His eyes grew tired.

Next thing he knew, it was morning. He sat up and pushed off a quilt. The top was covered with dew. Marcus must have thrown it over him during the night. Despite his gruff exterior, he was a decent guy. And calm under pressure.

Jacob shook out the quilt and hung it over the deck railing to dry. He walked into the house. Marcus wasn't in the kitchen or the living room. Maybe he was gone. Or still asleep.

The living room was a mess. In the light of day, it was apparent how close he'd come to death last night. The sofa where he'd been sleeping was directly under a large window, maybe five feet tall and eight feet wide. The shock wave had shattered the glass, blowing shards into the room and dropping huge jagged pieces onto the sofa, where they pierced the fabric like shrapnel. Now they stood there like jagged mountain peaks protruding from the cloth.

Jacob pulled a piece out of the cushion. It was buried deep in the cushion with its deadly sharp points.

How had he survived this?

He'd been thrown off the sofa, sure, but wouldn't that have been in the same instant as the glass shattered and fell? He must have been tossed out a moment earlier.

Maybe one moment had seen him tossed and the glass break, and the next had seen him hit the floor as the glass hit the sofa.

He swallowed. A single moment had saved his life.

Readers: you can buy Book 3 on Amazon!

LETTER TO READERS

Dear new friends,

Thank you for choosing this series. I hope you enjoyed it. Would you do me a favor and write a quick review on the site where you bought it? It will help me as an author, and it will help your fellow readers decide whether this book is for them. **Thank you very much!**

If you'd like to communicate with me, you can contact me at my website, www.JamieLeeGrey.com

May God's face shine upon you and bring you peace.

All the best,

Jamie Lee Grey

ACKNOWLEDGMENTS

Readers and friends – Thank you for reading, and for your support. You make it worthwhile. Special thanks go to my beta readers for encouragement and feedback; you're a great team! And to my "legal friends" (you know who you are!) – thanks for so many years of friendship and gentle nudging to get something published.

Candle Sutton – Everyone needs a friend like you, my amazing critique partner. Here's to the next decade together! (Hey, everybody, be sure to check out Candle's books at www.CandleSutton.com .)

My husband – You are the best. Thank you for your encouragement and support of this project, and all my other crazy ideas.

Jesus Christ – My life and breath, and the giver of all good gifts. Thank You.

BOOKS BY JAMIE LEE GREY

Holy War

Band of Believers series

Book 1: Dissent

Book 2: Duplicity

Book 3: Destruction

Book 4: Darkness

Daughter of Babylon series

Book 1: California

Book 2: New York

Book 3: America

Book 4: Oregon

ABOUT THE AUTHOR

Jamie Lee Grey is the author of numerous Christian novels, including the Band of Believers series and the Daughter of Babylon series.

For information on upcoming new releases, sales and giveaways, please sign up for her newsletter at www.JamieLeeGrey.com.

... ...

Made in United States
Orlando, FL
11 September 2024

51402416R00153